*Praise for Kathleen Kole's previous novel:*

"Written with sharp and witty dialogue."

7 out of 10
*Chick Lit Club*

"The entire cast of characters had me laughing."
*A Buckeye Girl Reads*

"I was really intrigued by the story."

4 out of 5
*Chick Lit Plus*

"Put this on your must read list!"

*Just Jump*

"A fun, fast read that will keep readers wondering."
*Chick Lit Bee*

"A fast, enjoyable summer read and lovable characters."
*Adventuring Through Life*

"If you're in the market for something light, fresh, and true to life, this is the book for you!"

3.5 out of 5
*Steph the Bookworm*

*Also by Kathleen Kole*

Breaking Even

# Dollars to Donuts

Kathleen Kole

Sublime Coyote Media

This is a work of fiction. Names, characters, places and incidents are either the product of the author's imagination or are used fictitiously, and any resemblance to actual persons, living or dead, business establishments, events or locales is entirely coincidental.

DOLLARS TO DONUTS



ISBN: 978-0-9868956-4-7

This book is published by Sublime Coyote Media. For more information please visit www.sublimecoyote.com.

To my family and friends, your support means more than words can ever say.

And, always, to Peter. My heart.

# CHAPTER 1 - Friday

5:55 a.m.

"Ahhh!" April yelled as she clenched the brakes on her mountain bike, trying to stop her momentum. She was too successful in her efforts and instead of just stopping, sent herself tumbling clumsily over the handlebars to land with a squishy thud, right in the middle of a copious mud puddle on her side lawn.

"Oh-my-God," April exhaled, shocked by the feel of the cold sludge seeping through the knees of her sweatpants and squishing through her fingers. Things had happened too quickly. One moment she was on her bike, the next there was a blur of fur charging across her path and then... Her brain was trying frantically to connect the dots and she was finding it a challenge to catch her breath.

A screen door creaked loud and long and April turned to see her neighbor, Carol, resplendent in a riotously flowered housecoat and beige, shaggy slippers, exiting her house.

"Oh, fudge," April muttered under her breath. She was splattered from head to toe with dripping, mucky water and now, this?

"April!" Carol called out, shuffling down her front steps and across the lawn, her hot pink rollers jostling merrily in her blonde hair.

"Hey, Carol." April gave a small, stiff wave, then grimaced when mud oozed from her hand down her arm. Gross. She had to get up off of her knees.

"What on Earth?" Carol's blue eyes were wide and her mouth flapped open, then closed, like a fish inside a glass bowl.

"Seems I had a bit of a mishap," April replied, through a tight smile, willing herself to stay calm. In the few months she'd lived in her new cul-de-sac, she'd had more than her share of neighbor encounters to inspire patience. She could just add this one to the list. If things kept up, she'd end up with the composure of a Monk.

"And then some," Carol added as she watched April lean toward the grass and try to wipe her hands clean. It didn't work. Instead, she was left with small bits of green grass stuck to her palms.

"When I heard you scream," Carol continued, her face contorted in a grimace as she pressed a hand to her ample chest and shuddered. "I thought the worst, I'm sorry to say. Maybe a hate crime... I've been watching the news."

*Oh, Jeez, not more talk of the news*, April thought. She eased herself up out of the muck and imagined she probably looked like some sort of movie creature, emerging from the ooze to terrorize the town. Judging by Carol's fast step backward, April guessed she wasn't far off.

"Do I have dirt on my face? It feels like it might be in my teeth."

"You're just filthy," Carol said, matter of fact, wrinkling her nose. "And, smelly."

"You think?" April spat a piece of grit from her mouth and wiped her nose with the back of her hand.

Carol took another small step backward and glanced at April's metallic blue bike laying inelegantly on the ground. She pursed her lips and shook her head. "And, your bicycle... I remember when my girls were young, Edward and I were adamant they take care of their belongings."

April blanched. Was Carol comparing her daughter's once-upon-a-time, childish negligence to what was in front of her? Unbelievable.

"We always told them," Carol blathered and wagged her index finger as she relived her memory. "It only takes a moment—"

"Sometimes you cannot plan ahead, Carol," April cut in, her words clipped, as she wiped her dirty palms on her soiled grey hoodie. "For instance, I could never have predicted, when I was innocently trying to leave my property, that *your* dog would be the reason I ended up in the mud at the crack of dawn."

"Peaches?" Carol's face lit up and she looked around expectantly.

"Over there." April pointed a grubby finger toward the flowerbeds in Carol's yard. The shaggy, blonde Cocker Spaniel was sprawled comfortably in the soft grass, watching the show.

"Has my Sweetums been playing with you?" Carol shook her head, making her rollers wobble, and giggled.

"Playing?" April echoed, flicking bits of grass from her sleeve to the ground. "Well, if you call dashing in front of a moving bicycle *playing*—"

"You may not know this," Carol confided, as she adjusted the sash on her flowered robe. "But, one of her favorite games is Chase."

"Yeah," April said, her voice laced with sarcasm. "I picked up on that." She shook each of her legs in turn, in an attempt to rid her navy blue sweatpants of muck. Nothing budged.

"It doesn't matter what it is," Carol added, tucking her hands into the pockets of her housecoat and smiling affectionately at her dog. "If she gets the notion in her head, look out."

April stared at her neighbor, at a loss for words. *How*, she wondered, *does one respond to such blind devotion?*

Carol peered at April's head. "Am I mistaken, or isn't it a law that you're supposed to be wearing a helmet when you ride your bicycle?"

*Shit*, April thought. She had completely forgotten about her head. She snapped her hand in the air, then exhaled in shaky relief as her fingertips made contact with the makeshift turban she had fashioned out of an old, beige scarf. Thank goodness, it was still there.

"I could be wrong, maybe Edward and I were over protective with our girls..."

"Well," April said, ignoring both Carol's question and commentary. "It's been interesting, but I should be going."

"Going?" Carol cast a skeptical look at April's soiled clothes.

April rolled her eyes. "It's just a little dirt. It'll come right off." She shook her arm to prove her point. The mud didn't budge.

"And, besides," Carol added, clearing her throat. "Isn't it a bit, um, early for you?"

Good God. Did these people keep time cards or something?

"I mean," Carol blustered, patting at her pink hair rollers. "Not that I'd know when you usually go out..." She tapered off and smoothed the folds of her robe.

April sighed and bent down to get her bike. She knew she couldn't win; better to quit while she was ahead. She wrapped her fingers firmly around the bike's handle bars and yanked, only to discover - too late - that she'd unintentionally delivered the final jostle needed to the scarf on her head.

"Good gracious!" Carol clapped a hand across her mouth, her eyes wide and round like saucers, as April's scarf rapidly unraveled to expose her hair to the summer breeze.

"Oh, come on!" April blurted. It was too much. At any minute, she was sure she would wake up. She had to, otherwise her once-blonde, shoulder length hair, currently a shocking shade of florescent orange and a mess of awkward frizz and tangles, would really be on display for the whole neighborhood to see. That wasn't an option.

"A-A-April!" Carol sputtered, like a can of empty whipped cream.

*Fudge it*, April thought. Good neighbor charade be damned. She had dressed in the most bland, least obvious clothes she could find in her closet for one reason: to get out of her cul-de-sac without being observed by any of her prying-eyed-nosey-neighbors. Did it work? No. Not even close. Apparently, leaving like a normal person, undetected by the people on her street, was not an option.

"What? How?" Carol began.

"Spit it out, Carol!" April's voice was menacing with barely suppressed rage. She tightened her grip on her handle bars, snapped her head in Carol's direction and stared her in the face. She'd hit the wall. "What is it you're trying to say?"

Carol leaned back sharply. Apparently, circumstances made it unimportant that April was only measured five foot two inches tall. Clearly, having a face streaked with mud, hair that appeared jolted by electricity and breathing like a half crazed dragon took precedent over anything else.

"W-w-well," Carol stammered and wrung her hands together. "What I meant to say is... Well, Dear, your *hair*..."

"Whow thare!"

Peaches, pretty much forgotten in the midst of the chaos, jumped to her feet at the sound of the booming voice and yapped a few times, ready for action.

"You have *got* to be kidding me," April groaned in disbelief.

It was Thomas, April's Scottish neighbor, his brogue almost as thick as the knee high grass in his yard. He popped his head out from behind some ratty, tangled shrubs and April wondered just how long he'd been there, before deciding to make his entrance.

"Aye, yur quite the sight thaur, arn ye lass?"

April pushed her kick stand down, leaned her bike on it and rubbed her temple as the first twinges of a headache threatened. "Friend of yours?" she asked Carol. Carol recoiled and April snickered. Apparently not.

Thomas ambled through his overgrown yard, ducking beneath the long, untamed branches of his oak trees as he moved toward them. He puffed on a cigarette dangling from his lips, causing a thin trail of smoke to follow in his wake.

As April watched him approach, she found herself briefly envisioning the man as a toddler, a cigarette tucked in his mouth instead of a pacifier. It was a reasonable notion - she'd never seen Thomas without his habit of choice in all the days she'd lived in the neighborhood.

"Goan thein," Thomas prompted, once he stood squarely in front of April. "Tell us, whot's this?" He jerked his chin in the direction of April's head. "Retro meets bairnyard chic?"

April scowled at him while he rocked back and forth on his heels, a glint of mirth shining in his eyes. She wanted so badly to tell him to flake off, but she didn't. All in the name of neighborly preservation.

Instead, she eyeballed his outfit with barely disguised contempt. He was sporting a pair of red plaid pajama pants, a stained, green sweater and a pair of yellow-tinted workshop glasses pressed against his forehead. Combined with his head of unkempt, salt and pepper hair and Van Dyke beard, the man looked like he was out on a day pass.

"I'm-sure-I-don't-know-what-you-are-talking-about." April punctuated each word with a flick of her hand to dispel the smoke forming a hazy cloud around her face. It wasn't just the smoke that was bothersome; the cigarette itself made April nervous. That fiery tip, so close to her highly flammable hair... Yikes.

Thomas didn't so much as flinch in the face of April's flapping. She stopped her ineffectual flailing and exhaled in defeat. Clearly, he'd missed her point and she was, quite frankly, exhausted. It was time to retreat and eat donuts. Besides, she mused while gazing at her mud caked clothes and reflecting upon her catastrophic hair, facts were facts - she wasn't fit for the public eye. Time to say Uncle.

"Well, I guess that's it, then." April flicked the kick stand on her bike with the toe of her dirty sneaker and firmed up her grip on the handle bars. Peaches stood up and wagged her tail, eager to see what April would do next.

"No, no, Sweetums," Carol cooed, while April scowled at the dog. "You can't play with April any more, today."

April pressed her lips together, repressing the urge to comment, and dragged her bike around the mud puddle. *Play, indeed.*

"Oh!" Carol blurted as April began to move away. "What about your scarf?"

"Don't need it, don't care," April called over her shoulder as she trudged across her lawn toward her yellow house.

Thomas looked up at the rapidly darkening sky. "Leuks like we might hae a bit 'o the lashing doan," he commented, the motion of his lips causing ash at the tip of his cigarette to scatter down across his green sweater.

*What?* April paused to look back at her neighbors. Judging by the confused expression on Carol's face as she retightened the sash on her flowered robe, she hadn't understood Thomas' speculation that they might be in for rain.

April cast an appraising eye at her quirky Scottish neighbor and wondered what his deal was. He had to be in his early sixties, definitely not new to the area and, yet, how was it he was still speaking like a countryman who had just hit dry land? She decided to test him and called back, "Yup, should get inside before it starts, or at least get an umbrella."

Thomas snapped his head in her direction and April snickered under her breath at the surprise on his face. *Curious*, she thought, nodding to herself as she pushed her bike across the remainder of the yard and leaned it up against the side of her house. Clearly, he hadn't expected her to understand him.

"Might even want to grab a Mac," she couldn't help adding, just to stir it up. Thomas furrowed his brow, making his shop glasses look like a second pair of yellow eyes on his forehead. April giggled.

*Let him stew on that*, she thought, then turned on the heel of her mud caked sneaker, sprinted across her lawn and up the wooden steps to her front porch. She slipped inside the house and, without a backward glance, slammed the front door so hard the white shutters on the windows rattled.

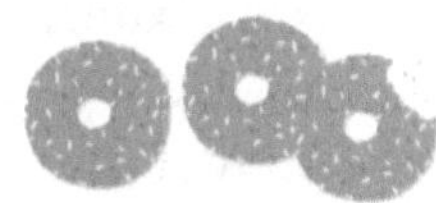

## 9:14 a.m.

April paced back and forth across the hardwood floor of her unlit foyer. She'd cleaned up and was dressed in a fresh pair of tan capris and a turquoise tee shirt, her mud-caked garments cast to the bottom of her laundry basket. Her hair she'd rewrapped in an old green towel, to disguise the obvious.

As she paced, April took large bites of a chocolate dipped, custard donut and silently cursed that she had been forced to abandon her plans and call for back up.

The back up in question was her sister, Jessica.

Jessica was a brilliant stylist with her own salon, *A Cut Above*, and April knew if she had any hope of correcting her hair fiasco, it was Jessica who was going to do it. Besides, she reasoned, who else would she go to in her predicament? Visiting another salon in the area would be like taking out a full page advertisement in the local newspaper. *'Newcomer To Boxwood Hills Makes*

*Spectacle Of Her Own Head. Elementary school teacher boyfriend in dismay. More on page 3"*. No thanks.

"I've Barbied my own head!" April blurted to the empty space around her, snorting so hard she almost sent custard up into her nose. The memory of how the expression had been born in her family gave her a fit of the giggles as she cast her thoughts back.

When they were children, at the tender ages of eight and eleven, both April and Jessica had loved Barbie. April, petite with freckles and honey colored hair, had loved to dress her doll in the sparkled flouncy outfits and tiny shoes.

Jessica, the older sixth grader, tall for her age with a mane of long, wavy brunette locks, had been passionate about Barbie for a different reason - her hair. Jessica would adorn Barbie's head with scrunchies and delicate barrettes, or weave multi-colored ribbons through the sunshine inspired strands. Whatever struck her fancy.

It would have been fine if she had left it at that, but she never did. Instead, Jessica was compelled to rub it in when she had styled Barbie's hair and smugly declare something like, "I've created a rainbow, just for Barbie".

It had infuriated April. Primarily because Jessica resolutely refused to give her hair the same attention - her reasoning being Barbie was better at sitting still.

The unfairness of it all.

April had tried to counter that, clearly, Barbie held a distinct advantage in the department of sitting still. She was a doll, whereas April was an eight year old girl. Jessica would not be swayed. She had stuck to her biased logic, case closed.

Finally, in an act of youth inspired retaliation, April had decided to permanently alter the appearance of her Barbie. It hadn't been all that difficult. With a small amount of Kool-Aid at her disposal, April had easily turned Barbie's golden locks a sickly pink and then, with a pair of safety scissors...

That simple act of rebellion had been Jessica's undoing.

Upon discovery of the newly transformed Punker Barbie, Jessica had flown into a fury. She had dropped the defiled doll onto April's bedroom floor and tore through the house, safety scissors in hand, intent upon hunting April down. It hadn't been much of a challenge, she'd just had to follow the smell of freshly baked, chocolate chip cookies - April's favorite - to the kitchen. Once she found her little sister, Jessica had advanced upon her threatening to create a "Barbie" for her young head. Thankfully, their mother had been home and intervened, sparing April the wrath of her own safety scissors in the angry hands of her older sister.

Good times.

There was a knock at the door and April stopped pacing the floor to press her eye to the peephole. She had learned, from hands-on experience, it wasn't just in the city where she needed to check who was on the other side of the door before pulling it open. In the Burbs, the same rule applied.

Jessica stood on the front step, her face distorted by the fisheye lens, and April grinned. Her savior had arrived. She squished the remainder of her donut into her mouth and hauled open the door. "Come in! Quick!" she gurgled through dough and custard.

"Ow!" Jessica frowned when April grabbed her forearm and attempted to bodily drag her into the house. "Leggo!"

April yanked harder, pulling Jessica across the threshold, then slammed the door forcefully behind her; narrowly missing catching her sister's purse in the jam.

"Jeez, April! What the heck is wrong with you?" Jessica scowled and flipped her green bag back and forth, checking to see it was okay. It was. She turned to her sister and her face twisted from a scowl, into a grimace. "And, what on Earth is that on your chin?"

April wiped at her chin, where remnants of chocolate had smeared in her haste to stuff the remainder of her donut into her mouth. "Chocolate," she said and licked her fingers.

"Eww!" Jessica rubbed at her wrist, making three gold charm bracelets jangle noisily against one another. "It's probably on me, too, thank you very much."

"Sorry." April apologized, then flipped her hands back and forth, checking for chocolate. "Really. But, my neighbors are always watching and waiting for any opportunity to breech the threshold. I didn't want you to encourage their gawking."

Jessica slipped off her royal blue sandals and set her purse on a wooden bench near the front door. "Why do you have it so dark in here?"

"I just said. The neighbors are watching."

Jessica raised an eyebrow. "You sound off your nut, you know that, right?" She shook her head and walked into the living room, her denim skirt brushing at her ankles, and sunk into a patchwork patterned chair adjacent to the couch.

April shrugged and followed behind her. "Maybe so, but it's still true. My neighbors are nutty and invasive." She dropped herself down into the coffee colored, microfiber couch with a satisfying 'whoosh' of the cushions. "Anyway, that's not why I asked you to come over. At least not directly. Maybe indirectly, but not directly."

Jessica tucked her feet beneath her and pointed at April's head. "What's with the towel? Did I get you out of the shower?"

"No," April frowned. "In fact, I've been up for bloody hours."

"You?"

"Yes, *me*," April huffed, from her prone position on the couch. "But, that's not the point."

"There's a point?"

"Tell me, this neighborhood looks normal, right?"

"Uh-huh." Jessica nodded.

"I know it does because, when I first saw it, I thought the same thing." April shook her finger. "News flash. It's not."

"No?"

"No."

"It looks fine to me," Jessica said and tucked a strand of her long, auburn hair behind one ear.

"Oh, no question," April readily agreed as she turned onto her side to face Jessica. "It does look fine. All of the houses are pretty, cottage-styled, cute. The yards are manicured and weeded to an inch of their lives. The mountains are practically in the backyard. The whole damned area looks like its been pulled out of a movie set." She paused as an image of Thomas' riotous property came thundering forward. "Well, okay, *most* of the homes are like that. You get my point."

"And, this is bad, because?" Jessica scrunched her eyebrows together, confused.

"Because," April insisted. "I can't so much as make a move without one of my neighbor knowing I did it. I can't walk outside in my bathrobe if I want to, I can't get the paper without being detected, it's like living in a fish bowl with a group of really nosey humans on the other side of the glass."

Jessica blinked and frowned. April waited. She knew her sister sometimes needed a moment to process what had been said. Jessica took a breath. "Okay," she clarified. "Let me get this straight. You called me here because you want to walk outside in your bathrobe? Why? Why would you want to do that?"

"Oh, for pity's sake! That's not what I was trying to get at." April sat upright on the sofa. "Forget it. Just take a look at this." With a flourish, she yanked her towel from her head and her florescent hair burst messily from its confines; as though it had been waiting eagerly to do just that.

"Oh-My-God!" Jessica stood up, her eyes wide with shock. She goggled at April's head. "What have you done?"

"Made a mistake."

"How?" Jessica blinked rapidly, her mouth opening and closing without sound, much as Carol's had done earlier that morning.

"I was trying to dye it red—"

"WHAT?" Jessica's face was incredulous.

"And, clearly, I failed."

"But, you have me! Why? Why would you...?" Jessica was having trouble completing her sentences. "It's what I *do*, for goodness sake!"

"I know!"

"My God, April, how old are you?"

April raised an eyebrow, but stayed silent.

"Thirty-two." Jessica pressed. "You're thirty-two years old and you still think it's okay to do something this drastic to your head?"

"*And*," April shot back. "You're thirty-five and still think it's okay to lecture me?"

Jessica began to giggle. April rolled her eyes and Jessica not only giggled harder, but threw in a few snorts, as well. "You've Barbied your own head!" She threw her head back and laughed raucously.

"Crap," April spat.

Jessica laughed harder. "You remember, right?" she asked, between giggles.

April nodded, her face a picture of annoyance. Yes, she had found it amusing when *she* had thought of it, but she still didn't enjoy being blatantly laughed at by her older sister.

"Oh God, my stomach." Jessica clutched at her sides and tears glistened in her eyes. "I'm going to wet myself, if I'm not careful."

"Oh, for goodness sake." April sighed.

"Whew," Jessica exhaled, trying to catch her breath. "Did you think the same thing when you saw it?"

April shrugged her shoulders. "Maybe."

"You did!" Jessica exclaimed and wiped the tears from her eyes. "Come on, April Showers, like it or not, it's funny."

"Okay, fine," April said. She knew if she didn't admit to it, Jessica wouldn't let up. "I did think it and, yes, it is a bit funny."

"A bit?" Jessica sniffed and pulled a tissue from her skirt pocket to blow her nose.

"It's true, though," April moaned and let herself fall haphazardly back into the couch. "I've gone and ruined it, just like I did to Barbie. It's the ultimate karmic go-around and I'm going to have to shave my head."

"Oh, shut up, no you're not." Jessica brushed her hair back from her face, took a deep breath and exhaled. "Believe it or not, I'm pretty sure I can fix this."

April jumped up and clutched at Jessica's arm. "Really? You're not messing with me? Can you do it before Kevin sees me?"

"He wasn't here when you did this?"

April released Jessica's arm and covered her face with her hands. The very idea of her boyfriend seeing her predicament was too much to contemplate. "No!" She spoke between her fingers. "I can't bear the thought. He'd never let me live it down. I don't know what it is, but it always seems when I screw up, Kevin is around to witness it. It's not right. I'm really much more stable than this."

"I can barely understand you, take a breath," Jessica counseled, and then added, a sly grin on her face. "*Barbie*."

April yanked her hands away from her face and sharply pointed her index finger at Jessica. "You see! I knew it! Even you, Ms. Professional, can't let it go. I *knew* I should have found another way."

Jessica was grinning, but she held up her hands in surrender. "Okay, it was a joke. Sorry. Just ignore me, I'm being an ass."

April nodded her agreement.

Jessica cut her eyes at April. "*Anyway*, obviously there's no way I can do anything here. We have to go to the salon."

"Perfect. No neighbors, no spying. Perfect."

"What neighbors?" Jessica waved her hands around and looked at April imploringly. "Have you even looked out there? It's as quiet as a ghost town."

Just then, the skies rumbled.

"Okay, a ghost town with rain threatening."

"Oh, yeah, *now* it's quiet." April gave her sister a penetrating stare. "But, trust me, these people are odd, Jess. Odd and nosey. And, you can't argue because you've seen it, too."

"Really? When?" Jessica challenged.

"Remember that time we were out to lunch and those two fake-friendly women came over to our table? And, after they left, you told me they had practically stalked you for the first six months you lived here? What were their names?"

"Denise and Heidi," Jessica mumbled, suddenly interested in the nail polish on her finger nails.

"Yes! Those two." April nodded smugly. "See? Odd."

"Okay," Jessica admitted. "Fine. They are a little odd..."

"Uh-huh," April pressed. "Face it, the people here do not know the meaning of minding their own business."

"What's your point, again?"

"My point is, I don't want to encourage my stalkers–—"

"Neighbors."

"Semantics. Anyway, I don't want to give them any more reasons to meddle in my life."

"Fine." Jessica sighed. "Whatever. Can we move on to what matters here, your hair?"

"Did you drive?" April asked.

"No, I walked," Jessica said, sarcastically. "Of course I drove. I'm parked in the driveway."

April nodded and rubbed her chin with her fingertips, thinking, as the sky rumbled for a second time.

"When are you going to get a car, by the way?" Jessica placed her hands on her hips. "If I recall, wasn't that one of the things on your To-Do list when you moved here?"

April waved away her question and ran her hands over her hair in an attempt to smooth it down. It did nothing. "Never mind that—"

"Said the woman who has to either ride her bike, or bum a ride, to get anywhere."

"I've had an epiphany." April rubbed her hands together and grinned.

"Epiphany?" Jessica smirked. "Don't tell me, you're going to get a tiny car and finally run off with your people of the Big Top?"

April narrowed her eyes at her sister, but refused to be baited. "You can go outside and create some sort of diversion to attract the neighbor's attention and then, when they're watching you, I'll sneak out and tuck myself into the Jeep." She gestured to her head. "Obviously, I'll put this under wraps, first."

"A diversion?" Jessica folded her arms across her chest and gave April a skeptical look. "What exactly did you have in mind, Ms. Fletcher?"

"Fletcher?" April frowned and shook her head, not following Jessica's lead.

"You know, from that show, Murder She Wrote? Angela Lansbury played the murder-mystery writer, Jessica Fletcher?"

"Oh." April shook her head. "Ha, ha. Very witty." She began to pace back and forth across the beige area rug on the hardwood floor, beneath the coffee table, and stopped when a third rumble shook the house. "Sounds like we're in for some serious weather."

Jessica sat back down in the cushy chair. "Uh-huh, I could smell it when I got out of the car, so I'd suggest, if we're going to do this, that you get ready before we get caught in it."

"I will, but first, I still have to tell you the most unsettling part of this whole situation." April stopped pacing and stood beside the black metal and glass coffee table.

"It gets more unsettling than you having hair to envy a circus clown?"

"Yes!" April insisted, vehemently. "Not only did my hair coloring attempt go awry, but I was basically hijacked this morning when I tried to leave."

"Hijacked? What do you mean, hijacked?"

"By a dog, of all things."

"Hijacked," Jessica echoed. "By a *dog*?"

"Uh-huh. My neighbor's dog. It's this little shaggy mop of a thing, wanders around the neighborhood. No collar, no leash, nothing."

Jessica nodded, unfazed by the information.

"See?" April held her hands out imploringly and sat down on the sofa. "Is it really so small town here that these people don't worry about possibly losing a pet?"

"Pretty much." Jessica shrugged her shoulders.

April blinked and gave her head a small shake. She had seen so many unfortunate animals in the city left to fend for themselves, or hurt, all because of their owner's negligence of the simplest things - like taking the time and consideration to make sure they had identification and were safe in their own space.

"I know." Jessica nodded sympathetically when she saw the look on April's face. She understood exactly what she was thinking. "Believe me, I think it, too."

April breathed deeply to regain her composure, there was no point in wasting her breath airing her issues on the subject. "*Anyway*, the damned dog snuck up on me when I was trying to cycle out of here and nearly got squished by my tires."

"Was it okay?"

"Oh, yeah, fine. Just scared the hell out of me and made me scream loud enough to rattle the windows. Which, of course, didn't go unnoticed and the next thing I knew, I didn't just have Peaches—"

"Peaches?" Jessica asked.

"That's the dog's name."

"Oh." Jessica smirked. "Does she look like a peach, or something?"

April grinned. "No, not that I've noticed."

Jessica shrugged. "Whatever floats your boat, I guess. So, you screamed, which alerted the dog and, then?"

April refused to share the information of how she had tumbled off of her bike into the mud. She knew Jessica would find it hilarious and her hair fiasco would become a *story*, hauled out at family functions. No thanks. She'd give her an edited version.

"My scream basically set off a domino effect and kept me from leaving to get to you. First Carol came barreling out—"

"Carol?" Jessica questioned. "Who's Carol?"

"The dog's owner. Although," April said, with a snicker. "She calls herself the dog's *Guardian*."

Jessica pulled a face. "God. I get the same type at the salon. All indignant that I won't let them bring their beloved pets inside when they show up for their appointment. Never mind I'm actually protecting them from the chemicals."

"Exactly," April agreed and relaxed back into the sofa cushions. "So, anyway, the domino thing. Carol came running out to catch the action and then Thomas appeared."

"Thomas? There's a Thomas, too? Jeez, talk about a cast of thousands."

"Uh-huh, that's what I've been telling you. I know you think I'm being over the top, but these people never mind their own damned business and they're everywhere. It's like, every time I step out the door, I'm playing another round of dodge the neighbor."

April cocked her thumb in the direction of Thomas's house. "As for Thomas, he's next door on the other side of the house and let me tell ya, he got a great big old kick out of my hair."

Jessica nodded, knowingly. "It's a small vanilla town, April. The only people who do anything off-beat to their hair are the teens, just to drive their mothers round the bend."

"Yeah, I got that." April yawned. "Anyway, the guy's a looney Scotsman and from what I've heard and seen, not necessarily dealing with a full deck. He's probably at home right now, cooking up some sort of haggis to turn into something else."

"Really?" Jessica grimaced.

April shrugged her shoulders. "No. I don't know. Maybe. The rumor is he's some sort of inventor, has made a killing on his work and is semi-retired; which would make sense since he's around pretty much all the time. I've heard banging and seen smoke coming from his workshop more than once, so it's just as possible as not it's true. All in all, comparatively speaking, he seems relatively harmless."

Jessica turned her head sharply toward the living room window.

"What?" April sat upright.

"Nothing, I just thought I saw something."

April stood up and moved forward, toward the window. "Ah-ha! Right there." She pointed her finger between the blinds and gestured to a spot just on the inside of Thomas's property line. "That's him. Don't be surprised if you see Carol next."

Jessica got up from the chair and joined April at the window, just as large drops of water began to fall from the sky. "That's Thomas?"

"Uh-huh."

"Huh," Jessica said, watching him walk in circles in his yard, a large stick in his grasp. "I don't know why, but I pictured him less, um, wild looking."

April nodded. "You get used to it." She frowned when Thomas stopped his pacing and stared up at the sky. "What the hell is he up to?"

"I mean seriously, look at the man's hair, never mind his beard," Jessica elaborated. "Does he even own a comb?"

"Oh!" April exclaimed, when Thomas suddenly spun around and hoofed it down the side of his house and out of sight. April turned to stare, wide-eyed, at her sister.

"What the?" Jessica said.

"The backyard!" April cried out and tore away from the window. "Come on!"

Jessica, close on April's heels as she ran toward the kitchen, began to giggle madly. "You look like a crazed Muppet!"

April laughed as they shoved open the kitchen door, skittered across the tile floor and lunged toward the window, edging aside cups and plants on the countertop and window sill.

"There he is." Jessica pointed her index finger at the window, when Thomas came into view. "Good God." She peered between the rain drops that were falling with increased velocity onto the glass. "What *is* he wearing?"

April recalled when she'd had the same reaction to the man. However, over the past few months, his uniform of faded pajama bottoms, funky colored sweaters and safety glasses had become pretty much the norm. She no longer gave Thomas' wardrobe a second thought.

Thomas walked with measured steps around his backyard, then looked up at the sky and shook his stick.

"What's with the stick?" Jessica commented. "Is he doing some sort of rain dance? Or, is that something he usually carries around?"

"Not that I've seen. But, then again, considering I try to stay *away* from the neighbors, that really doesn't say much of anything."

A cat, lean and the color of smoke, with large orange eyes and a kinked tail, appeared from around the side of Thomas' workshop situated at the back of his property. It stayed in the shadows, out of the steadily falling rain and slunk slowly toward the workshop's doorway.

"Ooh, look at that cat." Jessica pointed, her bracelets jangling together. "Let me guess. It's his, right?"

"Yup, good guess," April said. She'd seen the animal sunning himself outside on Thomas' property. From what she could tell, it didn't have a collar, either. Not that *that* surprised her whatsoever... "I think its name is Corkscrew."

Jessica laughed. "Of course it is."

"Oh, wait." April held up her hand. "He's changing tactics." They went silent and watched as Thomas suddenly dropped his stick, slicked his rain soaked hair back from his forehead and sidled up to the garbage can standing on his lawn.

"What's he doing now?" Jessica squinted at the window, trying to see more clearly through the rain smattered glass.

April shook her head. "No idea."

Thomas pulled the lid off of his garbage can, peered inside and then slammed the lid back down.

"Is he going to throw it?!" Jessica's voice held a note of incredulity as Thomas hoisted the container into his arms.

"What? Throw it?" April looked quizzically at her sister. "Why on *Earth* would you say that?"

"Because." Jessica raised her chin. "If he did, it could be a big mess to clean up."

"Okay, that makes no sense."

"Yes, it does," Jessica retorted.

"No," April insisted.

"Yes," Jessica shot back.

"Okay, stop." April held up a hand, then pointed at the window. "Look. He's not."

Thomas, although of lean build, was a lot stronger than he appeared. In his arms, the garbage can looked as though it weighed little more than a grocery bag. He charged speedily across his yard to his workshop and, with his shoulder, shoved hard on the door. When it swung open, Corkscrew skittered deftly out of the way and disappeared around the side of the building. Thomas dumped his garbage can inside, reached for the handle and yanked, slamming the door firmly shut.

"Yikes!" Jessica yelped when the sound reverberated off the house walls. "What the hell was that about?"

Thomas marched away and into his house. The show was over.

April shook her head, flummoxed. "You've got me."

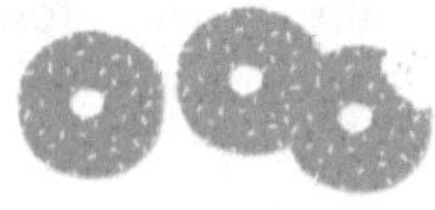

## 12:30 p.m.

"Okay, done." Jessica stood back and examined April's head, a satisfied expression on her face. They had sequestered themselves inside the staff bathroom at *A*

*Cut Above*, so Jessica could work her magic disguising April's tortured locks. Finally, the task was finished.

April coughed when she inhaled the aerosol mist that hung in the air, but was pleased by the end result. "This is fantastic!" she enthused, turning her head back and forth to see every angle. "I wish it could look this good naturally."

Jessica turned on the ceiling fan to clear the air and laughed at April's comment. She had spent the better part of an hour armed with a mauve silk scarf, a set of blond hair pieces, a whole host of styling products and about a hundred hair pins, transforming April's hair disaster into something fashionable.

"You'd never know the truth, you know," April stated. "Makes me wonder what's really going on under the hats and scarves of women who look like they have fabulous hair."

"Well, I'm hoping when I actually fix it, it looks better than this," Jessica told her as she started to clear away the remaining styling detritus piled up on the countertop.

"Here, let me help." April imitated Jessica's movement, gathering up the last of the pins and hair products and dropping them into an open drawer on the vanity.

Jessica reached into another, smaller drawer for a scarlet lip gloss and swept a layer of it across her generous mouth. April watched, her head cocked to one side, amazed as always at the differences between she and her sister. It was mystifying to her that they were even related.

Jessica was all about legs and curves and thick hair colored a deep, rich auburn, whereas she, April, was the antithesis - short, erring on the side of skinny with dishwater blonde hair... Genetics, she deduced with a sigh, could be a real bitch.

"Are you sure you can hang out for the day?"

April nodded and watched the reflection of her newly quaffed head go up and down in the mirror. The mauve scarf matched her ballet flats and upped the bar, making her tan capris and turquoise shirt suddenly look cute, instead of average. "Absolutely. I'm working on a column, but I can catch up the time later at the library."

"Procrastination still working for you, then?"

April stuck out her tongue and Jessica snickered. That was the trouble with family, they knew all of your quirks and weaknesses. A person couldn't get away with anything without being called out on it.

"For your information," April raised her chin indignantly and refused to meet Jessica's eye. "I no longer procrastinate. I now mull things over for a good long while."

Jessica snorted.

"*Then*," April said, pointedly ignoring her. "Once I've taken the time necessary to peruse all of my thoughts, I commit them to my column."

She was a bald faced liar. She did procrastinate and for good reason. Her column was such an effort to write, such a blood, sweat and tears sort of endeavor, of course April avoided it until she had no other choice except to face it. Hell, the fact that she completed it - at deadline once a week - was a testament to her willpower, if nothing else.

Why then, one could reasonable ask, if writing the column was so abhorrent, did she do it at all? The answer was simple: agony or not, she didn't have a choice. It had been April's dream, from the moment she started freelance writing, to have a column of her very own. When that happened for her, there was no turning back.

That being said, April would admit she did take one large misstep in the actualization of her dream. She'd let her excitement totally obliterate any possible attempts at keeping a level head. The moment she had heard, through the freelance grapevine, that a certain newspaper was seeking to add a new columnist to their roster, she'd hurled her resume into the applicant pile without skipping a beat. Instead of doing the smart thing, investigating the subject matter of the column, she'd jumped in with both feet. If only she'd taken a moment... April sighed at the memory.

She could see herself in the office of the Potential New Boss, dressed up in her best lady suit and hoping she was presenting herself as put together and ready for anything. A serious untruth. The reality was, she was anything *but* those things. Instead of being organized, April often found herself running around in last minute panic, searching for her house keys, shoes, wallet, whatever.

What irony it had been to discover none of her outwardly efforts had mattered. Potential New Boss had been kind and personable, not a shark as she had been led to believe. She probably could have arrived for her interview in faded jeans and a tee shirt for all he cared about such things. He had also been no-holds-bared-thrilled that she, "*a freelance reporter with so much experience under her belt*", was interested in the position.

April admitted, upon reflection, his enthusiasm about her interest in the position should have been a red flag. However, the expansive praise he had so willing lavished upon her, "*I think you would bring something unique to the position, April. Too often, this type of column ends up dry and predictable*", combined with the invitation of a steady paycheck, had dulled her natural skepticism. She should have hesitated enough to ponder his use of the words, *"this type of column"*, but ... she hadn't.

Instead, she had positively glowed with pleasure and recklessly declared, "Oh, of course! I like to keep things fresh, challenge myself to find a new angle, that sort of thing." It would not have shocked her if, in that moment, she had leaped from her seat and started tap dancing around his desk to further demonstrate her enthusiasm.

Potential New Boss had grinned from ear to ear and then, as they had paused for a moment to revel in the perfect kismet that had brought them together, he'd dropped the bomb.

"So, what kinds of crafts would you call your specialty?" he'd asked, leaning forward behind his large desk, his eyes bright and curious. "Do you have anything in particular you especially enjoy creating?"

*What?* April's smile had slid from her face, to be replaced with a puzzled frown.

Potential New Boss had swiftly elaborated, nay clarified, he was just trying to get a *thread* - pun intended! - of where her real passion lay with crafts. He wasn't trying to *pin* her down - again, with the pun - to just one thing, he was simply trying to get a feel for where she might begin the introduction of her column to her readers, should she get the position.

*Crafts?* April had been struck dumb. What the hell did she know about crafts? Nothing, zippo, that's what. If pressed she could sew on a button, but after that she was pretty much tapped out.

Observing her sudden silence, Potential New Boss had inquired, "Is there a problem, April?"

"No!" April had blurted; then laughed raucously, desperate to recover her poise. "No problem at all! I was just thinking I must have misheard you. You said *crafts*, not *rafts*, right? Because, I swear I heard you ask me if I have any particular *rafts* I'm passionate about! Threw me right off of my game!"

Thank goodness, Potential New Boss had found the mixed message idea funny and had laughed along with her because, in her next breath, April began to utter not so much half-truths, but out and out lies.

"I haven't really tied myself down to one particular area of crafty creativity," she'd blathered. Talk about an understatement. Then, she had gone further out on her already dangerously tipping limb to expand her bullshit, stating that not only had she outfitted her sister's entire house with window treatments, but just loved to make special, signature, one of a kind pillows.

Good golly, what a load of crap! If she would have been a Baboon, she would have been queen of the feces flingers! April so swiftly lost control of her own mouth that, by the time she had stopped to take a breath, she had half expected Potential New Boss to hand her a shovel to dig herself out.

Did it work? Did it ever!

Potential New Boss had been so pleased with April's enthusiasm he had offered her the position straight away. Just like that, while the air was still pungent with the smell of her verbal diarrhea, she had been given one week to submit her first column. And, providing it was everything Potential New Boss knew it was going to be, she would have a regular space, every Sunday, in their leisure section.

April had left the building that fateful day unsure as to whether she should rejoice, or weep. She finally had her desperately sought after column within her grasp, but didn't know a thimble from a bobbin. She had been sure she was going to be sunk, before she barely had a chance to master threading a needle.

She had also been wrong.

Three years later, she was the queen of the needle. She fuddled her way through every damned project, nearly killing herself and anyone around her unfortunate enough to stumble upon her when she was learning something new, and her readers loved her. It was absurd.

"Okay, Ms. Mill It Over," Jessica teased as she unlocked and opened the bathroom door, interrupting April's not-so-pleasant reverie. "Call it whatever name floats your boat."

April sighed and dropped her chin from its lofty height. Her sister knew the truth about her past, heck she had almost peed her pants laughing when she'd heard the news that April had been offered the column, aptly named *Pins and Needles.*

"You know," April told Jessica as she trailed behind her into the adjacent staff room. "I was poised to branch out again into metro news."

"Uh-huh." Jessica nodded, reaching into a small fridge in the corner of the room. "And then you moved here to small town central, gave up your dreams and the rest is crafting history." She pulled out two bottles of water. "Old news, April Showers. Time to move on."

April shrugged.

"Besides," Jessica continued as she closed the fridge door. "You've actually gotten pretty good at what you do, for all of the bellyaching you make about it."

"It only appears I've gotten good at it," April replied, taking one of the bottles of water Jessica handed to her and flopping down onto the green sofa that lined one of the copper colored walls of the staff room. "Trust me, it's still one hell of a ride between projects."

"Still, it's better than the alternative, right?"

April raised an eyebrow as she twisted open the plastic top on her bottle. "Meaning?"

"Going back to freelance?"

April shuddered. When she'd first started working freelance, it had amazed her she could make money from her writing. Her amazement hadn't lasted long. The reality of running her butt off around the city, juggling her assignments and effectively playing Beat The Clock - just so she could make enough money to make ends meet - swiftly put a halt to her enthusiasm.

"Point taken," she acknowledged.

"Exactly."

"So, tell me," April said, then paused to take a swig of water.

"What?'

April swallowed. "We've been going on about my stuff, what's been going on with you?"

Well," Jessica glanced at the clock on the wall and hesitated. "Maybe it should wait, I need to get out of here to my next client in about 10 minutes."

"Quickly, then," April encouraged, patting the green cushion next to her in invitation.

"Okay." Jessica sat and placed her bottle on the pine table in front of the sofa. "But, I'll have to give you the Reader's Digest version."

"Sounds ominous, about what?"

"My latest date."

"Ooh, goody." April leaned forward eagerly. "Spill."

Jessica laughed and shook her head. "What would you do for gossip, if it wasn't for me?"

"Probably go crazy. I live vicariously, after all." April looked at the clock. "Hurry, time's ticking."

"Okay, as I said, the Reader's Digest version. I met this guy—"

"How?"

"Through Donna. You haven't met her, yet."

April nodded. "Got it."

"So, anyway, the guy and I met at Bello Alimento–"

"You met up at the restaurant?" April interrupted.

"It was a first date."

"Okaaay." April shrugged her shoulders.

"Remember, before I moved here?" Jessica explained. "That guy, Julian?"

"Uh." April wracked her brain. "Oh, right!" She snapped her fingers as the memory unfolded and then frowned. "*That* guy."

"Exactly." Jessica shuddered. "Weirdo stalker guy who I foolishly let know where I lived. I'm not taking a chance on another Julian."

"So, what about this new guy?" April shifted in her seat.

"I don't think there's any chance we'll be calling him that," Jessica said. "More likely to be called, first-date-last-date-guy. Or, FDLDG, for short. Is that shorter? It feels longer."

"Does it matter? He's history. What happened before he was history?"

Jessica smoothed her denim skirt. "In hindsight, I probably should have left moments after I sat down at the table."

April winced. "Oh, boy, do I want to hear this?"

"You asked, I'm telling."

"Fair enough," April agreed.

"So, anyway, after we were seated at our table we ordered drinks," Jessica explained. "Then, first-date-last-date-guy started patting his pockets like a madman and announced he had forgotten his wallet."

"Oh, please."

"Just wait, it gets better," Jessica said, shaking her head. "I was taken so off guard, the next thing I knew, I was offering to pay."

"No you didn't!"

"I know, right? I didn't know what else to do." Jessica covered her face with her hands and exhaled through her fingers. "I've had a lot of crappy dates, trust me. But, forgetting his wallet? That was a first."

April shook her head. "I'm almost afraid to ask, then what happened?"

Jessica emerged from behind her hands, her expression grim. "It went from bad to worse. We ordered our food and another drink and then he started coming and going, to and from the bathroom."

"What?" April scrunched up her face, puzzled.

"It was like he was on some sort of timer." Jessica shrugged her shoulders and raised her hands, palms upward. "I don't know, really strange. We'd be talking for a few minutes and then, bam! He'd jump up and off he'd go. After the third or fourth time—"

"Third or *fourth*?" April repeated, incredulous.

"At least. I lost count," Jessica said.

"Did you ask him what his trouble was? Was he doing drugs, or something?"

"I thought the same thing, but if he was, there was no obvious evidence of it. And, to be honest, at that point I really didn't give a flying flip." Jessica smoothed her hair from her face. "It all seemed like an exercise in futility."

April nodded. "Did he eventually stay in his seat long enough to eat his dinner?"

"He never got the chance, at least not with me. While he was gone from the table I hailed the waiter and told him I had an emergency and would have to have the food to go."

"You didn't!" April said, her voice full of respect.

"Yes, I did," Jessica said, her face proud.

"What did the guy do?"

"When he came back from the bathroom I thrust his bag of food at him—"

"No!" April cut her off. "After all of that, you gave him his share?" She was gobsmacked at the thought. "And, for that matter, you actually waited for him to come back from the bathroom?"

"I don't know!" Jessica huffed and twisted the silver rings on her fingers. "I've never been in that sort of situation, before. I was in unchartered territory."

"Well, I have to say, I'm impressed. I can honestly say I don't know if I would have done the same."

Jessica shrugged. "At the time, it felt like a small price to pay just get the so-called date done and get out of there."

"So, what happened when you told him things were done?"

"He actually looked embarrassed."

"Points for that, I suppose," April said, a wry grin on her face. "Although not many."

"Then, he tried to explain himself and I told him to forget it." Jessica leaned forward and picked up her water bottle from the coffee table. "Here's the kicker, though. He wouldn't let it go and insisted on paying me back with a check!"

"What?" April's eyebrows shot up. "Was he for real? He didn't have his wallet, but he had his check book? For how much?"

Jessica started to laugh. "Fifteen bucks!"

April whooped and leaned back into the couch cushions. "No way!"

"Yes, way." Jessica giggled.

"Where do you find these guys?" April asked, dumbfounded. "Not to mention, what kind of friend would set you up with a guy like that?"

"Trust me, there are more of them than you want to know," Jessica replied, soberly. "You lucked out with Kevin."

April cleared her throat and sidestepped the comment. "Has he called?"

"Who, Kevin?"

"No, Mr. Money Bags."

"No." Jessica laughed. "Thank goodness. I'm hoping he took a hint and leaves it." She looked at the clock, stood up and smoothed her skirt with her free hand. "Speaking of which, time to get to work. Thanks again for filling in at the front desk."

April waved her words away with a flick of her hand and got up from the couch. "No trouble. Besides, it's good for me to get out from behind my computer once in a while and get my hand on the beat of the pulse." She waved her hands over her head and added, "Woo-woo!"

Jessica smirked as she watched April bob her head in time to a silent beat. "You are so not a woo-wooer," she said, turning on her heel. "Especially with the scarf," she added, over her shoulder, as she opened the staff room door.

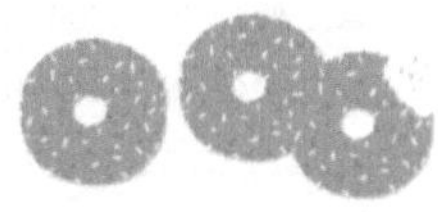

## 1:06 p.m.

There was an appreciable temperature rise when the sisters entered the salon. April's head began to itch beneath its layers of cover and she was surprised the sage green paint on the walls wasn't starting to peel from the humidity.

*Just a few hours to hair freedom*, she silently counseled herself, while resisting the urge to paw at her head like a dog forced to wear a stupid seasonal hat.

"Whew," Jessica exhaled, before checking the thermostat. "It's warm in here today, ladies. Time to kick it up a notch." She fiddled with the controls and April felt a whoosh of cool air flood from the vents on the walls.

Tara and Patti, the two stylists who worked alongside Jessica, waved across the room at April and she smiled in return - just before she sneezed. The hair dye, perming solution and styling sprays were a potent combination.

"April, bless you," a woman's voice called out, stopping April in her tracks. She turned to her left to see Denise Chang, the very person to whom April had been referring earlier that morning, grinning in a friendly manner from the chair at Jessica's station.

April was taken aback that Denise even remembered her. When she had first met the woman it had seemed she was more interested in talking to Jessica, than in acknowledging her. It came as news that Denise not only remembered her, but they were on a first name basis.

"How nice to see you, again," Denise offered as she pulled her hands out from under a magenta colored, nylon cape draped around her shoulders. She smoothed the nylon with her palms and watched April closely, her dark almond shaped eyes bright with curiosity. "Lovely scarf, the color really suits you."

"Thanks." April said and took a tentative stepped backward. Something about Denise's scrutiny was making her very uncomfortable. She wished she could just drift away, out of sight.

"What brings you here?"

April jumped at the sound of another voice to her right. She had been so focused upon Denise's radar-like gaze, she had completely missed the woman's best friend, Heidi Becker, sitting in an adjacent chair.

Heidi leaned forward, an expectant expression on her face, and April swallowed uncomfortably. "Oh, uh," she stammered. Her head began to itch in earnest and she wondered if the air conditioning had turned off. "Just here to lend a hand with the phones."

"Hey, April," Jessica interrupted the interrogation. "Could you please check the computer to make sure my three o'clock is still scheduled?"

*Bless you*, April thought, acutely aware Jessica was rescuing her from the double-teaming duo. She gratefully accepted the metaphorical life saver being thrown her way, blurted, "Right away!" and hightailed it out of the room to seek refuge in the reception area.

"Whew," April exhaled as she dropped gratefully into the safety of the padded chair behind the large stone and brick covered reception desk. Thank goodness for her big sister, still looking out for her no matter what their ages.

Jessica had been the epitome of a big sister. She could harass April all she wanted, but if anyone else dared to try, watch out. Jessica's protectiveness had carried on right into their teens and any boy interested in April knew he had to pass muster with Jessica, first.

One boy in particular came to mind and April snickered at the memory. Cam Stewart. Cam had ventured over to their house one afternoon, after his soccer practice, seeking out April. The poor boy, he was only fifteen after all, had failed to realize he smelled like old socks. He didn't stand a chance. Jessica had been merciless.

She'd told Cam to get his sorry, stinky butt home, take a well needed shower and then, *maybe*, he could come back - after he'd asked for permission to talk to April. The amazing part, in April's opinion, was he did exactly as he was told.

"I literally just about fell right over when I noticed it was Gerritt who was coming into the shop!" Denise's booming voice sailed through the salon, jarring April from her walk down memory lane.

She sat up straight in her chair and, despite her often judgmental thoughts about people who eavesdropped, cocked an ear to listen.

"Did you talk to him?" Heidi's voice joined the conversation and April shook her head as she imagined the woman's rapt face, eager to know the gossip.

"Well, *you* know," came Denise's reply.

April smirked, did she sense some hesitation in Denise's voice? *Think so.*

"We were both intent on our shopping and a person doesn't want to come on too strongly and give a bad impression."

*Right.* April rolled her eyes. She would have bet dollars to donuts Denise had chickened out.

"However," Denise said, her voice so bloody lofty April wished she had the guts to peek around the wall and see her face to get a visual assessment of what she was saying. "We *did* say hello and, well—"

"Sorry, Denise," Jessica cut her off. "Time for the dryer. You girls will have to put your conversation on hold."

Phooey. It was just getting interesting. Or, not. Who could tell. "Ah, well," April muttered to herself.

"Hmmm, talking to yourself. First sign of brain slippage, I've always heard."

"Oh!" April jerked in her seat and whipped her chair around to face the desk. "Kevin, hi! How crazy is it I didn't hear you come in?"

Kevin raised an eyebrow and his chocolate brown eyes flashed with amusement. "You seemed pretty intent upon staring at that wall."

April flushed. Her boyfriend was no dummy and she felt like a child, caught in the act of trying to hear the adult secrets. Time to change the subject. "Wow, I can really smell the rain. Is it still coming down?"

Kevin nodded and removed his jacket. The deep green color had turned almost black, it was so soaked with water. "Heavily. Like it doesn't plan to let up for a while." He walked over to the area rug at the salon entrance, vigorously shook the jacket and carried it back over to April. "Hope that's enough," he said, holding it out. "Could you hang onto that for me?"

"Sure." April took it from his grasp and draped it across the back of her chair.

"Jess isn't going to have to wash my hair to cut it," he said, running his fingers through his wet lock and grinning in amusement.

April watched his tight biceps flex beneath the fabric of his navy blue tee shirt as he leaned his elbows on the stone and brick desktop.

"So, how did this happen?"

"What?" April pulled her gaze from his arms and cocked her head. She had no idea to what he was referring, there were so many things to consider it was dizzying.

Kevin gestured to the room. "This. You. Here. I tried your cell but you didn't answer."

"Oh, sorry, I think I left my phone on vibrate and it's in the staff room."

"The last place I thought I'd find you was here," Kevin continued. "Maybe at the library—"

"Wait." April held up a hand and frowned. "Have I really become that predictable?"

"No." Kevin smiled, making his dimples flash. "Definitely not predictable." He looked at her grim face and laughed. "Look at you, all serious."

April looked down at her hands, clasped together so tightly her knuckles had turned white. She disentangled her fingers, flexed them and tried to relax her shoulders.

"I didn't mean anything by it," Kevin said, his eyes kind. "Simply that it's getting close to your column deadline and you seem to thrive on the last minute pressure thing."

"No, I don't," April argued. "It's like I told Jess, I need time to mull."

"Okay, fine." He chuckled and reached out to stroke a finger gently down her cheek. "I take it back. You win. You're a muller."

Before she could stop herself, April flinched and pulled back from the affectionate gesture. When Kevin's finger had barely a moment to graze her skin, his expression twisted from adoring to kicked in the stomach.

*Damn it,* April thought. Her head began to itch, again. The last thing she needed, or wanted, was yet another discussion about how he thought she had been growing distant with him. Good lord, couldn't the man just try to understand that sometimes a woman needed a bit of space? They lived together, didn't they? And, by her standards, they spent an inordinate amount of time together; was it really so unreasonable to want a bit of breathing room?

"So." April tried for damage control. "Do you like my scarf?" She gestured to her head with one hand and surreptitiously used the other to pick up a pen from the granite desktop and scratch at the edge of her hairline.

Kevin gave her a quizzical look and rubbed at the dark stubble on his chin. April held her breath and waited. *Please*, she silently prayed. *For once, let things drop.*

"It's cute," he finally replied and April exhaled. "I don't think I've ever seen you wear a scarf before."

"You see?" She smiled, attempting to be playful. "There's a lot about me you still don't know."

"Apparently," he responded, so tightly April would not have been surprised to see him spit out a diamond. "So, are you planning on staying here for the rest of the day?"

"Mmmm, I think so." She looked past him to the steadily falling rain outside the pane glass windows. Anything to avoid meeting his eye. "They're pretty busy here today and the new receptionist doesn't start until next week, so I'll probably stick around." She dared to meet his steady gaze. "You'll be okay thought, right?"

Jessica came out of the salon. "Hey, Kev!" She smiled cheerily. "How's my favorite grade school teacher doing?"

Kevin turned away from the desk. "Flattery. I like it," he bantered, his eyes softening from hard and steely, to warm and friendly.

April raised an eyebrow at the obvious transformation. *Maybe*, she mused, *I should consider being his friend, instead of his girlfriend.* A lot less pressure and a lot more easy-going interactions.

Jessica reached out to envelop Kevin in a hug and he returned her embrace with an affectionate squeeze. "So, tell me," she said when they'd separated. "Are you feeling ready yet for the back to school rush? Only a few weeks left before the rug rats return, empty vessels looking for a harbor."

Kevin laughed and leaned back comfortably on his elbows against the desktop. "As a matter of fact, I was just at the school today."

"Oh, right." Jessica snapped her fingers. "You weren't at the house."

"Pardon?"

Jessica's eyes went wide and April quickly twisted her chair around to face the computer. Her sister's face had taken on the expression she always affected when she was caught - blank and uncomprehending. It took all of April's self-control not to laugh out loud.

Kevin's eyebrows knitted together and he looked at Jessica, puzzled. "You knew I was at the school today?"

"Well, of course!" Jessica put her hands on her hips. "It's almost time for a new school year! Where else would you be?" She turned to April for back up. "Right, April Showers?"

"Oh, absolutely," April agreed, deftly avoiding meeting Jessica's eye straight on. God, her sister and her ability to put her foot in her mouth!

Kevin hesitated and glanced first at Jessica, then over to April. "So, now *I'm* the predicable one?" he asked.

April made a face and stuck out her tongue.

"Anyway, go on," Jessica prompted, attempting to move the conversation away from her blunder. "You were saying you were just there, at the school?"

Kevin took a deep breath and April let her shoulders relax. She knew that breath, it meant he had decided to drop it. Thank goodness, Jessica hadn't blown her hair disaster cover.

"Right." He nodded. "I was at the school because every year I try to get a jump on things in my classroom, before it all gets up and running. That way, I'm in the mode and ready to proceed with a whole new year of nine year olds."

"Brave man, I say." Jessica turned on the flattery and tucked a strand of hair behind her ear. She nodded at April. "You have a very brave man at your side, little sister. Willing to face year after year of grade school children, I shudder at the very thought."

April bit her lip to keep from laughing. Poor Jessica was making a valiant effort to regain control of her wayward mouth and Kevin was watching her with an amused expression on his face. Thankfully, the telephone rang and she was given the excuse to redirect her attention. She winked at Jessica and reached for the handset. "*A Cut Above*, how may I help you?"

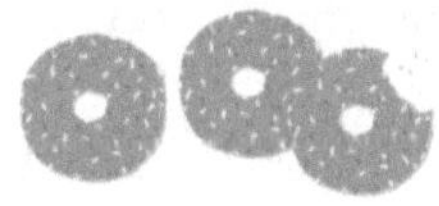

## 8:30 p.m.

"Thanks again," April said, as Jessica pulled her Jeep up to the curb in front of April's house. "For the hair, the dinner, the ride, everything." She reached across the dark interior of the vehicle to envelop her sister in a hug.

"Your driveway is empty," Jessica commented after they'd disentangled themselves.

April nodded and leaned back into the soft leather of the seat. "Kevin said he was going out to play darts with a friend. Gerritt somebody."

"Gerritt Bond? The new guy who's been running the antique shop for Max?"

"I guess so." April shrugged her shoulders and zipped up her hoodie. "Why? Do you know him?"

"He's been into the salon in the past couple of months. Seems nice, personable and definitely easy on the eyes."

"Wait. Was he the guy Denise and Heidi were eluding to this afternoon?"

"You heard them out front?"

"How could I not." April said, matter of fact, and then snickered. "Denise has a voice to envy a megaphone."

Jessica giggled. "God, those women. Anyway, yes, the same guy." She peered out through her windscreen. The street lamps illuminated the rain as it streamed in steady rivers across the glass. "It's seriously coming down out there. You'd better make a run for it, or you'll get soaked."

April pulled the thin hood on her sweater up over her head and reached into her pocket for her phone and house keys. "I wish I didn't have to cover my hair now that you've transformed it into something so fantastic."

At the end of the work day, after the doors to *A Cut Above* had been closed and securely locked, Jessica had addressed April's hair fiasco. The end result, achieved amidst much gossip, laughter and pizza, was a short, multi-colored cut, - no orange in sight. It made her look a lot like an elf.

Jessica yawned and fiddled with the vehicle's heat controls. "Well, I'll say one thing for sure, you gave me a challenge like I haven't had in a very long time."

"Glad to be of service."

"Yeah, that's what we'll call it."

"Okay, I'm going to brave the elements, I'll talk to you tomorrow." April stepped out of the Jeep and into the downpour. Jessica waved and pulled away from the curb, leaving April to tuck her chin into her neck and dodge puddles on the pathway to her house.

"Oh!" April yelped, when Peaches leaped from the darkness and cut swiftly across her path. She very nearly went face first into a large pool of water, and only managed to avoid it by stamping her foot down, sending cold water splashing up over her ankle.

"Peaches! For goodness sake!" April reprimanded the soggy canine smiling up at her. "What are you doing?"

The animal wiggled her entire body in glee when April spoke to her, making it very difficult to stay annoyed in the face of such irrepressible spirit.

"You are a goof-ball," April said, stuffing her hands into her pockets and hunching her shoulders forward as the rain drummed steadily down on them. "And, you're also soaking and should go home." She stepped around the dog, intend upon taking her own advice, when her neighbor's front porch light burst into life.

"I'm blind," April said, squinting into the glare. Her keys were still clenched in her fist, so she used her free hand to wipe away the rain water clouding her vision, just in time to see the Noble's front door nearly pulled from its hinges by a clearly distraught Carol.

"April!" Carol shrieked, with such volume April's ears range.

Great. Both blinded and deafened. What was next?

"Oh, thank goodness! You sweet, wonderful girl, you found her!"

"Pardon?" April replied, confused, as Carol stepped further out onto her covered porch, an enormous rose colored towel clutched in her hands. Was she offering it to her?

"I was worried sick about her!" Carol began to wring the towel as she told her tale. "I was on the verge of insisting Edward get up from that TV and you, April dear, you found my Poopsy."

Ah. Suddenly it all made sense. "No," April tried to explain, unsure if Carol could hear her over the pounding rain. "I didn't actually do anything—"

"Don't you dare start that!" Carol shook her index finger sternly at April. "No modesty, young lady. You've been caught, red handed, looking out for my little angel. You know what you did and *I* know what you did."

April raised an eyebrow. If Carol had uttered that statement under any other circumstances, it could have been interpreted as a threat. Maybe, April mused, it was. A threat that she was going to be embraced even more intently by her neighbor. Help.

I'll remember this," Carol added, before she turned around to lean through her open doorway, back into her house. "It's okay, Edward," Carol called. "April found her."

April sighed. She was soaked through, chilled to the bone and she had a sloppy mess of a shaggy dog at her feet. She opened her mouth to protest a second time and then closed it. It was too much to fight. Why bother.

Carol turned back and crouched down, fluffy towel held out in invitation. "Sweetums," she beckoned to Peaches. "You silly girl. You're soaked. Come to Mama and let's get you all dried off."

*Okay, well,* April thought. *That's my cue.* She turned back toward to her house, her shoulders hunched up around her ears, her footsteps making distinct squishing sounds with each step.

"That's a good idea, Dear," Carol called out. "You should get inside, you look like you're as soaked as

Peaches. I know you're young, but still, not a good idea to stay out in the rain for too long."

April reached her covered porch and glanced over to see Carol cuddling Peaches in the towel. The dog's furry face peaked out from the cottony folds and, if she didn't know better, April would have sworn the beast was smiling. She snorted derisively, then gratefully crossed the threshold into her warm dry house.

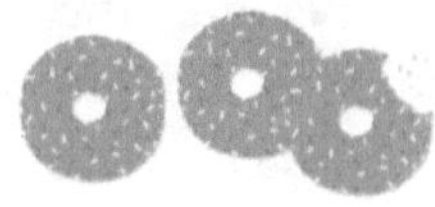

## 10:00 p.m.

"Stupid pillow," April muttered, while tentatively pressing down on the pad of her index finger with her thumb. She had been attempting to make progress on her latest craft venture - a pillow that was supposed to end up looking like a stuffed text book - and instead of going through the cloth with her needle, she had delivered a sharp stab to her thumb. It had made her so cross she'd abandoned her project in a heap and flounced into the kitchen to make a cup of tea.

Waiting for her kettle to boil, April leaned against the countertop and debated between continuing her project, or pushing it aside for one more evening and delving into her recently purchased novel. The novel idea was winning. Before she could come up with a valid counter argument in favor of her pillow, she was interrupted by the sound of the front door opening.

"Hello?" Kevin called out, just before a blast of cool, wet air rushed under the cafe-styled kitchen door. "April, you home?"

The kettle clicked off and April poured water over her tea bag. "In here," she called back, a surge of pleasure sweeping over her at the friendly tone of

Kevin's voice. Perhaps, for a moment or two, their crossroads might be ignored.

April added a dollop of honey to her chamomile tea and her eyebrows lifted in surprise when the sound of laughter echoed in the foyer. Curious. She picked up her mug, inhaled the sweet, citrus smell and crossed the kitchen to push the door open with her hip.

"Sorry, Kev," she began as she stepped into the short hallway just beyond the foyer. "I must have missed that. I couldn't hear what you were saying—"

"There she is," Kevin said, his voice laced with warmth and invitation.

April stopped in her orange, slipper clad tracks. "Uh," she faltered, when she saw Kevin wasn't alone. He was standing next to another man, someone she had never met, and they were removing their rain soaked jackets.

"Hey, you cut your hair." Kevin smiled tenderly and admired her messy locks. "Very cute. It looks great."

"Thanks," April squeaked, her eyes glued to the mystery man. She couldn't help herself, he was striking. Not necessary conventionally handsome - he was tall and lean, his nose a touch too long, his lips slightly too full - but, somehow, combined with his sharp cheekbones, mocha colored skin and electric blue eyes... *Whew.*

April had to avert her gaze to keep from blushing and the expression 'tongue tied' came to mind, something she had never understood until that moment. *Good God*, she thought, horrified at her reaction. *I'm acting like an unnerved teenager.*

"April," Kevin said, jarring her enough to remind her to clamp her slack jaw shut. "This is Gerritt." He turned to Gerritt. "Gerritt meet April, my girlfriend."

April took a bracing breath and looked up, gosh he was tall, to meet Gerritt's mesmerizing eyes. He smiled warmly at her and revealed straight white teeth that must have cost his parents a small fortune. "Nice to meet you."

April clutched so hard at the mug between her hands, she hoped it wouldn't shatter in her grip. *This* was the Gerritt that Kevin had told her about? *This* was the guy who had stepped in for a mutual friend to run the antique store in town? *This* was the guy those nosey women in the hair salon were talking about? And, for good measure, *this* was the guy that went to Jessica's salon and she'd casually said he was *easy on the eyes*?

"My sister cuts your hair!" April blurted, then blanched in horror. She could not believe she had said that out loud.

Gerritt's eyebrows knotted together in confusion and Kevin stepped in to clarify. "Jessica, from *A Cut Above,* is April's sister," he explained.

"Oh." Gerritt's face cleared as he rubbed a hand across his closely cropped curls. "Okay. Right." He observed her more intently and April had to steady herself not to flounder under his gaze. "I would never have guessed."

"That's usually what most people say," April mumbled and pulled her mug up to her face. "Jess looks more like our Dad, whereas I look more like our Mom."

Gerritt smiled politely, probably because he hadn't heard a word she had spoken into her cup, and April wished she could disappear. It was all too much. What was next, she wondered. Was she going to be struck by the desire to start sliding her foot back and forth across the wooden floor, only to look up demurely from beneath her eyelashes? Yuck.

To further add to her discomfort, April was uncomfortably aware she was wearing only a pair of baggy, grey sweatpants and a too-tight, pink tee shirt, sans bra. While she knew she no walking advertisement for babes with boobs, suddenly her unimpressive B cups felt like they were straining at the cotton fabric to be noticed.

April hunched her shoulders and snuck a quick look at Kevin. He seemed oblivious to her internal turmoil. She wondered if she should be relieved by his lack of awareness, or insulted. Probably neither. She just plain needed to get a grip.

"Gerritt's had a bit of bad luck," Kevin informed her, before shaking his head and sharing a wry grin with his friend.

"To put it mildly," Gerritt added.

A rumble of thunder shook the house, interrupting them, and Kevin glanced toward the ceiling. "Come on." He motioned to Gerritt to follow. "Let's go inside and get comfortable." He led the way into the living room and April watched them go. Kevin had only addressed Gerritt, so maybe she could sneak into the kitchen when they weren't looking...

"You coming, Hon?" Kevin asked her.

"Oh, sure!" April bleated in surprise, then attempted a breezy laugh. When she heard herself, she cringed. Her chuckle sounded more along the lines of maniacal, than breezy, and she was certain she was giving the impression of being a full-on ditz.

She walked into the living room, noticed the two men had settled themselves into the leather couch and club chair, respectively, and made a beeline for the end of the sofa, opposite Kevin.

"Sorry, about all this," she offered as she placed her cup on the coffee table and began to gather up the jumble of fabric and stuffing she'd left strewn across the middle couch cushions. "I was having some trouble, so—"

"No, no," Kevin assured her, vehemently, while she dumped her materials haphazardly on a side table. "It's fine."

April stole a glance at him, just in time to see his eyes dart toward the mound of materials she had stacked on the side table, then quickly snap away to somewhere else in the room. She perched on the arm of the couch and bit the inside of her cheek to keep from laughing out loud. Poor Kevin, he had regularly witnessed the profanity she was prone to uttering, not to mention the frustration she aired like dirty laundry, when she clawed her way through her various projects. His aversion to all things *crafty* was showing.

April often wondered what his thoughts were, when she was so clearly struggling to work through a project. Didn't it confuse him at all that she had no apparent aptitude for what she was doing? Or, for that matter, how had he refrained from pointing out the obvious - she could write her column without actually creating the project, saving them both a lot of cursing and grief? Maybe he thought was it was a part of the creative process?

If he would have had the gumption to ask, April would have told him the truth - she wasn't any sort of expert and it was only by doing the work that she felt confident enough to write about it. If she skipped the step of actually making the craft, she knew she would never come across as truthful, just a bunch of words on a page, and they - the Crafters - would never let her get away with it. They would out her in a minute, writing in droves to reveal her ignorance.

They were an interesting bunch, the Crafters. They would easily forgive any learning mishap, like gluing your fingers together with a hot glue gun - don't ask. But, dare to try and fudge your hands-on input and look out.

"So," April said, reaching out to retrieve her mug from the coffee table; then tucking herself into the corner of the couch, pulling her knees up to cover her not-so-well-hidden chest. "What's this bad luck about?"

"Right." Kevin perched his left ankle atop his right knee, ran his fingers through his damp hair and looked at Gerritt. "Do you want to tell it?"

*Score one for me,* April thought proudly as lightening flashed outside the living room windows and thunder rumbled in its wake. *Giving the impression I have an inkling of a brain.*

Gerritt cleared his throat and nodded at Kevin. "Sure," he said, turning toward April. She breathed deeply to keep from giggling. Oh, help.

"Kev and I were at my place, or rather Max's house."

Kevin chimed in. "You remember Max, right, Hon? My friend who owns the antique shop? I'm sure you've met him."

"Uh-huh," April agreed. "Once."

"Right." Kevin nodded. "I thought so. Anyway, Gerritt's running the shop for him, while he's on vacation, and staying at his house, as well."

April nodded and hoped when she looked at Gerritt she appeared interested in the story, as opposed to being ready to pounce. Bathed in the soft light of the imitation Tiffany lamp on the side table, she thought the man looked positively edible. Or, something like that.

"We'd stopped in at the house after playing darts at the pub," Gerritt continued. "And, it was only a few minutes we'd been there when a huge bolt of lightning sizzled really close to the skylight in the kitchen."

"Lit the whole room up like daylight!" Kevin enthused.

"Absolutely," Gerritt agreed. "And, right when we were commenting on how close it had been to the house, there was another one right behind it." Gerritt paused when the living room was suddenly illuminated and the house vibrated. "Exactly like that, actually."

April looked toward the windows and back again, only to find Gerritt watching her closely. Her breath caught in her throat.

"We're fine, now," Kevin said, interpreting April's silence as worry.

"Oh, sure," Gerritt said, while he locked eyes with April. "Where was I?"

"The second bolt of lightning," April offered, then dropped her gaze back down to her chamomile tea. For a blend that was supposed to be soothing, it wasn't doing its job very well.

"Right." Gerritt nodded. "Anyway, after that there was a movement outside the kitchen windows that caught my eye and almost before I could register it happening, the tree right next to the house—"

"A huge pine!" Kevin cut in. "Easily three times the height of the house."

"Huge," Gerritt agreed. "The tree started swaying - that's why it caught my eye - and I had a gut instinct it wasn't just the wind tipping it toward the house. There was something different, not quite right about the way it was moving—"

"It was amazing!" Kevin couldn't contain himself and was on the edge of his seat, his eyes wide. "In that split second, before the tree actually toppled forward to hit the house—"

"Oh my God!" April blurted, shocked. "It hit the house? Seriously?" She stared at Kevin, agog. "And here I was, thinking you'd lost track of time and forgot to call."

Kevin laughed and shook his head. "No, we were definitely busy, Gerritt mostly, being a ninja."

Gerritt burst out laughing and judging by the glint of mirth in Kevin's eye, April was certain he'd already said the same thing to Gerritt.

"He grabbed my arm," Kevin elaborated, clutching his left wrist with his right hand to demonstrate. "So fast I didn't even have time to react to what he was doing. Next thing I knew, he'd dragged us both down and under the kitchen table for cover."

"Wow." April looked at Gerritt with admiration.

"It was really something," Kevin enthused. "And, it's a damned good thing he did, because there was a second tree also hit by lightning—"

"What? Get out. Two trees?" April couldn't believe what she was hearing.

"No lies. There were two." Kevin shook his head as he exhaled. "The second one crashed into the living room windows, took them out completely and caved in a part of the wall and roof."

April placed her mug of cooling tea on the coffee table and looked at Kevin, amazed. "Two trees on the same house, one after the other, what are the odds?"

"I know, right?"

"My God, poor Max." April grimaced. "His house, I can't imagine. Have you spoken to him?"

Gerritt nodded. "Yeah, I got in touch with him after everything had settled down and we had an idea of the damage."

"How did he take it?" April asked.

"Pretty good, considering. He's a level headed guy, so after the first shock was over, he got down to practicalities and he's going to get things into place to fix the damage."

"And the sound," Kevin marveled, still caught up in the memory.

April snapped her head in his direction. She had been so focused upon what Gerritt was saying, she had momentarily forgotten Kevin was there. *Jeez, get a grip*, she inwardly chastised herself. *Quickly*.

"It had the energy of a freight train," Kevin added. "Busting through the house at speed."

"All of that and neither one of you got hurt?" April turned to Gerritt. "You're a hero."

"That's what I told him," Kevin said. Gerritt shook his head in protest and Kevin laughed. "Yes, you are," he insisted, blatantly proud of his friend. "Because of your instant, ninja-fast reaction time, we stayed clear of all of it."

"Too much." Gerritt rubbed his fingers across his chin, a wry grin on his face.

April watched him with unabashed appreciation. *Lordy*. She held back an obvious sigh. *What a smile. He probably gets his way, a lot, with that smile.*

"Anyway, all kidding aside, I'm just glad we're okay," Gerritt said, sincerely.

"Absolutely." Kevin stretched his arms above his head and yawned. "And, that's further reason why you're here with us."

"Because?" April leaned forward and waited for Kevin's reply.

"It's obvious, he needs a place to stay."

April nodded. "Of course." She had already assumed as much. A year and a half involvement with Kevin had given her a very secure understanding of his generous nature.

"I already told you," Gerritt cut in. "I'm fine grabbing a hotel room." He turned away from Kevin to face April and restate his case. "Really, I'm not lying. I'm just fine."

Kevin frowned. "No way. You basically saved my life, or at least kept me from a whole lot of possible injury. There's no way you're going to some faceless hotel room when we've got plenty of room here. End of discussion." He looked at April and raised an eyebrow.

"Kev's right." April picked up her cue. "You've had a rough night, you should stay with us. It's no trouble."

Kevin grinned. "You see? I told you she'd say so."

Gerritt sighed and leaned back in his chair. "All right, you win," he said, his lips curving into a small smile. "I'm too beat to argue."

"Good," Kevin said.

"Thank you." Gerritt nodded at Kevin, then looked across to the other end of the sofa at April, where he let his gaze linger. "I appreciate it."

April's breath caught in her throat and she wished she hadn't placed her mug on the table; it would have come in very handy to hide behind. It was time for her to make haste, she decided. She was obviously tired and not thinking straight. Good looks aside, she had no business making goo-goo eyes at a perfect stranger, right in front of her boyfriend.

"No trouble," she said, matter of fact, while getting up from the sofa. "But, listen, I'm beat, too, so if it's okay, Kev will show you the guest room."

"Of course," Gerritt said, taking the hint and looking away.

Kevin nodded. "Absolutely. I've got it covered. You go on up to bed, I'll be up in a bit."

April leaned across the sofa, dropped a small kiss on Kevin's cheek and walked swiftly out of the room. "Night," she threw over her shoulder, disappearing up the staircase to the safety of the second floor and her bedroom.

# CHAPTER 2 - Saturday

6:03 a.m.

April yawned, her mouth stretching into such an oversized oval her jaw cracked. Holy Dina, she was beat. She hadn't slept well at all and blamed it on having too much on her mind. Finally, when the sun began to cast its first rays through the gap in the bedroom blind, she'd given up and slipped out of the bedroom without disturbing Kevin.

April rested her elbows on the kitchen table, pulled her glasses from her face and dropped them beside her mug of slowly cooling Earl Grey tea. "Oy," she groaned as she rubbed her eyes. They felt gritty.

*I'll just lay my head down for a moment*, she thought, nudging aside her green mug to make space for her arms on the table top. *Just a moment*, she inwardly repeated, then sighed as she let her head drop into the soft, flannel folds of her pajamas.

"April?"

"Oh!" April jerked upright, so quickly she made herself dizzy and her left elbow sent her rectangular frames skittering away.

"Sorry!" Gerritt's hand shot out and he stopped her glasses at the table's edge, just a fraction of an inch before they went tumbling to the floor.

April, oblivious to the close save, rubbed her face and squinted at the clock on the kitchen wall. 6:30 a.m. Yikes, she'd drifted off there for a few minutes. She stretched her hand across the table for her glasses, then perched them on her nose.

"You're up early," she said, while attempting to swallow a yawn. "Unless, of course, that's your nature."

Gerritt didn't respond, instead he cocked his head to the left and studied her.

April looked up to meet his stare. God, even first thing in the morning the man looked inviting. Dressed in navy blue jogging shorts and a white tee shirt, that made his skin look so dark and silky she wanted to reach out and run her hand across his bare arm, April was almost put out by the unfairness of it.

"What?" she asked him, a touch forcefully, when he didn't turn his eyes away.

"Oh, sorry." He grinned, flashing her his impossibly straight white teeth. "I didn't realize you wore glasses."

April flushed and adjusted the magenta frames on the bridge of her nose. "I don't, usually," she told him. "Just first thing in the morning, or at the end of the day, when my eyes are done wearing contacts."

"They look really good on you, great color," he said, his blue eyes warm and appreciative. "A very different look, but really good."

April smiled and ducked her head. "Thank you," she muttered, then reached for her cup and pulled it toward her. "How did you sleep?"

"Very well, thanks."

"Good." April nodded. "Because, that furniture in the spare bedroom was mine, before I moved in here with Kevin. That bed used to be mine, I slept there and I just wanted to make sure you were comfortable because, um..." She swallowed and took a breath. God, she was rambling and had no idea where she was going with her chatter.

"It was fine," Gerritt said, kindly attempting to save her from herself. "Better than fine. Really."

"Are you going jogging?"

"Pardon?" Gerritt looked startled by the sudden change of subject.

April waved a hand up and down in his direction. "You look like you're ready to go jogging."

"Oh, right." Gerritt looked down at his clothes and laughed, a low intimate sound that made the hairs on the back of April's neck stand up. "No. This was the first thing I pulled out of my bag, so..."

"Where do the blue eyes come from?"

Gerritt's eyebrows shot upward on his forehead and April wished she could slither into her cup. What was it about the man that gave her such unstoppable verbal diarrhea?

"God, I'm sorry. That was too forward and too nosy," she hastily apologized. "You don't have to answer that, just ignore me."

"No, it's okay." Gerritt shook his head. "A legitimate question. We were talking about eyes, well eye *glasses* anyway." He smiled.

"You're generous," April stated, with a wry grin.

"The blue eyes come from my Mother's side," he explained, leaning back against the kitchen island. "She's Dutch. My father, on the other hand, is from

South Africa, so..." He raised his hands up and shrugged. "Here I am."

April nodded and took a swallow of her tea. Anything to keep her wayward mouth occupied.

"So, anyway," Gerritt hedged, covering his mouth as he yawned. "Would it be too much trouble if I made myself a cup of coffee?"

"Of course!" April exclaimed, then cringed at the volume of her voice. He really made her jumpy. She took a breath and tried again, softer. "What a hagberry I am, sitting here like a lump, practically interrogating you. I usually make it as soon as I get up. It's just this morning I was tired and distracted, so I made some tea. Easier to negotiate a tea bag--"

"No, that's not what I meant." Gerritt waved her words away, then paused and gave her a quizzical look. "Did you just say *hagberry*? As in the fruit?"

April lifted her eyebrows at Gerritt, surprised. "Yes and gotta say, I'm impressed. I've only met one other person who knew what it was and that's Kevin. Go figure, the teacher. Why on Earth do *you* know what it is?"

"I have a colleague in Russia who made reference to it once and I was curious, so I looked it up."

*A colleague in Russia,* April silently repeated to herself. A person didn't hear that every day. She didn't press him for more information, even though it was taking all of her self-control to keep from querying him as to what he did to warrant a Russian colleague. *Nobody likes a Nosey Parker,* she reminded herself.

"Anyway," Gerritt said, his voice becoming firm. "I don't expect you to run around serving me. Stay put and I'll find everything myself."

"Forget it." April stood up. "As I said, I'm not going to be a *hagberry.* One pot of coffee coming up." She smoothed her baggy, blue flannel pajamas and shuffled across the tile floor toward her coffee maker on the opposite counter top. "As long as you don't mind having coffee made by a Muppet," she added, offhandedly.

"A Muppet?" Gerritt repeated, quizzically.

April turned and pointed at her head. Her hair was standing out at every awkward angle possible. "In the dictionary, next to the word Muppet, there's a picture of my head."

Gerritt laughed. "No worries." He grinned. "I don't mind. I'm quite partial to Muppets, actually. Quite the fan. Always have been."

April swallowed nervously. She would have liked to believe he was hinting at something, but brushed it aside. It was an absurd notion, born solely from her pitiful ego and she needed to get a clue and focus.

"Okay then," she began as she grabbed for her can of coffee beans, eager for a distraction. "Whoops!" she barked, when her pajama pants conspired against her, tripping her up in their fraying hemline and making her careen into the countertop.

"Whoa!" Gerritt blurted, when the canister jerked violently from April's hand and the coffee beans launched themselves joyously out of the container, as though they had been waiting for that exact opportunity to do so.

April struggled to regain her footing and used her free hand to flail in a pathetic manner, striving to catch some of the beans in mid-flight before they hit the floor. She missed every single one.

Gerritt, moving with cat-like speed, also flew into action. He managed to catch some of beans before they hit the floor, as well as narrowly avoiding smacking his forehead into April's in the process.

"Whoa! Sorry." He jerked backward, avoiding a collision.

April froze.

Gerritt was perched close, very close, next to her on the floor and everything came to a sudden stop. She could smell him, a combination of fresh soap and a hint of licorice, and it made her want to press her nose to his skin and inhale. She lifted her eyes from the floor to meet his. "I seem to be making you say that a lot this morning."

"And yet," he said, not moving a muscle as he held her gaze. "I did take some English courses, once upon a time. Honest. I have a whole repertoire of words besides '*sorry*' just itching to be used."

"I'm sure you do." April giggled, then caught her breath when she registered the mischievous glint in Gerritt's eyes. "So, what's the deal?" she said, keeping her tone light and easy as she gestured to his hand. "Are you planning on eating those au naturel, or can I brew them for you?"

Before Gerritt could form a reply, Kevin pushed open the kitchen door, the telephone held to his ear. "Yeah, she should be right here," he said, then stopped short in the doorway. "What's going on?" he asked, his eyebrows raised as he looked from April to Gerritt, then at the coffee beans scattered across the floor.

"I spilled the beans, literally." April said, deadpan.

Gerritt burst out laughing at April's statement, a deep, contagious rumble from his chest, and she couldn't help but grin with pleasure.

"No, sorry, not you," Kevin spoke into the phone and stepped forward into the room. "Your sister."

Gerritt hadn't moved and was still dangerously close to April's face and lips, so she slowly stood up and brushed off her pajama bottoms, all the while avoiding eye contact with Kevin.

"That was Gerritt," Kevin said, into the receiver. "Hang on, I'll pass you over to April."

"Miraculously," April said, casually, as she reached for the telephone that Kevin held out to her. "I still seem to have some beans left in the canister. I'll sweep the rest of these off the floor first, then get a pot brewing in a minute."

"I've got it, Hon," Kevin offered, moving toward the broom closet.

Gerritt straightened upright and looked at the coffee beans resting in his palm. He held them out to April and let them drop, warm, from his hand to hers. "I'll help Kevin with the sweeping," he said, with a wink. "If you do the brewing."

"Deal." April grinned, then pressed the phone to her ear. "Hey," she said, giving her sister her attention as she brought a coffee bean to her nose and inhaled its earthy, nutty fragrance. "Yeah, same guy," she replied, leaning against the countertop. "Speaking of which, we need to talk—"

That was as far as April got. A scream, chilling enough to make the hairs on her arms stand upright, cut through the walls of the house and brought them all to a jarring halt.

April's eyes went wide. "What the HELL was that?" she exclaimed and pressed a hand to her chest. A coffee bean fell for a second time to the floor. Jessica, still on the line, was saying more or less the same thing.

"I have no idea," April spoke into the telephone. "It came from outside."

Kevin abandoned the broom and dustpan and was over to the window in a shot, trying to get a better look through the glass.

"Anything?" Gerritt asked as Kevin craned his neck back and forth.

"I should go," April said. "I'll call you back." Without waiting for Jessica's reply, she hung up the phone and dropped it, along with the rest of the coffee beans she was holding, onto the kitchen island.

"Forget sweeping, Kev," she said. "We'll get it after. We should go out and see what's going on." She thrust her feet into a pair of green flip-flops at the back door and grabbed a weather-worn, cardigan hanging from a hook on the wall.

"Come on," she insisted, and burst out the door.

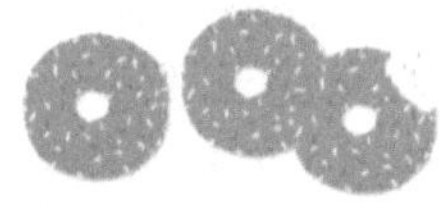

April tore down her cement steps, just in time to watch her neighbor, Carol, huffing and puffing her way across her backyard. She was headed in the opposite direction, toward her neighbor, Deborah, who was standing in her yard next to an open trash can.

April paused to push her arms into the sleeves of her sweater and Kevin and Gerritt came charging out the door behind her.

"Which way?" Kevin asked.

"There, I think." April pointed left toward Carol's middle-aged, shuffling backside, just as another set of neighbors, Matt and Cristina, approached from the opposite direction. Cristina held the couple's two year old daughter, Sofia, on her hip and the little girl waved wildly, her dark eyes bright and cheerful.

"Hey," Matt greeted them.

"Hello, Cutie." April grinned at Sophia and was rewarded with a sparkly smile.

"You hear the scream as well?" Cristina asked.

Kevin nodded and pointed across the yards. "Who didn't? I can't imagine anyone on the block missed it."

"Nearly made me jump out of my skin," April commented, while observing Matt covertly appraising Gerritt.

"Me, too," Cristina agreed, also checking Gerritt out from the corner of her eye.

April felt a wave of relief wash over her. She wasn't the only one who noticed the man's obvious charisma and Cristina was married, for goodness sake. Nothing to worry about after all. Just a normal reaction.

"Matt, Cristina," she offered, while enjoying the sweet scent of lilacs on the breeze and feeling decidedly more chipper. "Meet Gerritt."

"Oh, sorry," Kevin spoke up. "Where are my manners." He clapped a hand on Gerritt's shoulder and grinned. "Gerritt's staying with us for a good length of time, so get used to his face."

Gerritt laughed and shook first Matt's, then Cristina's hand, while April went still and blinked like a doe in headlights. A '*good length of time*'? Really? News to her.

"So, anyway," Kevin said, dropping his hand from Gerritt's shoulder and jerking his head in the opposite direction. "Carol headed over that way, toward Deborah, we may as well follow suit."

"Sounds like a plan," Matt agreed.

"That dog is everywhere," April mumbled under her breath as they began to move, en masse, towards Deborah's yard. Peaches was milling around the edges of Carol's flowerbeds and sniffing at the damp grass. "Maybe we should consider a fence for around our yard."

"Pardon?" Gerritt leaned into her.

April hadn't realized he was so close and the enticing scent of his cologne - or maybe it was just him? - threw her off and caused her to stumble. Kevin reached out a hand to steady her. "You okay?"

"Fine," she said, straightening her glasses on the bridge of her nose. "Just my flip-flops."

"It's okay, everyone," Carol stated, when they had assembled in Deborah's yard. She was patting Deborah's shoulder in a rhythmic manner, just as a person would do to comfort a fussy baby.

It didn't seem to be working, Deborah did not look comforted in the least. She stood rigidly beside Carol and, if anything, her face was like a mask of focused neutrality. *Curious*, April thought.

"Her hair doesn't move." Gerritt, still close, whispered in April's ear.

He was right. Despite the strong breeze blowing across them, Deborah's perfectly quaffed, brunette bob didn't have a strand out of place. April could only imagine how her own hair looked. She fleetingly wished she had thought to throw on a sweater with a hood and then sternly reminded herself she didn't care one iota about the opinions of the people in her neighborhood.

"Is she even alive?" Gerritt's voice was warm and hushed next to April's neck. Apparently, their kitchen conversation had moved their relationship forward into something resembling friendship.

April bit her bottom lip to keep from giggling. He had a point. Deborah was stick thin and it was uncomfortably noticeable in her black yoga pants and matching hoodie. *She makes me look curvy,* April thought. Which was saying something.

"Shhh," April hissed at Gerritt. He rewarded her attention with a sly grin.

"What?" Kevin turned to look at April and her face flushed like a child caught talking in class. Gerritt snickered beside her and it took all of her will power to keep herself from tattling on him to the teacher.

"Nothing," April muttered, before involuntarily straightening her spine when Deborah's unyielding voice sliced through the freshly washed morning air.

"No, Carol, you're wrong," Deborah stated, her words clipped. "Not one thing is okay here, at all."

"Not okay." Cristina's daughter mimicked Deborah, from behind April's shoulder. The edges of April's mouth curved up in amusement and she resisted the urge to turn around to see if Sophia had also adopted Deborah's rigid facial expression.

Carol dropped her patting hand from Deborah's shoulder and looked a little put out by her friend's tight lipped revelation.

April shifted her weight onto one hip, inadvertently moving her closer to Gerritt, and crossed her sweater clad arms. Gerritt placed a companionable arm - was it just companionable? - around her shoulders and April's breath left her lungs in a fast whoosh. What was going on?

"In fact," Deborah continued, narrowing her eyes and scanning the faces of her neighbors. "I don't know if anything is going to be okay - for any of us - for a good long while."

"Pardon?" Carol frowned.

"Oh, for goodness sake." Deborah frowned and pointed with short, stabbing jabs at her trash can. "Let's cut to the chase. There. Look in there."

"Wook in dare. Wook, wook, wook." Sofia imitated Deborah's command, her cartoon toned voice echoing around them. April pressed her fingers to her lips to avoid snickering.

Carol raised a skeptical eyebrow at Deborah and didn't move.

"*Look*," Deborah insisted, jerking her chin toward the can then cutting her eyes at Sophia. The little girl remained silent and Deborah pressed on. "I mean it."

Carol heaved a heavy sigh. "Fine," she said and took a small, tentative step forward. April felt the collective breath of her neighbors being held as one.

"Dear God!" Carol recoiled sharply from the trash can and shot a filthy look at Deborah. She reached down for Peaches, who was sniffing the ground around her ankles, and clasped the fluffy dog to her bosom. "That's repulsive. What *is* it?"

Edward, Carol's stocky husband, was standing just behind his wife. He placed a steadying hand on her shoulder. Sophia, spurred by the continuing theatrics, blurted out, "What is it?", with a note of alarm to match Carol's effusive outburst.

It was too much, April had to speak up. It was either that, or burst out laughing. "What's in there, Carol?"

Instead of Carol offering a reply, Deborah turned cold eyes toward April. The skeletal woman trailed her gaze from the top of April's unkempt head to the tips of her bare toes, before finally settling upon her face. April stiffened and reflexively clamped her mouth shut.

"If she knew, female companion of Kevin," Deborah said, her voice brittle and barely containing her annoyance. "Or, for that matter, if *I* knew, do you think I'd be out here yelling for all and sundry to hear?"

April inhaled sharply, as though she had been slapped. *Bitch.* She clenched her teeth together and glared at Deborah, the desire to slap back reining supreme. The woman was probably a Botox junkie. How else would a forty-something skeleton have a forehead as smooth as a baby's butt? April wanted to out her right then and there. Rudely. However, before she could find the words to effectively smack Deborah back, Kevin intervened.

"Okay, let's all just calm down a minute." He held his hands up, much as he did with his students and stared pointedly at Deborah. She raised her chin and looked away.

"Calm down," Sofia reiterated and April finally allowed herself to turn around and have a *wook*. She wasn't disappointed. The little girl was still perched on her mother's hip and was holding her hands out, palms down, patting the air in front of her. Cristina caught April's eye and grinned, while April, grateful for the distraction, giggled. Perhaps the child would make a good school teacher one day.

Gerritt tightened his grip on April's shoulder, his hand warm and solid and April looked up at him with appreciation. He winked. *Maybe*, April thought, revising her position. *I won't smack the Ice Queen, after all. Maybe I'll have to thank her.*

"Bob," Kevin addressed Deborah's husband, standing slightly behind his wife. "What's the score here?"

"Mama." Sofia's voice carried through the group of neighbors. "Thirsty."

Bob, a portly man, his brown hair cut short and neat, stepped forward. April hadn't even noticed him until that moment, he had been so silent. She observed him and thought, not for the first time, that he was the exact opposite of what she would have imagined in a husband for stick-thin Deborah. Not to mention, the man appeared to be rather easy going, personable and considerate - yet again, not what April would ever have imagined.

"Who's that guy?" Gerritt whispered in April's ear.

"Her husband," she replied, then almost laughed out loud at the look of surprise on Gerritt's face.

"No way, him? Really?"

"Yup."

"Wow."

"I know," April agreed.

Bob nodded at the collection of neighbors on his lawn and cleared his throat. "I wish I had something concrete to tell you, Kevin." He shrugged apologetically. "Deborah found something in our trash can this morning and it looks pretty vile. Truth be told, we're not even entirely sure what's in there—" Deborah coughed sharply and Bob rapidly wrapped up. "And, we don't want to disturb it, either."

"Not until the authorities show up," Deborah added, her arms laced tightly across her non-existent breasts.

"Authorities?" Gerritt straightened up and dropped his arm from April's shoulders.

Deborah cocked her head and fixed Gerritt with a haute stare. April repressed an impulse to step in front of him, her hands held out to deflect the dragon woman's evil glare.

"I'm *sorry*," Deborah said, in such a manner it was crystal clear she was anything *but*. "And, *you* are?"

Kevin, still in school teacher mode, raised his hand a second time. "Everyone, this is Gerritt. He's a friend and guest of both mine and April's." He looked pointedly at Deborah. "Not any sort of suspect for any sort of *authorities*."

Deborah gave a small, disdainful sniff. April looked at her boyfriend with respect. He definitely knew how to handle the woman. Bob, on the other hand...

April glanced over at Deborah's husband, awkwardly shuffling his feet in the grass as he stood next to her.

He made April want to do nothing less than implore him to call Kevin for lessons. It was painfully clear to her Bob had no idea how to handle his wicked witch of a wife.

"So, that being said," Kevin continued. "Are we going to talk of nonsense like authorities, or are we going to get a look at whatever it is in your trash can and see if we might be able to offer some information to help clear this up?"

Deborah tilted her sharp chin in the air and waved her boney hand. "Fine," she said, grudgingly. "Go ahead. Just don't change anything in case it's needed for evidence."

"Go," Sofia stated.

April could relate. She wanted to get lost.

Kevin took a deep breath and exhaled. The patient expression on his face - one he often used for his pupils - indicated to April that he was going to let Deborah's *evidence* comment slide. His trademark expression, '*choose your battles*', came to mind. He nodded confidently at the group and lead the procession moving toward the trash can.

April hung back, letting Kevin and Gerritt go ahead of her. Matt ran his fingers through his tousled, blonde hair and followed in their wake; Cristina held their daughter close and shook her head as she stood next to Carol; which left Edward and Thomas to bring up the rear.

"Where did *you* come from?" April frowned at Thomas. He must have snuck up on them, she hadn't seen him anywhere until that moment.

"Wag aboot, lass. Ye're neist." Thomas poked her in the arm, pushing her forward into the line.

"Say again?" April peered at him. Was he actually using Scottish slang to speak to her? He gave her another jab in the arm and she almost hauled off and smacked him. "I didn't want any part of this," she began and then turned to find herself right next to the open container. "Oh, good gravy!" she exclaimed and twisted away from the bin.

It wasn't the messy contents that set April off - which, upon reflection, looked as though some sort of animal had died inside the container. It was the piece of clothing - a red stained sweatshirt mixed into the jumble - that made her feel nauseous. Her stomach flipped so violently, it wouldn't have shocked her if she'd vomited right there on her neighbor's lawn.

Kevin rapidly stepped in beside her and wrapped his arm around her shoulders. "Are you okay? You're really pale."

What could she say? April thought. *No, in fact I'm not okay. That stained grey sweatshirt in there was mine, the very same one I was wearing when I'd messed up dying my hair red, which you don't even know about. And, now, somehow, it's been mixed up in that mess in Deborah's garbage can.* Not bloody likely.

"Do you need to sit down?"

April inhaled deeply, pulled her glasses from her face and rubbed her eyes. "No, I'm okay, really. I just wasn't expecting that. It startled me."

Gerritt came over, his face concerned. "Is she okay?" he asked Kevin.

Kevin nodded. "Just a bit taken off guard, I think."

"Um-hmm," April heard Deborah murmur. Her tone oozed so much smugness that April had a powerful desire to turn around and wallop the woman. Hard.

Gerritt coughed and ran a hand across his short curls. "I don't blame you, Showers. Whatever that is, it's not appealing."

April looked at him sharply. "What did you call me?"

His eyebrows shot up in surprise. "What? You mean, Showers?"

"Uh-huh." She pushed her glasses back onto her face.

"Oh." He grinned. "Sorry, I didn't mean anything by it. It just seemed fitting, you know? *April Showers* bring–
–"

"Oh, believe me, I know," April cut him off. "No worries, you just caught me off guard. That's my sister's favorite pet name for me."

"Can we continue this history lesson at home, please?" Kevin asked, a sharp edge in his voice as he began to practically frog marched April in the direction of their house.

"Sure." She wiggled her shoulder, taken aback by his sudden rigidity. "You okay?"

"Fine," he replied, loosening his grip, but still keeping them moving.

April let it drop. Kevin loathed melodrama and their morning had been thick with it. Looking at his grim expression, she was relieved she had kept her mouth shut about the stained sweatshirt. If he'd found out it belonged to her, who knew what sort of drama could have ensued.

She tucked her hands into her pockets and, flanked securely by the two men, silently counseled herself about the stained piece of clothing. Yes, the shock of possibly being connected to whatever was in Deborah and Bob's trash had momentarily made her loose her footing. However, with a bit of distance, she realized she'd probably over reacted. She was the only one who was privy to the information, t would blow over and no one would be the wiser, right?

April glanced over at Thomas' yard and noticed he was standing stock still in front of his own trash can. *What the heck is he up to?* she thought immediately. The last time she'd seen him that way was the day before, and he'd been very erratic. As she observed him, something didn't add up... what was it?

Then, it struck her.

Light bulb moment!

Thomas' trash can and lid didn't match! The can next to him was green, the lid in his hand brown, and April was certain that when he'd hurled the set into his workshop the day before, both pieces had been green.

She stared at him, willing him to look over and meet her eye. Her hope was that he would see her, *seeing him*, and give something away. He didn't. April sighed. She knew what she had to do. She squared her shoulders and, with much trepidation, whipped her head around toward Deborah and Bob's yard.

"Ah-ha!" She exclaimed. There, as plain as the nose on her own face, was Deborah's brown trash can and, laying adjacent to it on the lawn, Thomas' green lid. It was so obvious, and Deborah was so anal, April was surprised her neighbor hadn't made a Federal case out of it. She must really have been shaken up by the rodent in her trash.

"What? What's wrong?" Kevin asked. He and Gerritt had been deep in conversation and the two men looked around, alarmed.

"Oh, nothing, sorry," April apologized. She wasn't about to air her thoughts, especially not to Kevin. While she wanted nothing more than to rush across her yard and grab Thomas by the scruff and demand to know what he knew, she kept her calm and added, "Just thinking out loud." She turned back toward Thomas' yard for a second look, but the man had vanished. So, too, April noted, had his trash can and mismatched lid.

Very curious.

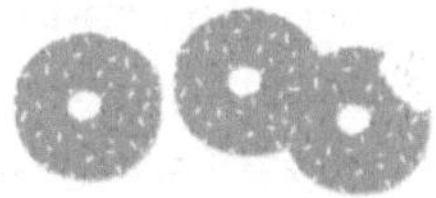

## 2:10 p.m.

"Check," April muttered under her breath, while giving a sharp tug on the heavy chain and lock she'd used to secure her mountain bike to the rack in front of Jessica's salon. It didn't budge. She was meeting Jessica in *The Bakery*, a pastry and coffee shop next door to *A Cut Above* and, since she didn't have a car, her only option was to arrive by bicycle.

April removed her front tire with a flick of her fingers, tucked it under her arm and hiked her purple backpack across one shoulder. *And, away we go,* she thought, striding purposefully across the sidewalk to the entrance of *The Bakery.*

The heady smells of fresh coffee and sugar enveloped her as she pushed open the door to the shop and April inhaled appreciatively. Jessica, sitting at a table at the back, waved to get her attention and April began to ease her way between the tables and chairs that littered the space; being careful not to accidentally strike anyone with her tire.

"You refuse to believe me," Jessica commented, when April arrived at the table. "Either that, or you don't listen."

April cut her eyes at her sister and leaned her wheel against the wall. "I've heard you," she said, while smoothing her tan, cargo shorts and dropping her backpack from her shoulder to one of the empty chairs adjacent to the table. "Trust me, every time you've spoken, I've heard you."

"Clearly not." Jessica crossed her legs beneath her calf length, blue cotton skirt and pointed at April's lone tire. "I've said it again and again. Not only do you not need to worry that someone is going to steal your bike - not that they could when you lock it up like Fort Knox - But, they certainly aren't going to make off with one lousy front tire."

April sighed while her sister laughed. Jessica was not a cyclist, so April forgave her her ignorance. "Call me overly cautious all you like," April said, straightening the hem on her green tee shirt. "But, I've known too many people who've had their bikes ripped off, just because they didn't take the extra precautions to secure them."

"So you say," Jessica said with a smirk and a nod, making her silver chandelier earrings sway. "But, need I remind you *again* we're in Boxwood Hills, not the inner city."

"I don't care," April stated, firmly. "It's a good habit and I'm not changing it."

"Fine." Jessica sighed and raised her hands in surrender.

"Hello, girls."

April looked up gratefully. Any interruption was welcome. "Hey, Phil." She smiled welcomingly at Jessica's business neighbor, the owner of *The Bakery.* "How're you doing? How's business?"

"Very well, thanks." Phil grinned at them, his brown eyes twinkling in his tanned face. "Business couldn't be better," he added, smoothing the apron covering his black golf shirt. "What can I get for you—" He broke off mid-sentence and his smile transformed into a look of concern when he noticed April's tire. "Oh, no. Did your bike break down?"

Jessica snorted under her breath and April shot her a filthy look before turning to Phil with a tight smile. "No," she told him. "My bike is out front. I just took the tire with me as an extra bit of security."

"Oh." Phil nodded slowly, his eyebrows knotted together in confusion as he shifted his weight back and forth in his brown, leather deck shoes. "Right. Of course..."

When Phil continued to nod, and the look of bewilderment did not transform into anything resembling understanding, April pressed on. "Could we get a couple of coffees, please? Black?"

"You bet!" Phil's face cleared and he smiled warmly. "Anything else?"

"I think that's it, for now. Thanks, Phil." Jessica grinned as he left their table.

"This is a really nice place, isn't it?" April looked around at the cafe and was pleased at what she saw. She loved the vibe of the shop, with it's pale green walls and dark wood wainscoting, the floors made of textured rock. Each dark round table, flanked by comfy chairs, displayed a pear shaped candle holder that cast a warm, yellow glow.

"Cozy. Homey," Jessica agreed, leaning back in her chair. "Just like Phil and his wife. In fact, when I first opened up next door, he and Annie were over in a shot with a platter of glazed donut holes, welcoming me and my staff to the area."

"Nice." April grinned, then gazed at the wall sculptures, created from unique combinations of wood, canvass and acrylics. "I really like the art work."

She found one piece particularly intriguing, made up of both sharp and smooth wooden shapes, lots of oil paint in primary colors and finished off with metal textiles - she had to stop herself from reaching out to touch it. "Do you know who the artist is?"

"Jade. Phil and Annie's daughter."

"Really?" April raised her eyebrows, impressed.

"She's wickedly talented. I'm thinking of commissioning her to create some originals for the salon."

Phil arrived at their table with coffee and two plates of cinnamon buns. "On the house, girls." He placed the treats on the table. "And, FYI, I couldn't help but overhear and I'm sure Jade would be thrilled to chat with you, Jessica."

Jessica grinned. "Does she have a card?"

"At the front."

"Okay, I'll take a few on our way out."

April took a sip of her coffee, then placed the cup back on the table. "Thanks, Phil." She smiled appreciatively, while pointing to the cinnamon buns.

"My pleasure." He waved over his shoulder as he went back to work.

"So, what's going on?" Jessica pointed at a beige baseball cap on April's head. "Things not working out with the hair? Is that why you called me in such a lather?"

"No. Definitely not. The hair is great. I just grabbed a hat because I didn't have a chance yet today to wash it and after the bike helmet..." April pulled a grim face and shook her head. "Not pretty."

"Ahh." Jessica nodded and lifted her mug from the table.

"I called about something else."

"Okay." Jessica waited.

"First, though, I have a question." April leaned forward.

Jessica raised an eyebrow while she sipped from her cup.

"Remember when we saw my neighbor the other day, the Scottish guy, hurling his trash can into his shop?"

Jessica swallowed her coffee. "Uh-huh."

"Did you happen to notice what color the can was?"

Jessica placed her mug on the table top and answered immediately. "Green."

"Both pieces?" April verified. "The can and the lid?"

"Yup. Why?"

"I knew it!" April slapped the table and nodded in a self-satisfied manner. "I knew I wasn't imagining they'd matched."

"Does this have any relevance to why you called? Because, I do have to get back to work, at one point."

"Yes, absolutely." April pulled a piece of her cinnamon bun from the doughy knot on her plate. "It's my neighbors."

"Again, with the neighbors? Seriously, April Showers, aren't you overdoing it, just a bit?"

April glanced surreptitiously at the other tables. No one was eavesdropping. "I only wish. You don't know the half of it. There are only a very select few in that cul-de-sac that appear normal."

"Okay, I'll bite," Jessica said. "What happened and which neighbor?"

April stuffed the gooey dough into her mouth. "There's been an incident," she said, blocking her mouth with her hand as she chewed.

"Incident?"

"Uh-huh." April swallowed. "With the neighbor that lives two doors down from us, on the other side of Carol."

"Which one is Carol, again?"

"The one with the dog."

"Right."

April wiped her sticky fingertips on a napkin and lifted her cup for a sip of coffee. "So, this morning," she said as she placed the cup back on the table. "The neighbor, Deborah, started screaming from her backyard."

"Was that when we were on the phone?"

"Yes, exactly. And, my God, the drama. All over something she found in her trash can."

Jessica furrowed her brow. "Say again?"

"And, it didn't stop there. I went over to her yard and, once she'd finally shut her yap, I had an actual *look* in her trash can—"

"Wait." Jessica held her hand up. "Back up. You *looked* in the woman's trash? Seriously?"

"Yup," April insisted. "We all did."

"*We*?" Jessica said, incredulous.

"Me and Kevin and Gerritt and some of the other neighbors." April sat back and watched her sister, amused by her disbelief.

"So, let me get this straight," Jessica said, blinking rapidly as she digested the information. "You all did *what*, exactly? Got in a line and had a look in the woman's trash can?"

Almost before April could fully complete her "Yup" a second time, Jessica blurted, "Get out!"

"I swear, I'm not lying."

Jessica pulled off a piece of her cinnamon bun and popped it into her mouth. "Okay," she said, between chews. "Admittedly, you're starting to convince me that your neighborhood is a little bizarre."

"Believe me, if it makes you feel any better, I tried to avoid the whole thing. But, then Thomas more or less shoved me into the line."

"God, I'm getting confused." Jessica swallowed and wrinkled her brow. "Thomas is the guy who was throwing his trash can around, right?"

"Yes," April affirmed. "And, even though I was angry that he pushed me into the line, it turned out to be a good thing because, when I looked into it, do you know what I saw?" April didn't wait for Jessica's reply. "One of *my* sweatshirts!"

"What?" Jessica's voice rose an octave.

"I know!"

"Come *on*. Are you absolutely sure it was yours? It didn't just look like yours?"

"Without a doubt. It was the one I used when I messed up my hair, so even the stain was still on it. And, even worse—"

"It gets worse?" Jessica laid a hand across her forehead. "How on Earth can it possibly get worse?"

"Like this," April said, matter-of-fact. "There was something gross mixed up in the shirt, like a dead squirrel body."

"Ewww!" Jessica dropped her hand onto the table, the charms on her bracelets aggressively smacking the wood, and scrunched up her nose. "Get out! That's disgusting."

"You're telling me," April stated bluntly. "How do you think I felt, actually seeing it?" She shuddered at the memory and dropped her voice to a near whisper. "I can't get it out of my head."

"My God, it's too much." Jessica leaned back into her chair.

"I know," April agreed. "It's totally playing with my head. The last thing I thought when I threw it out was that it would wind up as a part of some neighborhood craziness. Now I have to find out what's going on and whether or not I should be concerned that I'm going to get roped into something because of it."

"I don't follow."

"Oh, right, I forgot to add the lovely extra dash of crazy; Deborah was making noises about calling the cops about it."

Jessica gave her a skeptical look. "And say what, exactly? There's garbage in my trash can?"

"Maybe." April shrugged. "I don't know. She strikes me as the type who has experience at blowing things way out of proportion."

"I gotta tell you," Jessica said, leaning her elbows on the table. "This whole thing is making the story I was going to tell you seem positively dull, by comparison."

April cocked her head. "What story? You have a story?"

"Forget it." Jessica waved her hand dismissively, the silver rings on her fingers catching the light. "Just another date fiasco last Wednesday, but after your stuff, it's child's play."

"Another date? One after the other? Why didn't you mention it last night?"

Jessica gave April a stern look. "Hmm, let's see, probably because after I told you about first-date-last-date-guy, I wasn't sure I wanted to hear you say, *another date*, like you always do."

April had the good grace to look sheepish. "I don't mean anything by it," she said, shifting in her seat. "It's just that it sometimes seems there are a lot of dates." She shut her mouth when she saw the look of annoyance on Jessica's face.

"Listen, if I was willing to give up because of a bad date, I may as well go and join a convent." Jessica folded her arms across her chest. "I won't find someone to share my life with if I don't put in the work. You are so lucky, you don't even know—"

"Okay," April cut her off, she'd heard it before. "So I'll stop being judgmental and you tell me what happened, deal?"

Jessica sighed and tucked her hair back behind her ears. "Fine. Although, I have to admit it is getting a bit unsettling how many bad date stories I'm accumulating. Maybe I should write a book. How not to meet normal men. I seem to have a real knack for it."

April laughed, relieved she was able to make a joke about it. "How did you meet this one?"

"A friend of a client." Jessica ate another bite of her cinnamon bun. "He sounded really nice and since she knew him, I agreed to let him pick me up - at Lisa's house, of course."

April nodded, remembering Lisa from at a barbecue at Jessica's house.

"Everything seemed fine, he met Lisa, the usual." Jessica wiped her fingers on a paper napkin. "Then, before we started out, he told me he needed to stop at a friend's house."

"Oh," April commented. She had a bad feeling about the next bit to come.

"Yup, that's pretty much exactly what I thought," Jessica said.

"And?"

"And, when we arrived at the friend's place there were, of course, about a dozen of them there, drinking and hanging out. Pretty much your worst, or at least one of your worst, nightmares."

"*How* old was this guy?" April interrupted.

Jessica flushed slightly and coughed. "Um, he's a bit younger than us."

"A bit? How much is *a bit*?"

"Oh, like a couple of years..."

"So, we're talking what? Thirty?"

"Thirty-ish." Jessica busied herself with her napkin, smoothing it and folding it carefully in half.

April leaned forward and gave her sister a penetrating stare. "*Jess*," she said. "How *Thirty-ish*?"

"Ok, fine." Jessica huffed as she finally made eye contact with April. "He's twenty four. However—"

"Twenty four!" April shrieked.

"Shhh!" Jessica hissed, pressing her index finger to her lips. "In my defense, I didn't have that particular nugget of information when I agreed to the date."

"Still..." April's face scrunched up into a pained expression and she made an effort to lower her voice. "*Twenty four*. Jeez, didn't you notice he looked like he should be wearing diapers? Seriously, did he have a beard, or *something* that concealed the youth on his face?"

Jessica rolled her eyes. "Do you want me to finish this, or not?"

"I don't know," April shuddered. "Do I?"

Jessica laughed. "Yes, you goofball."

April took a bracing sip of her coffee and settled back into her chair. "Okay, I'm ready. Hit me. You were at the daycare, go."

"Ha-ha. Watch it," Jessica threatened. "Or, I'll hit you for real."

April held her hands up in surrender. "Fine, continue. You were at the friend's house and..."

"Before I could make heads or tails of all of the introductions, we were being invited to go out clubbing." Jessica paused, took a breath and added, "an *all-nighter*."

"Dear God, say it isn't so." April snickered, put her cup down and covered her mouth with her hand.

"Tell me about it." Jessica exhaled, shifted in her seat and recrossed her legs. "I haven't pulled an all-nighter in, I don't know, too many years to remember. Not to mention, I sure as heck had no desire to revisit my past with a bunch of strangers."

"So, you didn't go?"

"Hell, no." Jessica grimaced and smoothed her hair back from her face. "I made an excuse that I had to check in with Lisa about my dog."

"You don't have a dog."

"*He* didn't know that."

"Right you are." April tapped her temple, then pointed her index finger at Jessica. "Quick thinking, impressive."

"I'd say thanks, but..." Jessica shook her head and sighed. "Sadly, I've had to use the dog card a few more times than I'd like to admit."

A wave of pity for her sister rolled over April and she had to bite her lip to keep it from showing on her face. Maybe Jessica was right and she was lucky to have Kevin. Thankfully, the sound of a typewriter from her backpack saved her from having to come up with a response that sounded encouraging, instead of sympathetic, and April dived for her bag.

"My phone," she said, by way of explanation, averting her eyes and rummaging through the side pocket until she retrieved her iPhone.

"Who is it?" Jessica asked as April read the text on the screen.

"Kevin," April said, repressing the urge to apologize for having a normal boyfriend.

"Anything urgent?"

"No," April replied, feeling somewhat sheepish as she rapidly typed a response, then promptly tucked the phone back into her bag.

"What? What's wrong?" Jessica cocked her head. "You look weird. Is everything okay?"

"Yup," April said casually, attempting to sidestep her question. The last thing she wanted to reveal was that Kevin had been checking in, making sure she'd made it to *The Bakery* safely. It would have been like rubbing salt in an open wound. "Nothing important. Finish what you were saying."

"Oh, okay." Jessica nodded, then cleared her throat. "Where was I?"

"You fibbed about your imaginary dog."

"Right. Long story short, I made a big production that my dog wasn't well and I had to return to Lisa's, then deflected the guy's insistence that he would drive me back to her place and, finally, called a cab to get the hell out of there." Jessica snapped her fingers. "Oh, I almost forgot about the snake."

"Excuse me?" April's eyebrows shot up on her forehead. "Did you say a *snake*?"

"Just before I called Lisa for my escape route, my date's friend invited me to see his," Jessica lowered her voice, making it sound like a gravely surfer dude. "'*Seriously impressive snake*'."

"Oh-my-God." April's eyes widened considerably. "Was it a euphemism?"

"If only." Jessica snickered and dropped the inflection. "No, unfortunately he was talking about an actual reptile."

April slapped her hand back across her mouth to keep from laughing. "It just goes from bad to worse," she muttered through her fingers. "What did you do?"

"The only thing I could do," Jessica stated. "Peeked into the bedroom they kept the snake in, murmured some vaguely positive sounds and then bolted the hell out of there as fast as I could without tripping."

"Well," April said, inclining her head in a bow. "I concede defeat. You win. Your story trumps mine."

Jessica laughed. "Lucky me," she said and took a sip of her cooling coffee. "You didn't tell me, by the way, did you own up and tell your neighbors the sweatshirt was yours?"

"No way!" April said, emphatically. "There was a distinct mob mentality going on, who knows what they all might have done."

"You didn't say anything? At *all*?" Jessica said, taken aback. "Not even to Kevin?"

"No. He was really annoyed by the all of the drama and I wasn't going to add to it. Besides..." April hesitated.

"What?"

April searched for the words. "Well, Kevin and I..." She paused, especially hesitant after hearing her sister's date horror story. "Let's just say Kev and I, we're sort of going through a rough patch."

"Oh." Jessica cocked her head. "Meaning what exactly?"

April fiddled with the ends of her hair that stuck out from beneath her cap. She had hoped to avoid talking about it until she'd had a chance to think on things. She sighed and leaned her elbows on the table.

"Basically, we haven't been talking a lot and, when we do, it's more often than not to argue..." She wrinkled her nose as she tapered off.

"Why didn't you say something?" Jessica's face twisted with concern. "Is that why he sent you the text? Did you guys have a fight? How long has this been going on?"

"No, no fight," April assured her. "And, it hasn't been going on for long. Just the past couple of weeks.

Which is why I haven't said anything. I was hoping things would settle down."

"They haven't?"

"No, if anything, they've gotten worse." April shrugged. "He's been pushing me for more. More of my time and attention, more commitment than we already have—" April's phone trilled again and she winced. She pulled it out, read the text and stuffed it back into her backpack.

"How can you be more committed?" Jessica asked.

"Gee, I don't know," April said, her voice derisive. "Off the top of my head, I'd say one possibility would be *texting each other nonstop*."

"You're already living together," Jessica said, ignoring her sarcasm. She paused, then nodded as comprehension kicked in. "Oh, of course. He's pushing for marriage, yes?"

"Or, at least the first step, with an engagement."

"I'm sorry, but you'll have to educate me. The problem with that is *what*, exactly?"

Jessica sat back in her chair and folded her arms across her chest as she waited for April's reply. April watched as her sister's facial expression reshaped itself from concerned to irritated, and braced herself. She'd had the feeling Jessica's reaction was going to be sharp and it looked like she'd been right on the money in her hunch.

"I mean, come on, April. It's not like you're twenty years old and still figuring yourself out. You and Kev are both in your thirties and established, isn't marriage the next logical step? The goal of being together? Isn't that why you're with him in the first place?"

April shifted uncomfortably in her seat and avoided eye contact with Jessica. Her barrage of questions were legitimate and April had thought that was what she wanted, had even said that those very dreams and goals were the reason for moving from the city to Boxwood Hills. However, smack dab in the middle of it, suddenly she wasn't so sure.

"I thought so," April ventured, tearing at the edges on her napkin. "But, for the last while I've been feeling a bit claustrophobic and now, the idea of actually setting down permanent, no-going-back roots here in Boxwood Hills..."

"It would have to be here," Jessica interrupted, her words clipped. "You know that, right?"

April met her eye, nodded and bit her bottom lip to keep from reacting to her pushy tone.

"Because, Kevin's a teacher, April. He has a respected position that he's worked hard for at his school, not to mention his whole life and family are here."

"I *know* that." April clenched her teeth, her hands clutching the edge of the table. "Obviously, I do live with the man and have known him for a couple of years. I've met his Mother, his brother and sister..." April clamped her mouth shut, inhaled deeply through her nose and looked away. She didn't want to bicker. She'd had enough of that at home.

The front counter, with its large window displays of freshly baked pastries was busy, so April placed her attention there. Customers came and went and one woman, accompanied by a little girl of maybe three years old; all dark hair and shiny eyes as she pressed her nose excitedly against the display case, caught April's eye. She couldn't help but smile as she watched the child's naked delight at being offered a chocolate chip cookie by the shop girl behind the counter. Oh, to be so young and unencumbered.

"April," Jessica said, snapping her fingers and interrupting her sister's mental wandering. "Focus. You can't just brush this off and stick your head in the sand, you know. You're too old for this kind of thing—"

"Oh, for the love of God!" April exploded, not caring who heard her. "Why do you keep on saying that?"

"Because it's true!" Jessica glared at April, then quickly glanced around them to see if they were causing a scene. They weren't. *The Bakery* was busy and noisy enough; everyone around them stuck in their own conversations.

"You're not in your twenties anymore," Jessica said, insistently. "You need to grow up and start acting like a woman, instead of an overgrown school girl. I'm only saying what's true, Kevin clearly wants to move things forward and I, for one, think he deserves to be considered."

"I realize that, *Jessica*." April exhaled sharply, lowered her voice and glared back. "But, what would you have me do, tell Kevin I'm confused and get him all upset? Shouldn't I at least think about it first? Try and get my thoughts organized before I go shooting off my mouth?"

Jessica pursed her lips and tucked some wayward curls behind her ear. She looked at a loss for words.

"Besides," April added. "I just thought it was a phase and would pass. It wasn't until Gerritt showed up that I fully realized how seriously I felt about this. Talk about upsetting the apple cart."

Jessica frowned. "You're not making any sense."

"I'm talking about Gerritt Bond."

Jessica shrugged.

"The guy running the antique shop?"

"Yes, okay," Jessica said. "I know who he is, I've cut his hair. But, what about him? What does he have to do with this?"

"He's staying with us."

Jessica sighed. "Am I missing something here, some sort of code that only you know the words to? Are you purposely being vague?"

"*Jessica*," April looked directly into her sister's eyes and cocked her right eyebrow. "Have you looked at the guy? Because, I know that you have, you just said you've cut his hair. And, I also recall you telling me not so long ago that you thought he was *easy on the eyes*. A severe understatement, I might add. He's beyond gorgeous and you'd have to be dead without a pulse not to notice."

Jessica's expression hardened and she narrowed her eyes as comprehension dawned. "Oh-my-God." She sucked in her breath and exhaled harshly. "Don't you dare."

"What?" April straightened her spine, taken aback by Jessica's abrupt change of tone.

Jessica clenched her teeth and leaned across the table, her voice restrained. "This is *exactly* what I've been saying about your needing to grow up. So help me, April, don't you *dare* do what you always do, every damned time you get close to a guy. No way. Not to Kevin. Jesus, after the utter shit I tell you about the guys I meet..." Her nostrils flared. "I said he deserves consideration and I meant it."

April frowned. "Listen," she began, her voice nearly as tight as Jessica's. "I don't know *what* you're implying––"

"Oh, *please*." Jessica snorted and shot her a withering look. "You do, too." She sat back and crossed her arms across her chest. "God damn it, April, not again."

"*Again*? What again?"

Jessica paused one more time to cast her eyes at the neighboring tables. No one looked back. "Don't act like you don't know, April Pearl Patterson."

April clenched her jaw tight. All three of her names, those were fighting words.

"Every time you get close to a guy, something *happens*. It's like high school all over again. Either it's him, or you, or whatever. But, just when you start to really get into the groove of it, something *happens*. Then, you freeze up and the relationship hits the rails and goes off the tracks."

Jessica sat back and shook her head in disgust. "I cannot believe you would do this to a guy like Kevin. He's not like any of the other ones and take it from me, you'll be sorry if you make this mistake and can't backpedal from it."

April was about to defend herself, explain vehemently why Jessica was wrong when, outside the window striding purposefully along, was her neighbor, Thomas. "Oh my God!" she yelped. "There he is!"

Jessica's eyebrows shot up in alarm. "What? What's wrong?"

April jabbed her finger toward the window. "I have to catch him!" She jumped up out of her chair with a clatter and ran for the shop door. "I'll be right back!"

"April!" Jessica called out, too late. April was out the door, on a mission.

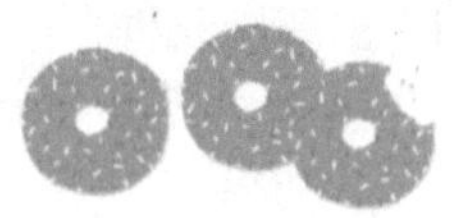

## 2:55 p.m.

"Hey!" April shouted as she half walked, half jogged along the sidewalk lining the front of the strip mall. "Hey, Thomas!"

Thomas stopped in his tracks and turned around, his face a picture of surprise and curiosity. April wondered how long it had been since anyone had called his name.

*Uh-oh*, she thought, when Thomas caught sight of her and his expression quickly reshaped from intrigued, to cornered animal.

"Don't even think about it," April yelled, when he darted his eyes back and forth, looking for an escape route. "I know where you live."

Her beige cap lifted from her head in a gust of wind and she dived to retrieve it from the sidewalk, barely missing scraping her knee. "I'm almost there," she told Thomas, closing the final few strides left between them.

Thomas pulled his cigarette from the corner of his mouth and exhaled a stream of smoke. "You dinna seem to have a muckle o' luck with yor hair these days, aye, lass?"

April plastered her hat back onto her head, straightened her tee shirt and fixed the man with a penetrating stare. "Okay, seriously, what the Hail Mary is it with the words?"

"Whot's that?" Thomas pushed his disheveled salt and pepper colored hair from his face and cocked his head.

"The *words*," April enunciated. "The whole 'just came from the old country' deal you're always selling. I know you're Scottish, but..." She cleared her throat and affected an over-the-top Scottish accent. "The juist aff the boat wirds, nay colloquialisms are a wee bit tiresome." She rolled her eyes and dropped the accent. "Come on."

Thomas' face twisted into a smirk and he took a long drag off of his cigarette while he studied April's face. He exhaled the stream of smoke through his nostrils and threw his head back, laughing.

April crossed her arms, taken aback. It wasn't the response she would have expected. She waited, one hip cocked to the side. Thomas finally stopped chuckling, ran his fingers through his windblown hair and looked at her with something akin to respect.

"Who'd ye knaw that was Scots, lass?" he asked, his cigarette bouncing up and down between his lips as he spoke.

"My great Uncle, on my Dad's side. He had a thick accent and kept his countryman way of speaking until the day he passed."

Thomas nodded and grasped his cigarette between the middle and forefinger of his left hand. "So, I'd best not be trying to gowk—"

April frowned at him and quickly clasped the brim of her cap between her fingers as another gust of wind tried to dislodge it from her head.

"Right. Let me rephrase that. I won't be fooling you with me slang, then."

"Nope," April agreed, releasing her hat and refolding her arms across her chest.

"Fair enough," he acknowledged, hooking his cigarette back into the corner of his mouth. "Lovely to 'ear a lass speaking with a homespun soond, though, so it is. Whot can I do you for?"

April turned her back against the wind and raised an eyebrow. "I think you know."

It was Thomas' turn to frown. "Whot's that?"

"I said," April started, before she was interrupted, loudly, by her sister.

"Jeez, April!" Jessica called out as she emerged from *The Bakery* and trotted along the sidewalk toward them, her blue skirt billowing around her. "You took off like a bat out of hell."

April turned to watch her approach.

"And this wind," Jessica grumbled, pushing her hair from her eyes as she came to a stop beside them. "Too much."

"You could have stayed inside." April pointed out.

Jessica didn't reply, instead she gave Thomas the once over. He was wearing faded brown cargo pants, a well-worn tee shirt that looked like it might have once been orange and his hair refused to lay flat, as though in tribute to Albert Einstein. Different from his usual cul-de-sac uniform, yet not.

Thomas took a step backward and April held up her hand. "Relax," she said. "This is my sister. She knows all about why I'm here."

Jessica reached into her skirt pocket and pulled out a crystal encrusted hair claw. "All about what?"

Thomas looked first at April, then shifted his gaze to Jessica and nodded. "Aye, I ken see the family resemblance."

"Really?" April brightened. She and Jessica were so rarely ever mistaken for sisters.

"Quite," he affirmed, his voice thick and smoky.

"Focus, April Showers," Jessica said, while disentangled her windblown hair from her earrings, then efficiently securing it back from her face with her clip. "Clearly, you chased this man down for a reason."

"Hey," April piped up. "My stuff, is it still in the cafe?"

"Relax," Jessica said. "I gave it to Phil to put behind his counter and told him you'd be back for it."

April exhaled in relief. "Good. Otherwise, someone might have—"

Jessica interrupted her by delivering a firm jab to her arm, with her index finger. "Blah, blah, get on with it."

"Ow! Jessica!" April scowled at her and rubbed her bicep. "I'm going to get a bruise from that. What's wrong with you?"

"What's wrong? Gee, let's see. We were having coffee and then, without so much as a backward glance, you took off like a fugitive." Jessica waved her hand in the direction of *The Bakery*. "And, I sure as heck didn't just run the length of this strip mall, in heels I might add, to be a part of a blustery outdoor tea party."

"Oh, boo-hoo, poor you," April said, matter of fact.

"Fine, big talker," Jessica shot back. "Let's see you try it. I'll even lend you my shoes."

"I could," April replied, her voice carrying inflections reminiscent of when she was a grade school child. "But, in case you didn't notice," she continued, while gesturing at Thomas. "I'm in the middle of something, not to mention the small detail that I'm not eight years old."

Jessica smirked and cocked her eyebrow. "Right."

"Anywaaay, as I was trying to say, before you interrupted," April said, returning her attention to her neighbor. "What was that all about this morning?"

Before Thomas could reply, Jessica butted in. "What was *what* all about?"

"God!" April exploded, flapping her arms in the air in annoyance. She loved her sister, but sometimes her timing stunk. "You keep interrupting!"

Thomas took another tentative step backward. "Well..." He shrugged. "Seems you lasses 'ave something ta wirk oot, I'll juist leave you to it."

"Freeze." April pointed a threatening finger at him and Thomas did as he was told. "We're fine. Just wait a minute." She took a deep break and faced Jessica. "I'm asking him about that trash can fiasco this morning."

"The weird conga line?" Jessica asked.

"Yes."

"What about it?"

"Well, I'm thinking that *Mister* over here." She jerked her thumb at Thomas. "Must have had a hand, or maybe more, in it."

"Hey, now," Thomas blustered.

April pointed her index finger at him, again. "Don't even bother. I *saw* you, Thomas. You were standing in your backyard after all of that drama and you were holding a trash can lid that was not yours. It was Bob and Deborah's."

"Who, again?" Jessica queried.

"The dragon lady I told you about. The fussy one who made the huge kerfuffle about the mess in her trash."

"Aye." Thomas scowled and ran his fingers through his hair. "She's a piece o' wirk, that one. Dinna knaw whot the problem is thare, but I do-nae envy her husband one bit."

"No changing the subject," April insisted, then crossed her arms tightly across her chest when the wind blew across her with force. "What did you do and, more importantly, how did my sweatshirt get involved?"

"Sweatshirt?" Thomas echoed.

"Yes, the red stained one in Deborah and Bob's trash can."

"That jumper was yers?" Thomas asked, his eyes lit up with interest.

"Yes!" April stamped her foot. "That's the reason I'm bloody here in the first place!"

Thomas paused, rocked on his heels and puffed on his cigarette. Jessica coughed, not delicately, in his direction. He didn't so much as flinch. "I must tell ya, I did 'ave a passing thought aboot who's jumper that was before I used it."

"So it was you, then, who took it from my trash? I was right?"

"Aye." He nodded.

"So, does that mean you're going to clue me in as to what the heliotrope is going on?" April pushed. "Like, off the top of my head, why did you have the neighbor's trash can lid? Why was there something dead looking in Deborah's trash? How did it get there? And, most importantly, why the heck did you involve my sweatshirt in whatever weirdness you were cooking up?"

Thomas had reflexively taken a step back with each question April fired at him. She followed alongside him, and Jessica followed her, until they found themselves two shops further down the strip mall, in front of an athletic apparel shop, next to the hardware store.

"Whew, that's a lot of questions, lass," he offered. "What makes you think I know the answers to any of them?"

"Gee, I don't know," April said, sarcastically, and placed her hands on her hips. "Maybe because you're the only one who didn't seem all that surprised by the chaos this morning. And, you just admitted you took my sweatshirt!"

Thomas' eyes widened when both April and Jessica glared at him accusingly. "At least we're closer to where

I was headed," he said, in an attempt to diffuse the situation.

"I want answers, Thomas." April wouldn't be swayed and her voice became menacing. "Don't make me have to resort to hounding you nonstop until you decide to give up the information."

"Aye." Thomas finger-brushed his beard, a thoughtful expression decorating his face as he regarded her. "I reckon you'd do that."

Jessica snorted and April cut her eyes at her.

"The truth of the matter is," Thomas began. "When I was thare oot—"

"Excuse me?" Jessica interrupted. "When you were *what*?" Her eyebrows knotted together and she shook her head at April. "Did you understand that, or is it just me?"

"Stop it!" April demanded of Thomas, restraining herself from slapping him across the shoulder in her annoyance.

He held a hand up, pulled his cigarette from between his lips and nodded. "My apologies. Auld habits and all that."

"What's going on?" Jessica asked, turning her head back and forth between them.

"He's still falling back on his usual, keep-them-at-arm's-length, tactics," April explained.

"Say, again?" Jessica rubbed at her temples and her rings glinted in the sunlight. "Either it's my ears, or the wind, but now you're not making any sense."

April elaborated. "Thomas has a well-developed habit that keeps the neighbors in our cul-de-sac away. He lays on the Scottish slang, fast and furious, just like Uncle Stewart used to do when we were kids, remember?"

Jessica's face lit up and she laughed appreciatively. "Right. I'd forgotten all about that. God, that was funny."

April gave her attention back to Thomas. "Continue, please," she asked.

"Where was I?"

"At the beginning."

"Right." Thomas tucked his cigarette back between his lips, stuffed his hands into his pockets and rocked back and forth on his heels. "The whole thing started when I was ootside yesterday mornin' and I happened upon a dead rodent in my rubbish." He shook his head at the memory. "It startled me 'alf oot me wits, didn't it? So, I did the first thing I could think of."

"Dump the whole thing into your workshop?"

Thomas' eyebrows shot up in surprise and April could have slapped herself. Out of the corner of her eye she saw Jessica's incredulous face and made quick work of her explanation. "*Because*," she elucidated. "I thought I heard your workshop door slam quite loudly yesterday. Didn't you Jessica? When you were over?"

"Uh-huh." Jessica nodded, her face like a blank slate as she smoothed down her skirt. "Oh, look," she said, pointing to a candy wrapper on the ground. "Trash. How apropos." She picked up the wrapper and tossed it into a large, round, black metal garbage can on the curb.

"Well, you lasses are a couple of cracker jacks," Thomas said, his voice full of admiration. "That's exactly whot I did with it."

"*Amazing*," Jessica murmured, biting her lip to keep from snickering.

"Excuse me." A woman pushing a jogging stroller exited the shop door around which they had unintentionally congregated.

"Pardon." Thomas nodded politely and moved aside.

April waved at the toddler inside the stroller and also stepped out of the way, whereas Jessica's face lit up and she cooed at the child with unabashed longing.

"Jess," April said, pulling her sister by the arm when it was clear she was so enamored she wasn't going to get out of the way. "Sorry," April apologized to the woman as she maneuvered her stroller around them.

"God," Jessica gushed, her eyes shining as she watched them walk away and disappear into *The Bakery*. "Aren't little ones so cute you just want to squeeze them tight?"

April shrugged and Thomas continued telling his tale, not missing a beat. "Later that evenin'..."

"A simple *no* would suffice." Jessica frowned at him.

"Right." Thomas nodded briskly. "No, I don'na have the desire to squeeze anybody's children. Good Enough?"

"Fine." Jessica shrugged. "Can we continue this inside? This wind is killing me."

Thomas needed no further invitation. He took a last drag off his cigarette, dropped it to the pavement and ground it out with the toe of his boot. Before Jessica could comment, he looked at her and said, "It's biodegradable," then headed toward the hardware store. He reached for the door, swung it wide and gestured at them. "Ladies? After you."

Jessica pushed past April into the shop and April trailed behind her. "Okay," she said, then adjusted her cap on her head. "We're inside. Can we please get back to the story?"

Thomas raised a hand in greeting to an older man behind a cash desk in the corner. The man nodded back and Thomas began running his eyes over the shelves, scanning and searching for who knew what. "Right. Where were we?"

"You found a dead rodent in your trash and put the container in your workshop. Then what?"

"Simple," Thomas said, then turned away from her and walked purposefully toward one of the overflowing aisles. He seemed to know his way around the place, which didn't surprise April. He spent so much time in his workshop, it only stood to reason he had to get his wares from somewhere. She scurried after him to hear the rest. "I knew I had to get rid o' the rodent and I did, once the coast was clear,"

"Clear of what?" Jessica asked as she followed behind he and April, fingering switches and cables, funnels and paint brushes. The shop didn't seem to have much organization, as though things were just set out as they arrived in their inventory. It was all very haphazard and piecemeal, much like Thomas.

"The neighbors. They watch." He stopped to examine a hand held torch.

"Oh, boy," Jessica muttered, then picked up a yellow, flower shaped solar light from a loosely stacked pile on a wooden table.

"Uh-huh," April agreed, her expression smug as she folded her arms across her chest and shared a knowing look with Thomas. "I *told* you they do that."

Jessica raised an eyebrow. "I have nothing to say," she stated and set the solar light back on the pile. "Whoops!" she exclaimed as the unsteady mound shifted and solar lights began to tumble to the floor.

"Jess!" April reprimanded, while slapping her hands down on the lights and leaned her upper body across the heap in an attempt to stop it from unsettling completely.

"Sorry!" Jessica insisted, also leaning into the mound. "I didn't realize they were so unsteady."

Thomas kept on walking and browsing, paying them no mind.

"Thanks for helping," April commented, dryly, over her shoulder. Still nothing. "Thomas!" she barked, annoyed at his blatant lack of attention. He turned around and waved his hand dismissively. "Don't worry aboot it, just pile them up best you can and leave it."

April raised an eyebrow and exchanged a look with Jessica. "I say we do as he says," Jessica offered. "This is his world and we're just visitors."

April shrugged, slowly straightened upright and caught any strays threatening to follow the others off the table. "Ridiculous," she muttered under her breath, while bending to retrieve lights that had made it to the floor, then helping Jessica shift the pile so they no longer continued to fall like grains of sand in an hour glass. "Okay." She breathed a sigh of relief. "I think that's got it. Where did Thomas go?"

Jessica jerked her thumb in the direction of the neighboring aisle. "That way," she said.

"This is getting tedious," April stated, bluntly, when they'd caught up to him. "Can we please get this whole story finished? I have stuff to do and need to get back to my day."

"And, me back to work," Jessica added, then reached out to pick up a child's wooden alphabet puzzle.

"Sure, sure." Thomas nodded, before he started pulling vinyl coated, wire rope cable from a large spool and began measuring lengths. "Where were we?"

April clenched her teeth. If he asked that once more... She took a breath and released it. "You were getting rid of the rodent, making sure there were no watching neighbors *and*...?"

"Right. So, I did the easiest thing I could think of. I waited 'til after dark, wrapped up the carcass—"

"In my sweatshirt," April cut in, reproachfully.

"Here's a question," Jessica piped up, placing the alphabet puzzle back on the shelf and slapping her hands together to get rid of dust. "How did you get a hold of her sweatshirt, in the first place?"

"From her rubbish container."

"Ewww!" Jessica exclaimed and stepped back from him as though he was contaminated.

Thomas frowned at her. "Now, dinna go gettin' any strange ideas about me and diggin' through rubbish containers." He finished measuring his length of rope cable and pulled a pair of wire cutters from the depths of his cargo pants pocket.

"Still," Jessica insisted. "Poking into someone else's trash—"

"Which I dinna normally do," he reiterated, firmly, then waved his hand at them, shooing them away. "Back up a few paces there."

They simultaneously stepped back and April watched, slightly agog, as he efficiently snipped the wire rope with his cutters. What kind of person walked around with wire cutters in his pocket? She wasn't sure she wanted the answer.

"Okay, drop it, Jessica," April demanded. "Obviously he had to have taken it from my trash can. That's where I left it and it didn't magically throw itself out onto the lawn."

"Fine." Jessica shrugged.

"Besides, I have to get back home and this story is threatening to take a week to tell," April told her, while sliding the brim of her cap back and forth across her scalp to scratch her head beneath. "Please, just let the man finish."

Thomas had gone back to ignoring them and had wandered away, again, down the aisle. April pushed past Jessica and beetled after him. "So," she said, when she caught up to him. "You wrapped it in my sweatshirt and, then?"

"I cast the whole mess into Deborah and Bob's rubbish bin," he said, over his shoulder, as he stopped in front of large plastic container filled to bursting with household nick-knacks.

"But, why! Why would you do any of that at all?" April blurted and hung her head. Another customer, a man, pushed open the door to the store, causing the bell above the entrance to jangle. If she had cared at all about anyone overhearing their conversation, April was long past it. She practically whined at Thomas as she asked, "Why on Earth didn't you just do as a normal person would and leave it alone to go out with the rest of your trash on pickup day?"

Jessica's head was going back and forth, again, as though she was watching a tennis match. She took a deep breath and plowed into the middle of the conversation. "She has a valid point." She cocked her head at Thomas. "What in the hell possessed you to go to all of that trouble?"

Thomas sighed and smoothed his hair back from his face. "Listen." He turned to April. "You're new to the neighborhood, agreed?"

"Yes."

"Right. So then, I'm willin' to bet ye'v already taken notice of the fact that our neighbors aren't all on the mark, yeah?" He shook his head. "Someone more guidwillt—"

"Eh-hem!" April cleared her throat sharply and frowned at his backslide into slang.

"Someone with more *goodwill* in their nature," he clarified, heeding her scowl. "Might call them 'unique'.

"Ha!" April barked. "That's a good word, unique."

Thomas rubbed at his beard. "So, I'm spot on, then. Ye'v noticed."

"And then some."

Jessica shifted her weight from one foot to the other. "But, their gardens are nice."

Thomas paused. "Whot?"

"Your neighbor's gardens," Jessica repeated, picking a lemon zester with a black handle out of a bin. "They really do a nice job on them, is all I'm saying."

April cocked an eyebrow at her sister. "Point?"

"Oh," Jessica held the zester up in front of her like a sword. "Nothing really. Just had the thought."

"Aye," Thomas agreed as he reached into his pocket and pulled out a cigarette package. "They do take an inordinate amount of pride in their greenery."

"Okay," April said. "That fun fact aside, what were you saying about our unique neighbors?"

"Deborah," he continued. "Or, *the dragon lady*, as you've so aptly coined her, has been out for me bollocks for a good long while."

Jessica looked like she wanted to counter him, but stayed silent and stuck to rolling her eyes.

"Be skeptical all you want, lass," he told her, then reached back into his pocket and fished out a lighter. "As crazed as it may sound, it's still a fact."

"It doesn't sound crazy to me at all," April threw in. "She's scary."

"What does any of that have to do with the trash cans?" Jessica asked, dropping the zester back into the slew of household gadgets.

"It had ta go. That mess couldna' been anywhere near my rubbish," Thomas stated. "It would 'ave been exactly the sorta thing that daft woman could 'ave used to set me up for all sorts o' trouble." He pulled the last cigarette from the package in his hand. "There was no way I needed all of that headache."

"She didn't know it even existed until you dropped it into her life," April pointed out.

Thomas nodded, lit his cigarette, inhaled deeply and exhaled with a flourish. "A valid point, lass. However, as I keep saying, this town isn't half that large. Someone would have noticed it, to be sure, probably those trash guys. They love to talk long and loud about what people throw out."

"Oh, please," April said, skeptically.

"No." Jessica defended Thomas. "He's right, it's true. It totally blew me away to have the women in the salon talking about the trash tales. It's still weird."

Thomas pointed at Jessica. "You see? Your sister knows. And, let me tell you, there's nothing that woman down the street likes more, than to stick her nose in other people's business. Especially mine. I, on the other hand, keep to meself, keep out the way. The last thing I was aboot to do was set meself up for a heap o' trouble, all because of a dead critter."

But, why her trash of all people?" April asked. "If everything you're saying is true, why her container?"

Thomas tucked his empty cigarette package and lighter back into his pocket. "I was of the mind to keep it with her. Let her deal with it, no one else. That way, she'd have no gossip on anyone else, would she?"

"Yeah, but..." April started to point out the obvious.

"Aye," Thomas agreed, before she'd even had a chance to finish her thought. "I'll grant you, it did'na work out the way I'd planned. She made a bigger fuss than I might have imagined."

"Okay, well, now that I know how my sweatshirt got moved out of my trash, there's just one more thing I need to know. Does anyone *else* know?"

Thomas shrugged and puffed on his cigarette. "I can'na say for sure, lass. I highly doubt it. I moved the trash after dark."

Jessica waved a hand in front of her face to dispel the smoke wrapping itself lazily around their heads. "Can I pose an obvious question before we wrap this up? One that doesn't involve asking you if you're actually *allowed* to smoke in here."

Thomas let smoke trail in wisps from his nostrils and nodded. "Go on."

"Where did the dead squirrel come from?"

He raised his hands in a "search me" gesture. "That, I don'na know. One day it wasn't there and the next, it was. How it got there in the first place is an utter mystery to me."

"Well, all I can say to any of this is, I think you both need to come clean. Get this all out in the open and move on."

Thomas and April looked at her as though she'd gone off the deep end.

"No way," April said bluntly.

"I second that." Thomas chuckled, making his cigarette dance up and down between his lips.

"What's so funny?" Jessica asked.

"You, lass. You haven't a clue what you're on aboot."

Jessica looked insulted. "Well," she began.

"It's been a right treat, gels." He cut her off. "However, if that's all you needed me for, I've got more items to find."

Before either April or Jessica could utter a response, Thomas saluted them with his cigarette, turned and sauntered away down the aisle, leaving them blinking and staring at each other in surprise.

April watched him disappear around the far corner and sighed. She had her answer as to how her sweatshirt had become a part of the equation, but was still uneasy about the possibility of being implicated in something to which she had no connection.

Maybe Deborah was right and the dead squirrel was a part of something more sinister. Maybe they'd need to start watching the neighborhood for suspicious activity. Or not. Either way, it gave her the willies to think her sweatshirt, no matter how indirectly, was a part of any of it.

"He's rather abrupt, wouldn't you say?" Jessica commented as they made their way back to the entrance of the hardware store.

April nodded, at a loss for words. She'd had another shudder-inducing thought. Only a day ago, she had more or less labeled Thomas as stranger than fiction. Then, via their conversation, she'd discovered that, while he definitely seemed to dance to the beat of his own drum, he wasn't nearly as odd as she had originally believed.

Had she been mistaken about the wild-haired Scotsman, or heaven forbid, was she able to relate to him because she was more like him than she had initially realized? Chilling stuff.

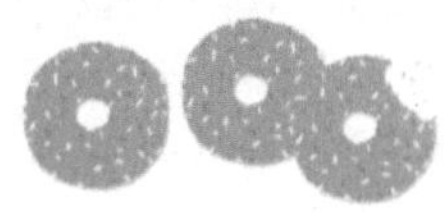

## 6:03 p.m.

April wiggled the toes of her foot perched atop an adjacent kitchen chair and admired the rich, purple polish glittering back at her. Very pretty. She leaned in to finish her last two toes, trying to give her full attention to the task, but Jessica's last words to her, before she'd disappeared into her salon, rang in her ears.

"*We still have to talk, April,*" she'd said, with corny, over-emphasis; as though April was some sort of moron and wouldn't understand she was making reference to their conversation about Kevin.

"Puh-lease." April snorted derisively and she closed the lid on her polish with a couple of firm twists. She should have known better than to open her yap in the first place. While she loved her sister, the woman could win an award for meddling.

She placed her foot back onto the kitchen floor, just as the front door opened, and April sent out a silent prayer that it was Kevin, as opposed to Gerritt, and he was alone.

"Hey," Kevin called out. "We're back."

Nope. Not alone. Damn it.

April admitted to herself that she was holding onto the desperate hope they were going to tell her Max's house was miraculously fine. That, in the light of day, it was discovered the house wasn't nearly as damaged as had been originally thought and, miracle of miracles, Gerritt would be able to move right back in without skipping a beat.

It would have been so much easier that way. No Gerritt to stir up treacherous hormones and she could deal with whatever was happening with Kevin, with a clear head.

"April? You home?"

Blast. Even if she wanted to hide, she wouldn't stand a chance. They'd be able to smell her out by the sharp fumes from her nail polish. "In here," she called and took a deep breath to ready herself for whatever was to come.

Kevin pushed open the kitchen door and entered the room, a large grin on his face. "Good news!"

Hope fluttered in April's chest. Good news? Perhaps her prayers had been heard. She smiled encouragingly.

"The house isn't nearly as bad off as we had thought it might be."

"Really? That's fantastic!" she blurted, enthusiastically.

"I know," Kevin agreed as he walked across the kitchen to the fridge, talking over his shoulder. "We met with the contractor this morning and it looks like the repairs won't take quite as much time as originally thought."

He pulled an apple from the fridge and carried it to the sink. April processed the information. "So," she asked, while he washed his fruit. "Does that mean Gerritt can go back to living there while the repairs are being done?"

"God, no!" Kevin replied, with a laugh. "Not even close," he added, turning off the tap.

April's face fell in dismay, just as Gerritt pushed open the kitchen door and walked into the room. She ducked her head and focused her gaze on her nail polish bottle, hoping he'd missed her expression.

"I was just telling April the good news," Kevin said, before taking a large bite out of his fruit. "Apple?" he asked, around his mouthful.

"Sure, thanks." Gerritt nodded. "In the fridge?"

"I've got it," Kevin offered, placing his apple on the counter and reaching into the fridge a second time.

April watched them, staying silent. After Kevin's 'not even close' comment, she was at a loss as to what to add to the conversation. She certainly didn't think her out and out dismay would liven the mood.

"So, anyway," Kevin continued as he washed another apple for Gerritt at the sink. "What they thought would take at least a month to repair, looks like it may only be a couple of weeks." He dried the apple on a towel and tossed it over to Gerritt.

April worked to keep her expression neutral as the two of them chomped loudly on their fruit. Her dismay was giving way to annoyance at the casual manner in which the information was being dispensed; allowing her no opportunity to process it without an audience in attendance.

A couple of weeks, while better than a month, was still a long time. Or, it could be if she was having to avoid her feelings the whole damned time. April stretched her neck to keep slowly growing tension from getting worse.

Kevin opened a cabinet door under the sink and tossed his apple core into the garbage can. He leaned up against the countertop and folded his arms across his broad chest. "We're going to go back and pack up some of Gerritt's stuff—"

"Listen, Kev," Gerritt interrupted. "I already told you, while I really appreciate both of your hospitality." He nodded at April to include her as he spoke. "I think it would be better if I just grabbed a hotel room for the next couple of weeks, until I can get back into the house."

Kevin straightened his back and the muscles in his folded arms flexed. Not a good sign. April's had no doubt her boyfriend was about to dig in his heels. She stretched her neck some more.

"Man, how many times do we have to go over this?" Kevin replied. "I told you, I'm still not buying it. It's completely ridiculous for you to spend money on a hotel, when we've got a room right here in our house that no one is using, anyway."

He turned to April for backup. "Help me out here, Hon. Tell the man."

April stopped stretching and swallowed, trying to find her voice.

Gerritt watched her face and took his opportunity. "Of course she's going to say it's fine, even if it's not. I'm right here."

Kevin frowned at April. "What's the problem? Why wouldn't it be okay?"

"Hey, hey, slow down. I didn't say it wasn't okay," she said, raising her hands up, palms forward. Suddenly she was defending herself? Even though she hadn't uttered an opinion?

"So, then it *is* okay, right?" Kevin persisted.

"Still here," Gerritt stated bluntly and folded his arms across his chest in much the same manner as Kevin.

"Yeah, but April's honest," Kevin insisted. "If she didn't think it was a good idea, she'd say so. Even if you were in the room." He looked at her. "Right?"

April, feeling cornered, kept her hands up. "I surrender. Just stop the interrogation. Whatever you guys want to do - Gerritt stay or not stay - is fine with me. I'm good either way."

Kevin shot Gerritt a triumphant look. "Told you. It's settled. You stay."

Gerritt sighed, unfolded his arms and stuffed his hands in the pockets of his jeans. “All right, fine, I guess I’m out numbered. But, I’ve got one condition.”

“Name it,” Kevin said.

“I’m not staying without paying my way. And, I like to cook, so I’d like to do my share of the meals as well.”

“Deal,” Kevin replied, then laughed. “Drives a hard bargain, doesn’t he?”

April flashed him a weak grin. She was speechless. Let the games begin.

# CHAPTER 3 - Sunday

8:04 a.m.

An insistent ringing battered at the edge of April's subconscious. She groaned, rolled over beneath her blue sheets and tried to wrap her pillow around her head to tune it out. It was no use. It wasn't stopping.

"Kev," she croaked, reaching out a hand to nudge him awake. Instead of his body, April found empty space. "What the heck *is* that?" she grumbled when the ringing finally stopped, started, then stopped again.

"April?" Kevin called out, his footsteps hitting the stairs, announcing his imminent arrival.

April pulled the pillow from her ears, heard muffled voices from downstairs and turned to squint at the clock on the mahogany bedside table. Eight in the morning on a Sunday? What on Earth was going on?

The bedroom door opened and Kevin poked his head inside. "Hon?" he asked. "You awake?"

April sat up and yawned. "Uh-huh. What's going on?"

"Put something on, the cops are downstairs."

"What?" April exclaimed, wide eyed. She threw back the sheets and quilt and scrambled from the bed. "What happened? Is it Jess?"

She started tugging agitatedly on the neck of her oversized blue tee shirt, trying to pull it over her head. Instead of freeing herself, she became tangled and frustrated. "Oh, God, is she okay?"

"No, no, stop." Kevin stepped into the room and grabbed her flailing arms, pulling her into a hug. "Sorry, I didn't deliver that well, at all. They didn't say exactly why they're here, just that they needed some questions answered. Nothing pertaining to anyone being hurt, or anything."

April stopped squirming, sighed and slumped against him. "Thank God."

"But, I do need to get Gerritt," he added. "If you're okay."

"Right," April said, pulling away from him and smoothing down her shirt. "You go."

He turned to leave and April called him back. "Wait. Were they ringing the doorbell a lot?"

"Uh-huh," Kevin paused in the doorway. "I didn't hear them at first, so they were really leaning on it."

April nodded. "I'll be right down."

Kevin closed the door and April dashed over to the dresser that matched their bedside tables. She grabbed her glasses, then pulled a pair of navy blue sweatpants and a lime green hoodie from a drawer - there was no way she was getting caught out again on the thin tee shirt embarrassment issue.

She tugged on the clothes and sprinted across the beige carpet into the on-suite to dash some water across her face; all the while, her mind racing. What could be so important, beside a tragedy, to bring the police to their door first thing on a Sunday morning?

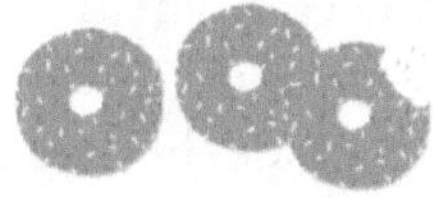

## 8:22 a.m.

"Thank you for giving us your time," the female officer said. She was a brunette, her hair pulled back into a tight ponytail beneath her black hat, and held herself confidently in the middle of their living room. "I'm Officer Moore and this is my partner, Officer Fitzpatrick."

The man standing next to her gave them a brisk nod. They both carried pens and notepads in hand and looked ready for business.

"No problem," Kevin said, sitting back comfortably in their multicolored armchair and gesturing to the sofa. "Please, have a seat."

Gerritt settled into an adjacent leather armchair and April flitted around the room, pulling back the window curtains, straightening objects on the bookshelves, giving the impression she had ants in her pants.

It wasn't April's fault she was so restless, she was afflicted with a not-so-positive childhood memory of the police; when she was only eleven years old. She had been at the mall with two of her best girlfriends and they had suggested stopping into a shop to look at costume jewelry. It had all been seemingly innocent, until April was rudely awakened to the fact that, to her friends, "looking" meant "taking". As in, choosing a bracelet or set of earrings they would like to *look at*, which translated to, *steal and bring home.*

April had been aghast! She had never so much as accidentally lifted a pencil from a classmate at school and was seriously out of her depth. Unsure as how to handle the turn of events, she'd decided her best option was to hightail it and ditch her *looking* friends. Unfortunately, she made her decision a moment too late. The two girls were caught out by mall police and April, by association, had been roped in with their crime. Guilty by association, the horror!

Her connection to the delinquent act hadn't lasted long; however and was quickly swept under the rug for two reasons: she'd weeped and wailed and insisted they search every one of her pockets for evidence and... her mother had shown up to take things in hand and put things right.

Unfortunately for April, the memory stuck. And, even though the experience was long past, she could still easily recall the thudding of her heart in her chest when those mall cops had given her their hard, judgmental stares.

"April?" Kevin broke into her thoughts and April started, realizing she had stopped dead in the middle of the room, lost in her memories. "You okay, Hon?"

"Oh!" she exclaimed and grinned widely. "Sorry, still half asleep I guess!" She pushed her glassed up on the bridge of her nose and forced herself to make eye contact with the officers. "Can I get you anything, a coffee, tea...?"

"Thank you, Ma'am , but no." The male officer... what was his name again? Fitzpatrick? shook his head.

"We don't want to take up any more of your time than necessary," officer Moore added.

April took her cue, they wanted to make it quick, and perched on the arm of Kevin's chair. All she had to do was focus and keep her breathing calm and even.

The last thing she needed was to hyperventilate and pass out. Awkward.

"So, just a few questions and then we'll be out of your hair," officer Moore informed them.

Kevin, Gerritt and April all nodded, mute bobble heads.

"As I told you at your door," she said, speaking to Kevin. "We had a call from one of your neighbors about a disturbance." She paused to open her notebook.

Her nerves forgotten, April sat up straighter and leaned forward to listen. The woman couldn't be serious, could she?

Officer Fitzpatrick picked up the thread. They were like a well-oiled machine. "Your neighbor gave us information," he said, also flipping open his notebook, then reading from whatever he had written on the page. "About something in her trash can that she believes may have resulted from foul play."

April's jaw dropped. No way. It had to be a joke, right?

"Oh," Kevin said and nodded. "Right. The trash can."

Officer Moore addressed Kevin. "You *know* about the trash can?"

"We all do," Gerritt said.

The officer shifted her attention to Gerritt and April could not believe her eyes. The no-nonsense, straight laced expression the woman was wearing, softened. "Please explain," she said, nearly simpering.

"Oh, well, I don't know if I should be the one..." Gerritt cleared his throat and shot a questioning look at Kevin and April.

"Go ahead," Kevin prompted. "It doesn't matter which one of us elaborates. We were all there."

"Definitely," April agreed, thoroughly amused by the way the tides were shifting.

Both officers leaned toward Gerritt, their pens poised. "Okay." Gerritt nodded. "Well, we were all in the kitchen—"

"We?" officer Moore interrupted.

"Me, Kevin and April."

"When was this exactly, Sir?" officer Fitzpatrick asked.

"Yesterday," Gerritt told him, then waited as the two of them scribbled down the information.

"In the morning," April added, then wanted to kick herself for pulling any of their attention her way. She clamped her lips together - the more she disappeared into the furniture, the better.

"Before we continue taking your information," officer Fitzpatrick commented, while studying April in such a focused manner she had to resist the urge to squirm under his steady gaze.

The words "Mall Cops!" were flying around inside her head and she clenched her teeth together so she wouldn't blab something she couldn't take back. She held herself stone still and silently pitied the people he interrogated. Finally, he glanced down at his notebook and April exhaled the breath she'd been unintentionally holding, in shaky relief.

"I don't believe we've clarified exactly who the home owner is here?" he stated.

"That would be me," Kevin said, raising his hand slightly, like one of his students. "I live here with April." He patted her thigh affectionately. "And, Gerritt is our guest."

"His house was hit by a tree," April blurted, then wanted to stomp on her own foot to tell herself to shut up. Kevin looked at her in surprise and she shrugged apologetically.

Officer Moore's eyebrows shot up on her forehead. "Pardon?"

"Oh, it's nothing." Gerritt grinned and the officer practically batted her eyelashes when he spoke. "The house I was staying at was damaged by a couple of trees that were struck by lightning—"

"Oh, right!" Officer Fitzpatrick snapped his book shut and nodded enthusiastically. "During that storm a couple of nights ago. I was one of the guys called out on that. I thought you looked familiar."

Fitzpatrick's partner cleared her throat and nudged him with her knee. "Right. Pardon me." He composed his features. "Off topic."

"So, you were saying, Gerritt," officer Moore encouraged.

"Right," Gerritt said. "We were all in the kitchen, making breakfast, and heard a scream from outside."

"A scream," officer Fitzpatrick reiterated, while rapidly flicking open his book and jotting something on the paper inside.

"It was their neighbor," Gerritt added, while pointing first at Kevin, then at April. "Deborah, I believe is her name?"

"Yes," Kevin confirmed, looking at April for back up. She did nothing more than offer a stiff nod. "Deborah McCaffey. She and her husband, Bob, live a couple of doors down."

The female officer refocused her attention upon Kevin. She looked reluctant to shift her gaze away from Gerritt and April had to resist the urge to roll her eyes. "So, when Mrs. McCaffey began screaming, did you leave the house to find out the reason for her distress?"

"Of course," Kevin said. "We all did. And, a number of our other neighbors did, as well."

April found herself growing impatient with the back and forth of it all. It was a straight forward story, not to mention a ludicrous one, and they were positively laboring over it. She took a deep breath, kept her knees together to stop them from clattering against each other and jumped in.

"We all went out," she said, firmly.

The officers looked up from their notebooks in tandem and April squared her shoulders to finish up quickly. She could do this. "We went over to where Deborah was in her yard with her trash can." She pointed at herself, Kevin and Gerritt. "Us three, and all of the neighbors close by who'd heard."

"And, Deborah's husband," Gerritt added, an amused smirk on his face as he recalled his incredulity over the surprise Bob McCaffey had been. "Don't forget her husband was there."

April cut her eyes at him and nodded. "Yes, Bob was there with her and that was when we all found out she'd screamed because she'd found some sort of dead rodent in her trash."

Officer Fitzpatrick glanced at his notes and nodded, as though in agreement with April's story. "Would you say," he asked, and looked up to meet her eye. "As her neighbors, this a fairly normal thing for Mrs. McCaffey to do?"

*Finally*, April thought. The truth could come out and she could get a bit of well-deserved revenge, ripping apart Deborah's character. "You mean make a mountain out of a molehill? Oh, yeah. Absolutely. I think so," April replied, resolutely, and turned to Kevin. "Wouldn't you say so, Kev? Deborah has always had a flair for the dramatic and you've noticed it more than a few times since you've lived here, right?"

"Yes," Kevin agreed, reluctantly. "I suppose that's true."

April knew he didn't like to cast disparaging remarks against anybody, but that was too darn bad. The woman had to be outed for what she was, an overbearing and nosey busy-body, or she could end up a danger to them all.

"How long have you resided at this residence?" officer Moore asked Kevin.

"Oh." He thought about it for a moment. "Well, it's got to be about ten years now."

The officers nodded and jotted down the information.

"So, that being said," officer Fitzpatrick surmised. "And, without putting words into your mouths, would you say the McCaffey woman is one who has shown herself to over react, even in situations that may not have called for such a reaction?"

*Come on, Kev,* April thought. *Back me up.*

"Yes," Kevin, ever truthful, nodded and April silently cheered. "I'd say that in the time I've lived here, Deborah has definitely made a lot of issues out of nothing. She comes across as a very tightly wound woman."

"I have a question," April ventured, hoping she would hear a positive reply. "Do you actually think there might be something more to this trash can thing?"

Officer Fitzpatrick cleared his throat. "While we cannot divulge case information, I think we do feel comfortable informing you that, thus far, we haven't yet garnered any information to cause neighborhood alarm."

The female officer nodded her agreement and April exhaled shakily. She wished she could share the news, right then, with Thomas. She felt certain he would be pleased to hear it, too.

"The only piece of possibly *evidence*, which we are as of yet reluctant to even claim as such," officer Moore elaborated. "Was some sort of garment of clothing."

April blanched and felt light headed. *Oh, Dear God,* she thought. *Don't say it.*

"Piece of clothing?" Kevin asked, while April did her best not to swoon.

"Yes, there was a piece of clothing in amidst the refuse," officer Fitzpatrick confirmed. "Mrs. McCaffey said it didn't belong to her and insisted we consider it. So, while we will take it in for further inspection, we highly doubt it will amount to anything more than what it is; a piece of discarded clothing."

Further inspection? April's stomach churned and she swallowed uncomfortably, worried she might vomit.

Officer Moore looked up from her notes and her eyebrows knotted together in concern when she saw April's face. "Are you okay? You look a bit off."

Kevin and Gerritt both turned their heads. "She's right, Hon," Kevin said, reaching out a hand to steady her on the arm of the chair. "You okay?"

"Oh, I'm fine." April tried to regulate her breathing, so it sounded more even and less ragged.

"I understand this sort of thing, in your own neighborhood, can be a shock," officer Fitzpatrick offered, kindly.

April nodded, appreciatively. "I think that's it," she managed to utter.

"That's true," Kevin agreed. "When we all saw the mess in the McCaffey's garbage, April was extremely unsettled then, too."

"A delicate stomach, I suppose." April smiled weakly and held onto the back of the chair for support.

"Right, then," officer Fitzpatrick stated and rose in unison with officer Moore. "We've got all we need. We won't take any more of your time."

"Thank you for being so cooperative," officer Moore said, while smiling up at Gerritt.

April gave a small, silent thanks that he was there to engage the woman's scrutiny. She didn't need any more inquiry than she'd already endured.

Kevin stood up to see them out and April stayed put. She listened closely for the sound of them being physically gone from the house and exhaled in relief when it was clear they were chatting with Kevin outside on the front porch. She slide down the arm of the chair that he'd vacated, suddenly spent. Maybe she would just curl up right there and go back to sleep.

"Are you okay?"

April jolted from her dreamy state. Gerritt was in the doorway, watching her intently. "Sure, fine," she said and pulled herself upright, so she didn't look so much like she was trying to hide.

His expression was quizzical as he sat down on the sofa. "You look a lot less green, at least."

April smiled and then, before she could over think it, blurted, "There is something."

Gerritt didn't say anything, just leaned forward and rested his elbows on his knees.

April shot a quick glance toward the foyer, making sure Kevin hadn't also snuck up without her notice. It was empty. "It's a long story, maybe best left for another time, but it has to do with that piece of clothing they found in the neighbor's trash."

"Yours?" He asked and April gaped at him. How did he know? How did he guess?

"Jeezus," she said, dumbfounded. "Was I that obvious?"

"No, no," he insisted. "Not at all. In fact, I just put it together, right now while you were talking."

"What does that mean, 'put it together'?"

"Well," he hedged and looked at bit uncomfortable.

"What?" April pressed, her voice rising in panic. "Oh God. Do you think someone else put it together as well?"

"No," Gerritt reiterated, his hands out in the classic 'calm down' gesture. "Don't worry about that."

"Then, what?"

"Well..." He paused and cleared his throat. His reluctance was making her jittery. "I just noticed, after watching you on Saturday when you looked in the trash can, that you were really out of sorts. And then, when I was watching you while the cops were talking about it you looked the same way and watching your reaction now—" He tapered off and looked at the rug, the walls, anywhere but at her.

April leaned back into her chair. It hadn't gotten past her that there had been a lot of watching going on. "Listen," she said, imploringly, changing direction. "The thing is, Kevin doesn't know about any of this."

Gerritt raised an eyebrow and looked puzzled by April's revelation. "Okay," he said, giving her his full attention.

"I'm well aware that sounds odd," she added. "But, I haven't said anything because he hates drama and, on top of that, we're kind of going through a strange patch. Basically, I want to keep it under wraps right now and I'd really appreciate it if you could do the same." She swallowed and watched his face, hoping he'd agree and leave it alone. "Okay?"

"Sure. Yeah, of course." He nodded and April grinned, relieved. "Actually," he said, smiling warmly. "I'm really flattered you'd tell me."

April paused and stared at him. That *was* saying something, wasn't it? That she would tell him her secret, but not Kevin? Before she could figure out a response, Kevin came strolling back into the living room and cut their conversation short.

"Okay," he said, running his fingers through his dark hair. "That's that, I think. Everything okay in here?"

"You bet," Gerritt responded casually, leaning back into the sofa.

"Yup," April agreed.

"You feeling okay, now?" Kevin asked, his eyes kind as he regarded her.

"I'm fine, much better," she assured him, covering her mouth with her hand as she yawned widely.

"Was it the mall cops flashback thing that set you so on edge?"

April bit her lip and looked sheepish. "Yeah. I don't know why that still happens."

"Mall cops?" Gerritt queried.

"She had an incident as a kid," Kevin shared with him, a grin on his face. "Involving mall cops. Nothing bad or anything—"

"No," April agreed. "They were just doing their job and I was a victim of bad timing."

"Anyway," Kevin finished. "Sometimes those memories rear their ugly heads when the police are around and make her all jumpy." He bent over and planted a kiss on the top of April's head.

Gerritt, still thinking about what April had told him about her sweatshirt, just nodded and said, "Ahh."

"I just hope I didn't chase them away before they got all of their questions answered," April commented, attempting to steer the conversation away from her nervous reaction.

Kevin sat down in the other arm chair. "Nah, I talked with them out on the porch and they seemed satisfied with what we told them. Basically, it comes down to the fact that Deborah is doing what she does, making an issue out of nothing. In fact," he confided, leaning forward. "They actually admitted this isn't the first time, by a long shot, that she's called them with some sort of complaint, or issue. She's actually getting a rep down at the station."

"Seriously?" April asked, amazed.

"Yup."

"What is wrong with that woman?" April shook her head.

"Who knows." He shrugged. "Attention, maybe? I think the whole thing will just blow over like the rest of the things we've never heard about."

Gerritt got up from the sofa. "Listen, now that that's done, I'm going to grab a shower, if that's okay?"

"Sure, go ahead," Kevin agreed and ran his fingers through his hair. "But, listen, I'm sorry about all of this. Some impression you must have of our neighborhood."

Gerritt started to laugh and both Kevin and April joined in. It was like the ending of a cheesy seventies sitcom.

"Truth be told," Gerritt said, once he'd caught his breath. "I'd have to say it's the most entertainment I've seen in a while. It's hard to believe this sort of stuff actually happens outside of fiction."

"You know," April cocked her head as a thought came to mind. "It occurs to me, if they came here, does that mean they're going to the other neighbor's houses, as well?"

Kevin yawned, then nodded. "Yup. They told me they'd just come from next door."

"Carol and Edward's?"

"Uh-huh. And, they were off to the other side of us."

"Thomas." April shared a knowing grin with Kevin.

Gerritt looked back and forth between them, confused. "What? What am I missing?"

"Thomas is what you'd call *eccentric*," Kevin said.

"To put it mildly," April chimed in.

"I'm sure he'll give them a run for their money when they ask him any questions." Kevin shook his head. "Don't envy them."

"That's if they can understand him with that thick Scottish accent." April snickered. "When he wants to be difficult, he lathers it on even thicker, making it almost impossible to understand what he's saying."

"Oh, I don't know," he said, skeptically.

"Maybe *you* don't," April stated, confidently. "But, believe me, I do."

Kevin didn't counter, leaving April to ponder another thought. Her sweatshirt. Thomas knew it was hers. The sudden, foreboding possibility that he might let it slip about where it came from made her pulse kick up a notch. Would he? He'd said he didn't need any trouble cast his way by Deborah, would he be willing to throw her under the bus to avoid suspicion?

"I'm going for a run," she declared. Things were getting way too complicated and she needed space to clear her head.

"That's fine," Kevin said, then turned to Gerritt. "We'll probably head over to your place to get some of your stuff, right?"

Gerritt nodded and April pulled herself out of the arm chair. She left the room to go and change clothes and didn't look back.

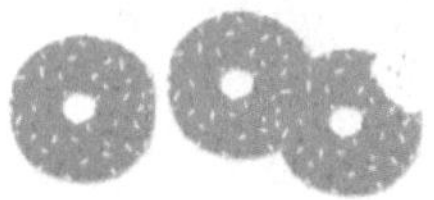

## 11:14 a.m.

April wheezed as she walked on jelly legs into her backyard. She had pushed herself throughout her entire run, hoping to rid herself of her jumble of thoughts. It had worked while she was running, but as she caught her breath and wiped her face with the hem of her sweat-soaked, blue tee shirt, she found herself returning to exactly where she'd left off - wondering what had happened with Thomas and the cops.

*Damn it*, she thought, irritatedly, as she pulled her earbuds from her ears and released the velcro fastener that strapped her iPhone case to her bicep. *Why did things have to get so complicated? Wasn't life supposed to get easier, the older you got?*

April slide the black phone case down her arm and placed it with her earbuds, next to her water bottle, then took a few long strides away from the cool shadow of the house; back into the hot sunshine in the yard. *Time to see if I'm having a lucky day,* she thought, while readjusting her beige baseball cap; then purposely making a show of stretching; in case any of her neighbors were feeling the need to be nosey.

With each dip, she sidled closer to the edge of her house, her goal being to peek around it and spy on the empty space. If she was having a lucky day, Thomas might venture into his side yard and then she could grab a seemingly innocent moment of his time...

"What are you doing?"

April nearly jumped out of her silver and blue running shoes. "Gee, whiz!" she exclaimed and whipped around to face the owner of the voice in her ear. "What are *you* doing, sneaking up on me?" She raised her palm and slapped Gerritt, hard, across the shoulder. "Trying to give me a heart attack?"

Gerritt, dressed in black jogging shorts and a green tank top that looked fantastic against his coffee colored skin, pulled back and glanced at the spot where April had slapped him. "Of course not."

"You could have fooled me." April frowned, her heart pounding erratically in her chest. "What are you doing out here, anyway?"

"I decided to take a run before your *boyfriend* and I go to Max's house. You made it sound like a good idea." His eyebrows knotted together and he looked puzzled. "You didn't leave the house that far ahead me, how did I miss you?"

"I don't go the street way." April ignored his *boyfriend* inflection and pointed to her left, away from the entrance to the cul-de-sac. "I take a path that goes around the back, so I can have some solitude before I hit the street for the last leg home."

She looked him over and noticed that he, unlike her, didn't seem nearly so sweaty and disheveled. "Are you sure you were jogging?" she asked, making a show of eyeballing his clothes and raising a skeptical eyebrow. "Or, maybe just doing a bit of speed walking?"

Gerritt grinned and his eyes flashed as he regarded her lean legs with blatant appreciation. "I usually run a lot longer than that, so..." He left his comment hanging and changed the subject. "You didn't answer my question."

April narrowed her eyes at him. *I could run circles around you,* she thought, before her phone jangled and interrupted her. She sighed, walked over to the back step, tugged her phone from its case and took a quick glance at the screen.

Yup, Kevin.

*Good God!* she inwardly raged. *I can't even take a simple run without him checking up on me.* Clenching her teeth, April typed a short, stabbing reply, "*Finishing up, home soon*", and suppressed the desire to slam the phone, touchdown style, back onto the step.

"Everything okay?" Gerritt asked, observing her swift change of mood.

"Fine," she replied sharply, before shoving the phone roughly back into its case and marching over to sit, with a firm thud, on the grass.

Gerritt raised an eyebrow, but said nothing.

"What question?" April said, looking up at him from beneath the rim of her hat.

"Pardon?" "You said I didn't answer your question, what question?"

"Oh, right." Gerritt grinned, amusement glimmering his eyes. "What was that you were doing, just before I startled you?"

"Oh, that? Just cooling down." She waved her hand vaguely in the direction of the yard. "I always stretch out here, more room than in the house."

"Really?" He remarked, no longer just looking amused, but sounding it as well. "Because, you didn't look like you were stretching. You looked more like you were nosing about."

"Nosing about? Did you just say 'nosing about'? Really?" April snickered. "And, besides, who do you think I would be *nosing about* for?"

"You tell me and then we'll both know." He sat down next to her on the grass, his face expectant.

April rolled her eyes and stood up. She wanted to slap his arm for a second time for being both charming, and too astute. Not that she was about to tell him that. It was bad enough she'd told him her secret about her sweater. He'd had enough insider information.

"Okay, this is getting a bit half-baked for me," she said, brushing stray bits of grass from the back of her shorts. "I'm going inside. You can stay out here and do ... whatever it is you're going to do, for as long as you'd like."

Gerritt smirked and April stopped in her tracks. "What? What's with the face?"

"Nothing." He leaned back on his elbows and stretched out his long, well-muscled legs. "You look cute when you've been caught."

"Caught?" she argued, taken aback. "Caught at *what*, exactly? Boy, for an antiques guy, you have a lot of theories. I'm not caught at anything."

Gerritt laughed at her dig, stood up and brushed away grass stuck to his forearms. "Okay." He shrugged, still smiling. "If you say so."

"I do say so," she began, then had her train of thought interrupted by Thomas, poking his head around the side of her house. "Oh!" she blurted in surprise and slapped a hand on her chest, over her heart.

"Something I can help you kids with?" Thomas said, eyebrows raised in curiosity.

Gerritt grinned. "You must be Thomas."

"Must I?" Thomas replied, then rubbed a hand across his wayward beard. "I don'na think we've met, lad."

"No, we haven't." Gerritt extended his hand. "I've just heard about you."

"Ah." Thomas grinned and wiggled his exaggerated eyebrows. "My reputation precedes me, aye?"

"Yeah, yeah," April cut them off. "Details. Anyway, Gerritt meet Thomas, our neighbor. Thomas meet Gerritt, our..." She paused to think and then smirked. "Boarder."

Gerritt straightened his shoulders, pointed his index finger at her and tried to be stern. "Hey, I don't think that *boarder* is exactly the term—"

"*Potato, po-tah-to,*" she interrupted, her tone lofty.

Gerritt laughed.

April ignored him and turned to look at Thomas. "I need to talk to you."

Thomas took a step backward and April had a flashback to their interaction at the strip mall. "Freeze, Scotsman." She narrowed her eyes at him. "Don't make me say it all over again."

"*It?*" Gerritt asked.

"I know where he lives."

Gerritt furrowed his brow, not following.

"Never mind," she replied. Telling him the backstory would just draw him further into things. Not a good idea. "Look, if you're going to stay, please just do me a favor and do so quietly."

Gerritt looked at Thomas. "Man, she can be a tough one, huh?"

Thomas grinned. "Aye. She's a city lass, no doubt aboot it. Strong mind of her own." He winked and stroked his beard. "Not that I disagree with it. Can be quite an attractive quality in a lass."

Gerritt nodded. "Oh, no doubt."

April listened to their banter and her ears perked up. Did Gerritt just agree he found her attractive? *Stop it. Focus*, she thought and gave her head a small shake.

"Okay, okay, ha, ha," she dead panned and took her legitimate opportunity to slap Gerritt's upper arm, again. "You're hilarious, the pair of you."

"Hey," he protested, raising his hands in the air.

"So," Thomas said to Gerritt, ignoring their carrying on. "You've been exercising, I see. Do you like it?"

"Exercising? Sure," he began.

"I used to do a bit o' runnin' meself—"

"Wait!" April stamped her foot. "Stop!" Then, like a doe in the headlights, she paused and glanced around, hoping her loud voice hadn't drawn the unwanted attention of the neighbors.

"Listen," she whispered, before moving a couple of paces over; back into the shadow of the house. Thomas and Gerritt silently watched her and April had to jerk her head at Thomas to inspire him to follow her over. Gerritt, to whom she did not motion, also followed. Whatever.

"There was something I really needed to ask you," she said.

Thomas nodded and rocked back and forth on his heels. "Goan, then."

"Did the cops ask about, um..." She hesitated, lifted her eyebrows and inclined her head. "You *know*, the sweatshirt."

"Aye."

"Did you tell them?"

"Are you mad?" he barked.

"That's a no, then?"

Thomas shook his head and chuckled.

Gerritt listened to their clipped conversation. "What are you talking about?" he asked, glancing from one to the other, then back again. "Does he know about your sweatshirt, too?"

April groaned.

"Well, I should hope so," Thomas said, matter of fact. "Seein' as I was the one who put it in the can." He turned to April. "Didn'ya tell the lad?"

"No," she said, quietly.

"No, she didn't," Gerritt reiterated, while processing the information. "She told me the sweatshirt was hers, but that was all. This is new information, that you put it in the neighbor's trash. How did that happen?"

April held up her hand before Thomas could speak. "May I?" she queried.

Thomas shrugged and pulled his cigarettes from his pant pocket. "By all means." He rattled the package at them. "Cigarette?" In unison, Gerritt and April shook their heads. "Suit yourself," he said and pulled a silver Zippo lighter from the same pocket, lit his cigarette and inhaled with a flourish.

April waved her hand to dispel the smoke that instantly begun to wrap lazily around the three of them. "Okay," she said, to Gerritt. "The Reader's Digest version is, I threw away my sweatshirt because it got stained. Meanwhile, in Thomas' world, he found a dead rodent in his trash can and wanted to get rid of it. He needed a rag to dispose of it, so instead of using something of his own, he took it upon himself to use my sweatshirt and deposited the whole mess into Deborah's trash."

"Seriously? Why?" Gerritt said, taking advantage of April taking a breath.

"Why did he use my sweatshirt?"

"No." He shook his head. "Why move from his trash to hers?"

"He has some sort of neighborhood thing with Deborah," April told him, while Thomas rocked on his heels and listened. "So, he figured it would be better to throw the dead rodent into her trash, than have her *hear* about it being in his and risk her getting all twitter-pated over the information."

Gerritt was ready for April to take her next breath. When she did, he turned to Thomas. "What's she got on you?"

Thomas puffed on his cigarette. He didn't look at either of them, just into the distance as though choosing his words. Finally, he sighed. "I get the feeling you're gonna keep pestering aboot this until you have your answer."

April piped up. "You're probably right."

Thomas licked his lips and nodded briskly. "Right. So, here is it. A while back, before you became a part of this neighborhood." He paused and took a drag off of his cigarette. "Deborah and I had a bit of, wit you might call, an *altercation*." Smoke trailed from his nostrils as he explained. "She had issue with Corkscrew and—"

"Corkscrew?" Gerritt's eyes widened and he grinned. "Is that code for something?"

"Corkscrew is his cat."

"Oh, okay." He nodded and dropped the smile. "Smoke colored, skinny, orange eyes?"

Thomas pointed at Gerritt. "That's him." As though sensing they were talking about him, Corkscrew appeared, poking his head out from around the side of the house in much the same manner as Thomas had done.

"Speak of the devil." Thomas grinned and gave a brisk nod to the cat. "Must have known we were chatting about him."

Gerritt appraised Corkscrew as the cat sauntered over and sat smoothly on his haunches to survey the yard. "He is one interesting looking cat," he said, with appreciation.

"Moving along." April wanted more details. "Did something happen?"

Thomas nodded. "It did. Your woman across the way had the daft idea Corkscrew was using her flower beds for his toilet." He sneered.

"Was he?" Gerritt asked.

"Absolutely not!" Thomas snorted derisively. His cigarette was clamped between his teeth and ash dropped from the end of it to swirl in lazy circles to the ground like snow on a windless day. "The lad has more manners than that. Was probably the cat up the way, the thing looks like he's not given much mind, nor has much brains in his tiny head."

"Did you tell her that?" April asked.

"Wouldn't have done a muckle bit o' difference. Ms. One-Woman-Militia had already gone round the bend and decided she had to stop him from placing even so much as one paw into her yard."

April leaned in closer and Gerritt followed suit. She had become immune to the smoke of Thomas's cigarette and judging from the neutral expression on Gerritt's face, figured he also had decided to ignore it for the greater good of hearing the rest of the story.

"What did she do?" she pressed, almost afraid to ask.

"She went and bought one of those wireless electronic yard sound barriers, you know the thing, yeah? To keep animals contained to certain areas?"

"Like those horrid shock things," April stated, feeling less and less charitable to Deborah by the moment.

"Right," he agreed. "Only with sound. She told me she choose the sound type because she figured it was kinder to use sound than shock—"

"Wait," Gerritt said. "You talked to her about it?"

"After it was all said and done, yes."

"After *what* was all said and done?" April's eyes widened.

"I'm getting there." Thomas took a final puff on his cigarette, dropped it and ground it out fiercely with the tip with his boot.

"Hold on" Gerritt raised a hand. "Don't those only work if the animal is wearing a special collar?"

"Aye." Thomas nodded and his face became grim as he gazed first upon his cat, then toward Deborah's property. "She set a humane trap for Corkscrew—"

"Get outta here!" Gerritt balked. "What kind of nut is this woman?"

April just swallowed and stared, lost for words.

"Rancid," Thomas declared. "And, once she'd caught him, she somehow got the damned collar around his neck and set him loose ootside the perimeter of her yard."

"This is too much," April said, clenching her hands into fists and shifting her weight from foot to foot. Her neighbor was a crack pot, it was official.

"How she did it, I din'na know. The lad's a fighter."

"You've gotta be making this up," Gerritt said, astounded.

"I swear to you, no word of a lie," Thomas replied.

"Jesus," Gerritt blanched and April knew exactly how he felt. It was unnerving to what lengths some people would actually go.

"I did'na realize she'd even done it," Thomas told them. "The beast is here and there, we can go for quite some time before we cross paths."

"How did you find out?" April asked, even though she was hesitant to know the answer.

"The first time Corkscrew stepped across the boundary of her yard, the sound, my God." Thomas grimaced, as though he could still hear it. "It ricocheted off of the houses in a terrible manner, louder than you can imagine."

"Good lord." April was floored.

"And then some. The critter lost one of his lives, I swear it."

"What did he do?" Gerritt was equally absorbed in the tale.

"He ran home like the devil himself was after him. Nearly took the door off when he burst through his flap."

"Flap?" Gerritt said.

"In the door, to let him come and go on his own steam."

"Right." Gerritt nodded. "A cat door."

"That's it."

"Did you figure out that he, or rather, the collar had set off the noise?" April tensed and pressed her palms together, waiting for the reply.

Thomas took a deep breath and his nostrils flared. "Aye, lass, once he came out of hiding I found it. And, I was bloody gobsmacked."

"What did you do?"

"No." Thomas sidestepped April's question and briskly shook his head. "We'll end this miserable story by sayin' that madam over yonder had to survive a wee bit o' backlash for her choices. It's done. Best leave it lie."

"Oh, come on," she protested. "You can't leave us hanging like that."

Thomas ignored her. "So, now, Gerritt," he said and stroked his beard. "You might have a better understanding of why I wanted ta keep anything remotely suspicious - like a dead rodent carcass - as far away from meself as possible."

"I believe it," Gerritt acknowledged. "But, wouldn't you want to get it out of the neighborhood, altogether?"

Thomas nodded. "I do understand whot you're saying. I do." He bent over to pick up his cigarette butt from the ground and tucked it into his pocket.

While impressive that he did so, April couldn't help wonder what else he might have hidden in his pockets. Best left to the imagination.

"However." Thomas gave a sharp nod of his head. "At the time, all I could think aboot was getting it away from my trash, as fast as possible, and logic said to toss in hers." He gestured toward Deborah and Bob's house. "I had the idea it would keep it at home, keep the mad woman from focusing upon her neighbors."

"How's *that* working out for you?" April said, sarcastically.

Thomas ran a hand through his unruly hair and Gerritt patted April's shoulder. "He did have the best interest of the neighborhood in mind."

April brushed his words aside. "So, long story *not* short, the cops mentioned the sweatshirt to you, just like they did to us, and that was it?"

"That was it," Thomas agreed. "They did'na seemed all that bothered by it, either. I'd say if you were ever in the water on that one, you're well oot of it now."

"So, that's that." April was pleased at how optimistic she felt.

"Looks that way," Gerritt agreed, then snapped his fingers and pointed at Thomas. "One more thing, at least from me. How did you get April's sweatshirt out of her trash without being seen?"

"I waited 'til after dark."

"After dark?"

"Right. Friday night."

"Jeez." Gerritt raised his eyebrows, incredulous. "During the storm? Wasn't that a bit tricky?"

April considered what he said. It had been horrible weather.

"Twas," Thomas agreed. "By the time I was done, I was soaked through right down to me socks. My shoes were like small sunken boats."

"Are you positive you weren't seen, at all?" Gerritt pressed.

Thomas shook his head. "No, no way. It was raining something fierce. Not to mention, it was so dark I could barely see to find me way."

Gerritt thought about the rain damage at Max's house from that storm and nodded.

Thomas fished his cigarette pack and lighter from his pocket a second time. "As a matter of fact, I almost stepped on your neighbor's wee shaggy dog." He lit his cigarette, inhaled with a flourish and gestured to the Noble's house. "The daft thing darted out at me in the dark."

"Me, too!" April laughed, watching the smoke trail from Thomas' nostrils. "I was coming home and she came charging out from the shadows and almost tripped me up."

"That was you, then?"

"What? You saw me?" Her eyes widened in surprise.

"I did. I was just aboot to cross over from your yard into the next, when a car parked itself at the front."

"You didn't see him?" Gerritt asked April.

"No, she didn't," Thomas replied.

"He's right," April agreed. "It was dark and there was way too much rain and then, of course, the dog."

"I was quick," Thomas said. "I pulled myself in tight to the house and stayed in the shadows until the car was on its way."

"Whoa, hold up." Gerritt held up his hand like a traffic cop and started to chuckle. "Let me get this straight. You were out in the backyard." He swept his arm in an arc to indicate the space around them. "In the dark and rain, hauling around your garbage can of dead rodent." He snickered and shook his head as he painted his verbal picture. "And, all the while, April was out front being tripped up by a dog, completely unaware of the your presence?"

"Sounds aboot right." Thomas nodded in agreement.

Gerritt ran his fingers across his hair and glanced at April, mirth making his eyes dance. "Too much," he said, with a grin.

Thomas said nothing, just looked past April and narrowed his eyes. She glanced over her shoulder to see what had caught his attention.

Oh.

Carol.

"Brace yourselves, mates," Thomas commented.

"Yoo-hoo," Carol called out and waved as she ambled down her steps.

April plastered a smile across her face, took a deep breath and turned her body in Carol's direction. "Hi, Carol," she said as Carol strolled across her yard and came to a halt in front of them.

"Hello, all." Carol grinned, her blue eyes positively sparkling with curiosity. "Am I interrupting something? Are you off for a run?"

Thomas didn't so much as flinch when Carol spoke. He stayed mute and puffed on his cigarette, rocking back and forth on his heels as though waiting for a bus. Gerritt also remained quiet and raised an eyebrow at April.

April shot them a scathing look, then squared her shoulders and took the lead. "No, just returned, actually. We were just chatting, catching up."

"Ahh," Carol murmured and batted her eyelashes at Gerritt.

April frowned at her neighbor. Dressed in red shorts and a white cotton blouse; bright orange Crocs on her feet and strawberry blonde hair in a disarray of messy curls; she was staring at Gerritt in a manner that jumped the border from uncomfortable, to downright rude.

"Have we met?" Carol asked him, while letting her gaze traverse his running gear and barely covered physique beneath it.

"This is Gerritt, remember?" April piped up. "Kevin introduced him yesterday, when we were all in the backyard?"

"Right, of course, yesterday," Carol said, her face transforming from open and curious, to guarded and miffed. April remembered how efficiently Deborah had cut her off, too.

"Nice to meet you." Gerritt extended his hand to Carol. Like magic, she swiftly dropped her put-out expression and simpered at him.

"So, Carol." April loudly cleared her throat. "What brings you outside this afternoon?"

Carol pulled her gaze from Gerritt, in what could only be described as a reluctant manner, and brushed her hair away from her cheeks. "I was just going to check on my tomatoes and maybe pop in on Deborah."

At the mention of their other neighbor's name, Thomas's expression darkened. He looked a bit like an untamed, scraggly dragon. Carol saw his face and her eyes widened in alarm.

"Hope she's feeling better than yesterday," April muttered, flatly, while adjusting the cap on her head.

"Me, too." Carol, for once, looked genuine. "In that regard, I wanted to ask you a question, April." She shuffled the Croc on her left foot back and forth on the ground, then cleared her throat. "It may sound a bit odd, but did you by any chance receive a visit from the police this morning?"

"Yup." April nodded, then pointed at Thomas. "They showed up at both of our houses."

Carol played with the white, Peter Pan collar of her shirt and chewed her bottom lip. "I thought as much. I insisted to Edward, after they left, that it wasn't just us who received a visit."

"Actually," Gerritt threw in. "We were just talking about that, before you arrived. Do you have any idea why she'd call the police?"

Carol pulled at the edge of her blouse and looked uncomfortable. Finally, she blurted, "I have no idea. Her actions seem, to both me and Edward, highly over reactive."

April couldn't help herself, she felt slightly sorry for Carol. Deborah was the woman's friend. It couldn't be easy for her to speak out against her in any manner without feeling guilty.

"Maybe she's under a lot of stress?" she offered.

Thomas snorted and April cut her eyes at him. He raised a bushy eyebrow, but kept quiet.

"That's exactly what I said to Edward, but he wouldn't have it." Carol sighed. "He said he thinks it was a long time coming and she finally went off the deep end."

Thomas coughed and pulled a blunt-sided, tin lid from his pocket. April watched him extinguish his cigarette on the metal, then flick the butt into the dirt beside his house. "Well, this speirin has been great dafferie," he said.

April shook her head at him. "Oh, *puh-lease.*"

Thomas tucked the lid back into his pocket and turned on his heel. "Mar sin leibh," he said, over his shoulder, and sauntered away in the direction of his workshop.

April laughed out loud.

Gerritt raised a hand to wave. "No idea what he said," he commented. You?"

April shrugged her shoulders. "I could hazard a guess, but it would still be a guess." She continued to chuckle, then noticed he'd stopped short, eyes wide as he looked across the yard. She followed his gaze and clamped her mouth shut.

"What?" Carol asked, her face baffled by the sudden change in their demeanor. "What is it?"

April jerked her head sharply to the right. Carol raised her eyebrows and glanced in the direction indicated, then exhaled a loud, "Oh!" Deborah was standing, still as a statue, only a few yards away on her back lawn.

"When did *she* get there?" April hissed at Gerritt, from the corner of her mouth.

"No idea," he replied. "I just looked over and there she was. Like she'd appeared out of thin air."

A shiver ran up her spine and April shuddered.

"Well, it was lovely talking to you!" Carol trilled, her voice loud and friendly. "Really, just lovely to catch up! Who knows, perhaps I'll take you kids up on the jogging offer some day soon."

Gerritt and April exchanged bemused looks and watched Carol practically skip across the grass, her curls bouncing, back to her own yard.

"Oh, Deborah!" They heard her say, her voice laced heavily with surprise as she performed an exaggerated, hand slapped on her chest, double-take. "I didn't SEE you there!"

"*Okaay*," April commented. "Don't even want to know what that's about. Let's get out of here."

"Right behind you," Gerritt replied.

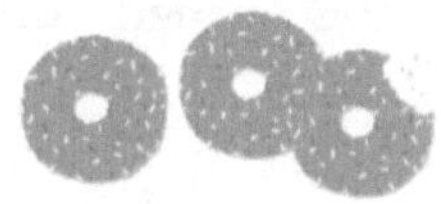

## 1:46 p.m.

"Do you want olives?" Jessica held up a large jar of oversized green olives for April to inspect.

April glanced at the jar and shook her head, making her gold, dice-shaped earrings sparkle in the overhead lights. Her thoughts were muddled and she was having a difficult time focusing her attention. "No. Maybe. I don't know. I think I'll just get a few dessert type things, maybe include some cheese to go with it."

The sisters were in the grocery store, the deli section, picking up a few odds and ends for later that evening. They had arranged a dinner outing- more accurately Kevin had arranged it - a double date where Jessica was being paired off with Gerritt. Once they had finished dinner, the intention was for the four of them to go back to April and Kevin's for a nightcap.

Jessica placed the olive jar into the depths of their shopping cart. "Well, I'll get them," she said. "They look tasty."

April nodded and moved toward the bakery section.

Jessica straightened the hem of her peasant blouse, the teal green and grey of the fabric bringing out the highlights in her hair. "So, what's the deal, now?" she said, matter of fact, as she pushed the cart forward to catch up with April.

April raised an eyebrow. "What? What are you talking about?"

"Oh, please. There's definitely something going on." Jessica scanned the shelves of sweets before them. "May as well be out with it." She reached for a package of sugar cookies and turned them over to read the ingredients.

April smoothed her navy blue skirt and sighed. "Fine." She sidled up close to Jessica, so they wouldn't be overheard. Not that it was really an issue; the only other shoppers in the section was a woman, accompanied by two, chatty toddlers. "My life is getting too complicated."

Jessica set the package of cookies back on the shelf and moved on to look at the cakes displayed behind the glass at the bakery counter. "These can't hold a candle to *The Bakery*, you should go there on the way home."

April nodded and twisted a silver, lace patterned ring on the index finger of her left hand. "We'll just get the cheese, and maybe some crackers, too."

"Complicated, how?" Jessica asked as they each placed a hand on the cart and simultaneously pushed it toward the cracker aisle.

"I know you're going to hate to hear it, but having Gerritt around is really shaking things up with Kevin and me."

April stepped ahead, reached for the front of the cart and pulled it to the right as they turned down the aisle.

"I don't necessary hate hearing it," Jessica argued. "I just don't want you to jump in any one direction too quickly, then regret it. You know the adage, act in haste, repent at leisure."

"Isn't it 'marry in haste'?"

"Whatever. You get what I mean. Don't do anything drastic without thinking it through, first."

April nodded. "I know that." She stopped in front of a selection of gourmet crackers. "But, I'm not the only one who needs that advice. Take this evening for example."

"What about it?"

"It was all Kevin's idea, right from the word go."

Jessica looked confused and April elaborated. "He suggested it *after* he found Gerritt and I together in the kitchen this morning. Instead of being rational and not acting in haste, he jumped. He doesn't trust me."

"What were you doing?" Jessica picked up a box of multigrain crackers and placed them in the basket.

"That's the point!" April hesitated a fraction of a second. "Nothing."

Jessica came to a halt and gave April a penetrating stare. "*Nothing*?"

"Well..."

April cleared her throat and became very interested in the crackers Jessica had chosen. She stared at the box, to avoid looking directly at her sister.

"Okay, fine," she huffed, giving up. "Gerritt and I had been outside and we ran into Thomas."

"What were you guys doing outside?"

"Running," April replied. "Only not together; separately. We just happened to arrive back at the house at the same time.

"Was that the problem? Kevin misunderstood and thought you guys had been together, without him?"

"No." April shook her head. "He didn't even know we'd both been outside at the same time until we started telling him about running into Thomas and some of the wacky stuff we found out - which, I might add, is information I still don't know what to do with."

"Uh-huh," Jessica said, waiting.

April exhaled and rubbed the back of her neck. "I'm actually getting a bit worried, you know. I think I'm starting to actually like the guy. I don't even want to think about the implications of what *that* could mean."

Jessica placed her hands firmly on her hips and frowned. "Um, hello? Does this stream of consciousness about your neighbor pertain in any way to what happened with Kevin not trusting you? Because, if not, you're getting seriously off track."

"Right!" April chose a package of stone ground wheat crackers and dropped it alongside the other box in the cart. "So, anyway, before Kevin found us in the kitchen, Gerritt and I were discussing what happened with Thomas. And, the more we hashed it over, the funnier it became. I didn't realize how much of a sense of humor he has. Gerritt, not Thomas. It's like he's an onion and keeps on revealing more and more layers..."

"Off track!" Jessica said, her voice steely between clenched teeth.

April took a breath and quickly got back on track. "So, long story short, I was laughing pretty hard when Kevin came into the kitchen and—"

"He didn't like what he saw?" Jessica finished.

"Sure seemed that way." April huffed petulantly and made to push her hair back. An old habit from before she'd had it cut and one she was trying to break. She massaged the tension in her shoulder, instead. "He went all tight and rigid, how he always gets when he thinks he's outside the loop."

"Can you blame him?"

April grimaced at the memory of Kevin's tense face. "but, that's the thing. He wasn't out of the loop, truly.

At least not for very long, anyway. Gerritt and I brought him up to speed on what happened, but clearly it wasn't enough, because all of a sudden he was rabbiting on about us all going out on a double date."

"Huh."

"Huh?" April echoed. "That's it? That's your response, 'huh'?"

"Well, it's none of my business and it's your affair," Jessica began and then, when April blanched, amended, "your *situation*, I mean. But, looking in as an outsider, I have to say I can see Kevin's side, too."

She pushed the cart away from the cracker section and April followed. "There's a whole lot of *we* going on there and none of it is about you and Kevin."

"That's only because of what I was telling you," April said defensively, her jeweled flip-flops sounding angry as they thwack-thwacked the floor sharply beneath her feet. "How else was I going to say it?"

Jessica nodded. "I know," she acknowledged, leading them toward the dairy section. "But, I'll bet there was the same *we-ness* vibe going on between you and Gerritt when you told Kevin about your adventures."

April went quiet and considered what she'd said. Jessica had a valid point. Since Gerritt's arrival in their lives, she *had* been finding herself being almost forced to address some of her own inner demons. They weren't pretty and it was just as likely as not Kevin was sensing the turmoil and reacting accordingly.

April opened her mouth to tell Jessica some of her thoughts, when her sister stopped abruptly in her tracks, stepped back and frantically signaled her to follow.

"Oh my God!" Jessica breathed, grabbing April's arm.

"What?" April looked around, alarmed.

"In the next aisle over." Jessica started to giggle. "It's Gerritt, and he's not alone."

April caught her breath. "What do you mean?" She wasn't sure she wanted to know, but then, *had* to know. *Please don't let it be a woman,* she thought.

"Denise Chang." Jessica bit her lip and jerked her head for April to follow her lead. The two of them peeked cautiously around the end of the aisle and, sure enough, there they were. Denise, looking as though she was feeling out her prey, and Gerritt, looking decidedly ill-at-ease.

"I wish we could get closer," Jessica began.

"But, I want no part of *that*," April finished.

"Agreed." Jessica nodded and snickered, again. "But, my goodness, doesn't Gerritt look uncomfortable. Almost makes me think we should rescue him."

April grinned. From what little she had learned about Gerritt, he didn't strike her as the type of guy who needed to be rescued from anything. Although, as she watched him lean backward when Denise pushed her chest toward him, she almost had a change of heart. Almost.

"Whoops!" Jessica leaned a touch too far and lost her balance, reflexively swinging her hand out and making direct contact with a carefully arranged row of potato chip bags. The bags teetered. "Oh God," she said, and then, before she could utter anything further, the bags began to fall like dominos to the grocery store floor.

"Run!" April blurted, wild eyed as she spun on her heel.

Jessica, jarred by April's outburst, reacted in an instant and whipped their cart around with the finesse of a race car driver, tearing off in pursuit of her rapidly disappearing back.

April's flip-flops slapped hard against the grocery store floor, making her feel the exact opposite of stealthy. She may as well have had a huge "LOOK NO FURTHER, IT WAS ME" sign plastered across her back and she felt sick at the thought she might have been spotted by either Gerritt or Denise, running from the scene. Ugg, it was too much. She didn't look back to find out. Instead, she ducked into an aisle a few rows down, then watched as Jessica slid in behind her and fought to catch her breath.

Jessica panted, one hand on the cart, the other clutching the edge of a shelf stocked full with cereal. "Jeez, that nearly killed me, trying to steer and stay upright in my shoes. Do you think they saw us?"

"I don't know," April replied, looking at Jessica's magenta, two inch heeled, cork wedge sandals. Suddenly, the overhead speakers came to life, a loud squawk calling for, "clean up on aisle five".

April twisted toward the cereals and grabbed a box, pretending she was studying ingredients on the back. "I really hope not," she added. "We'd look like a pair of crazy stalkers if they did. I don't know what the hell we'd say as way of an explanation."

It was too much. The whole situation was so absurd, Jessica dissolved into giggles. April tried to ignore her, but Jessica's squeaks and snickers were contagious.

"How old *are* we?" April asked, incredulously, as she, too, cackled so hard tears leaked from her eyes. She thrust the box back onto the shelf and swiped at the tears before they rolled down her face.

"Oh, my stomach," Jessica moaned between giggles. She reached into the pocket of her beige linen skirt for a tissue to blot her eyes and wipe her nose. "I cannot believe I did that. There were a lot of bags there. I feel badly for the person who's going to have to set it all back up."

April took a deep breath and exhaled. "Well, as callous as it sounds, better them that us. Let's get outta here."

Jessica nodded and pushed their cart to the side. "God, all of our stuff." She grimaced. "Should we put it back?"

"No way, I'm not risking it," April said, firmly. "It's bad enough we decimated a snack food display, if we run into Gerritt all bets are off. I know I won't be able to contain myself and he'll think we're a couple of sneaky, stalking, wing nuts."

Jessica snickered. "Okay, you have a point. We'll just go simple and stick with dessert from *The Bakery*."

"Sounds good to me."

April lead the way, shuffling toward the exit doors of the grocery store. She didn't want the sound of her flip-flops to draw attention to their departure, increasing the risk of she and Jessica being stopped and instructed to clean up the mess they had created on fateful aisle five.

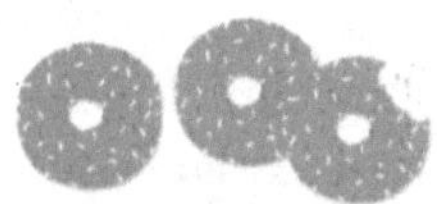

## 10:34 p.m.

"That was a really great idea," April said, lounging on the sofa in their family room. She, Jessica, Kevin and Gerritt had returned from their double date at an intimate restaurant called "*La Cucina Della Famiglia*" and she was feeling particularly mellow. A nice change from the past few days.

"I agree," Kevin piped up as he and Gerritt walked into the room.

April could hear the forced enthusiasm in his tone and silently counted to ten in her head. Kevin had been anything but chipper when they had been alone in the car, driving home. He had been downright pissy, accusing her of drinking too much wine and then having the audacity to tell her that, instead of coming off as charming, he believed it was possible Gerritt may have mistaken her friendliness for flirting. Strong words.

"So," April said, ignoring him. Even though Kevin's fake upbeat attitude was no less than she had expected, still, it grated on her nerves. "What can I offer you all?"

She pulled herself awkwardly upright from the depths of the sofa and headed, on slightly wobbly ankles, in the direction of the kitchen. "We've got coffee, tea and of course, *wine*." She leaned her weight against the swinging kitchen door, letting it carry her away from the room, and left them in her wake. Or, so she thought.

A moment later, Jessica came barreling in behind her. "I think we should definitely choose coffee," she said, tightly, before turning to rummage through the cupboards. Her bracelets jangled aggressively as her hands danced around the dishes and April rolled her eyes.

"Oh, for goodness sake. Not you, too."

"What?" She paused and twisted away from the cupboard.

April's feet were beginning to hurt, so she elected to sit down at the table and let Jessica continue doing the work. "Oh, just Mr. Serious Face in there. On the drive home he decided that I needed a *talking to—*"

"He didn't actually say that, 'a talking to', did he?"

April snickered. "Yes, he actually used those words."

Jessica raised an eyebrow, but reserved comment. Instead, she pulled forest green mugs from a cupboard and placed them on the granite countertop. "What was it that you needed the *talking to* about?"

"How much wine I drank at dinner." April slid off her purple sandals and let them drop to the floor beneath the table. "Whew, that feels better." She sighed with pleasure as she wiggled her toes. "Who does he think I am, one of his students?"

Jessica started measuring coffee into the coffee maker. "Maybe he was just thinking of you—"

"Bullshit," April stated, flatly. "He was thinking of himself."

Jessica poured water into the coffee maker and turned it on. April watched from her seat at the table and smiled. "You're so pretty," she said, appreciatively. "Look at you with your red ringlets, your swishy sparkly skirt and funky boots, and all of your shiny jewelry. You look like you stepped off the pages of a magazine."

She glanced down at her own outfit, a printed, sleeveless blouse and a pair of tan, gaucho pants. Her only bit of pizzazz were the purple sandals residing beneath her seat. "Whereas *I*, on the other hand, look like—"

"Stop." Jessica shook her head and folded her arms across her chest.

"What?" April asked.

"*What* is going on?"

"Nothing," April said, flippantly. "Nothing is going on with me, except that I was out for a lovely evening and it seems both my boyfriend, and now my sister, are having a hard time with the fact that I had fun."

"Talk about a load of bullshit," Jessica scoffed, then turned to open the fridge. "If you're not ready to talk about it right now, that's fine." She pulled out a carton of cream and placed it with the coffee cups. "But, remember, it's *me* here, okay?"

Kevin pushed open the kitchen door, making further discussion impossible. "How are things going in here?" He was still in peppy teacher mode, which made April want to gag.

"We're fine, just making coffee," Jessica answered, closing the fridge door.

"Can I help with anything?"

April stood up. "Sure. You can help Jessica get the donuts for dessert. Banana cream, your favorite. They're in the box there on the counter."

She pushed by him, forcing him to step aside, and walked out the door he'd just come through. "I'll be in the living room with Gerritt."

She didn't wait for a response, just left them to it and walked out.

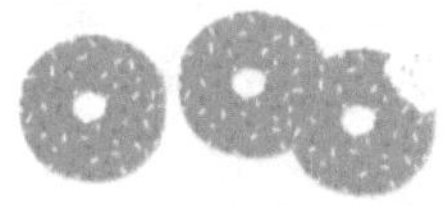

Gerritt was crouched by the entertainment center, perusing the selection of CDs. He looked up and smiled at April when she came in and the tension she was carrying across her shoulders released.

"Whatchya doin'?" she asked, easing herself into the same spot on the sofa she had vacated earlier and enjoying the view.

He was dressed in a pair of charcoal, pin-striped chinos and a red, long sleeved, polo shirt that gave just a hint of his strong, muscular body beneath it and April would have been content to sit there forever and watch him.

"You guys have some interesting music," he commented, joining her on the couch.

"Most of it's mine," she offered, bluntly. "Kevin's taste tends to be more mainstream, a bit more vanilla. I brought a lot of the other music with me when I moved in."

Gerritt nodded. "I guess he wasn't exactly raised in an eclectic environment."

April laughed. "That's a kind way of putting it." She tucked her feet up beneath her legs. "Not that his family aren't lovely people, they are. They just happen to be very much of the same small town vibe." She had a sudden revelation and added, "*Boxwood Hills*, how appropriate. Welcome to the box."

Gerritt looked at her quizzically and she clamped her mouth shut. The wine had loosened her tongue. She chastised herself for her sharp words and reminded herself that, while she was annoyed with Kevin, it didn't mean she needed to cut down his relatives. They had always been very kind to her and she wasn't going to forget it because their son needed to get the pole out of his ass.

"Sorry." She cleared her throat. "That might have come out a bit harsh."

He left it alone and changed the subject. "So, should I be safe to assume that means you grew up differently?"

April looked up to meet his steady gaze. It was the first time he'd asked her anything personal. "Yes." She nodded. "I'd say Jessica and I grew up in an environment that was almost the polar opposite of Kevin's."

April purposely threw Jessica's name into the conversation, just in case her judgment was off from the wine and he was actually fishing for info about her sister, *his date*, instead of her.

"You and Jess are so different," he remarked, leaning back into the sofa cushions. The movement shifted him slightly closer to her. "I mean, don't get me wrong, your sister is great, a very nice person—"

"I'm sensing a *but* coming."

Gerritt smiled and reached out to gently squeeze her shoulder. "*But,*" he said. "Even though you're sisters, you seem a lot more..." He paused, as though searching for the exact word. "Daring, I guess. More willing to get into it and experience life."

April digested his comments. Was that the impression she gave? Because, she certainly didn't feel daring. Just the opposite. She also wondered what he meant by getting 'into it'.

"I'm sorry, did I offend you?"

April blinked and realized she hadn't said anything. "No!" She laughed. "Not at all. I was just contemplating what you said. I guess I don't think of myself as daring—"

"Okay!" Jessica came bustling through the kitchen door, a tray in hand, putting a definite stop to their conversation. "Coffee and donuts for everyone."

Kevin trailed behind her, looking decidedly distracted. April watched him, his eyes distant in his handsome face, and wondered what had gone on in the kitchen after she had left. He helped Jessica with cups and napkins and April had a surreal moment where she felt as though she was a guest in their home, instead of the opposite.

"This looks great," Gerritt enthused, straightening upright in his seat. "Thank you."

April sat up as well and tried to help distribute... something. Too late. It was done. "Yes, thank you." she said, with a nod, while refusing to make eye contact with Kevin. "*Jess.*"

Jessica smiled and reached out to pat April's arm affectionately. "No worries. I know your kitchen as well as my own." She smoothed her skirt and sat in one of the chairs across from the sofa.

Kevin took the chair adjacent to Jessica and, as he reached for the carafe to pour coffee, April finally looked directly at him. She had to admit to herself that, despite her irritation, the man cleaned up well. His black dress pants flattered his trim torso and firm backside, the burgundy dress shirt he had paired with them brought out the richness of his thick, chocolate brown hair and his dark eyes seemed to smolder as he paused to look at her. April broke eye contact and shifted in her seat as the silence around them deepened.

"So." Gerritt cleared his throat and deftly cracked the silence. "Did Kevin happen to tell you guys about what happened at my place, when we were there this afternoon?" He leaned forward to retrieve a coffee cup from the tray, handed it to April, then took a second to give to Jessica.

"No." April shook her head and the room tipped slightly. Perhaps coffee was a good idea, after all.

Jessica took a sip from her cup, tucked a stray ringlet behind her ear and smiled encouragingly at Kevin. "No, you didn't. Tell us."

"Go ahead." Gerritt nodded at Kevin and leaned back into the sofa, his shoulder so close to April's she could feel the heat radiating from his skin.

Kevin chuckled, took a cup for himself and placed it on the table in front of him. "Okay." He rested his elbows on the arms of his chair and rubbed his hands together, ready to begin. "Gerritt and I were at the house, checking out the damage in the light of day."

As annoyed as she might have been with him, April couldn't help but be amused. Kevin loved to weave a tale and she was sure it was part of what made him so popular with his students.

"We were pretty much done," he told them. "Just had a couple more things to check on, when the doorbell rang."

Jessica raised her eyebrows and looked at Gerritt. "Who'd be way out there, ringing your doorbell?"

"That's exactly what we thought," Kevin agreed. "It's not exactly close to anything." He picked up his cup, took a sip, then set it back down. "Fantastic coffee, by the way," he said, to Jessica.

"Thanks." She grinned.

"So," Kevin continued, his eyes flashing with amusement. "Gerritt went to the door and you'll never guess who was on the other side."

"Mickey Mouse?" April blurted, then snorted in amusement at her own joke. Kevin paused and looked at her strangely. April clamped her mouth shut.

"Noooo," he replied, with exaggerated patience. "Not Mickey Mouse. But, someone almost as unexpected." He took a pause for dramatic effect, then dropped the bomb. "The local gossips, Denise Chang and Heidi Moore."

"Get outta here!" Jessica sat up, ramrod straight.

"I know, right?" he said. "Of all the people to show up at that house."

Jessica looked at Gerritt, turning her head so fast her earrings danced wildly beneath her earlobes. "Do you even *know* them?"

April perked up and took a sip from her coffee cup. Considering what she and Jessica had seen in the grocery store earlier that afternoon, she was eager to hear his reply. Things were starting to get interesting.

"No, not really." Gerritt frowned and shook his head. "I met one of them, Denise, at the grocery store earlier in the afternoon." He shuddered involuntarily. "*That* was a bit of a nightmare—"

"Not in *her* eyes," Kevin threw in, his voice filled with mirth. "She worked her butt off to remind him about their enchanted encounter."

April, her mouth full of coffee, started to choke. Gerritt turned sharply in his seat and began to pat her on the back.

"Are you okay?" He leaned in, his face genuinely concerned.

Jessica jumped out of her chair and edged Gerritt aside with her hip as April nodded and squeaked, "I'm okay." She coughed and wiped at her eyes with a tissue Jessica offered her from her pocket. "Just swallowed wrong."

"Jeez," Jessica said, rubbing April's back. "I thought we might lose you there."

April sniffed and began to laugh. The grocery store incident was still fresh in her thoughts, so any excuse to laugh out loud was welcome. "Sorry," she said, breaking into a grin. "Didn't mean to stop things so abruptly." She took a deep breath and exhaled. "I'm okay, now. Kev, finish you story."

Jessica stood up and moved back to her seat, smoothing her skirt beneath her as she sat down. "You sure?" she asked.

"Absolutely."

Kevin watched April, his expression unreadable. "You were saying?" she prompted, when it appeared he was stuck. "Denise Chang was at the door?"

"And, she was determined to make me remember our meeting at the grocery store," Gerritt supplied, picking up the slack when Kevin didn't jump in. "As though I'd forget it."

"Right," Kevin said, coming out of his momentary lapse. "I was in the living room, but man, that woman has a voice that carries. I could hear their whole interaction, plain as day."

April laughed, remembering hearing Denise at Jessica's salon.

'Yeah, and a fat lot of help you were, too." Gerritt shook his head at Kevin, while he grinned back, cheekily.

Jessica looked from one to the other and asked, "What? What happened?"

"This bastard didn't make any attempt to come and help me out, at least not until I was really squirming."

Kevin laughed out loud and as April watched him, she was reminded of why she had found him so attractive - once upon a time. They used to have fun. It suddenly seemed like a long time since they had enjoyed being together.

"Oh, come on," Jessica bantered. "I have a hard time believing that of Kevin." She turned toward Kevin and cocked her head. "Really? Did you really leave him to his own devices?"

Kevin grinned and took a sip of his coffee. "He's exaggerating," he said, dismissively. April felt as though she was on the sidelines, watching the show.

"Yeah, that's it," Gerritt threw in and laughed, shaking his head.

"What happened was, once Denise had finished insisting and insisting that she and Gerritt were long lost friends." Kevin continued, ignoring Gerritt. "She started offering him a place to stay until the repairs to the house were done—"

"She *came on* to you?" Jessica said, her voice laced with mirth.

"No," Gerritt balked, vehemently. "I don't think it was quite like that—"

"It was one hundred percent like that, my friend," Kevin cut him off. "You girls should have been there, she practically offered to pre-warm the sheets for him in her bed."

Jessica burst into giggles and caught April's eye. April bit her lip to control her snicker.

"*Oh, my, the devastation, Gerritt,*" Kevin mimicked Denise, his voice high and squeaky. "*You must come and stay with me, I have lots of room and no one to disturb us.*"

While Gerritt and Jessica laughed at Kevin's impression, April's humor began to slip away. She sipped at her cooling coffee and couldn't help but wonder if Kevin was making a poorly veiled jab at her, about her friendly behavior at dinner. Granted, she may have been being paranoid, but, then again, maybe not.

"How did you get rid of them?" she questioned Gerritt, pushing her muddled thoughts aside.

"After Denise commented that they had been driving by—"

"Driving by," Jessica said, with a scornful snort. "*Please.* Do either one of them even live around that area? Isn't it fairly secluded?"

"I'll say," Gerritt agreed. "When Max bought that house, there's no question he did it with the intention of being well away from anyone. I've never lived, or house-sat, in a home so quiet."

"So, after she *lied* and said they'd been driving by, then offered you lodging," Jessica recapped. "Then what?"

Gerritt chuckled and jerked his head toward April. "*Her* schmuck of a boyfriend, no offense intended—"

"None taken." Kevin laughed.

"*Finally* decided to show his face and help me out."

"Oh, man," Kevin protested, the grin back on his face. "You're making me out to be the bad guy. I didn't leave you hanging that long."

"No? You don't think so?" Gerritt retorted, then leaned into April and laid a hand on her arm. "Honestly, hand on my heart, if he'd left it any longer I don't know what would have happened. I was concerned those two women were going to try and drag me off with them."

While Jessica giggled, April observed Kevin out of the corner of her eye. He was gazing steadily at Gerritt's hand. She felt like a doe, rigid, caught in the headlights. If she only had some sort of distraction to help her...

"Hey!" Jessica blurted and pointed at the living room window. "Look out there! Something just went flashing by!"

April could have clapped with glee. Her prayers for a distraction were answered. Gerritt dropped his hand from her arm and leaned forward, while Kevin spun around in his seat.

"What *was* that?" Jessica questioned, then stood up and moved across the room, closer to the glass. Kevin was out of his seat in a hurry as well, joining her at the window.

"Is that Deborah and Bob?" Kevin speculated as Gerritt and April got up from the couch.

April sidled up beside her sister and peered outside. "Sure looks like them," she agreed. "What are they doing?"

As the four of them watched, Deborah ran from the sparse hedges bordering Thomas' yard, then beetled through Kevin and April's front yard toward her own. She began pushing into her shrubs with her hands then, lickety-split, darted into the Noble's yard to peer into their foliage. A second later she sprinted past the front window for a second time, a blurry skinny streak, making them all reflexively lean back from the glass.

"What on Earth?" Jessica exhaled, flabbergasted, while they watched Bob trudge behind his wife, desperately trying to keep up. "Has she lost her mind? Is she having some sort of episode?"

"No idea," Kevin replied, while Deborah spun on her heel and dashed back to her own yard. Bob stopped, methodically turned around, and attempted a heavy footed jog to follow in her tracks.

"She looks like she's on speed," Gerritt offered, when Deborah disappeared in a flash around the side of her yard.

"Look at poor Bob." April grimaced and shook her head. "He looks like he's hurting." She winced as Bob practically dragged himself after Deborah. He shouldn't have bothered. Just as he cleared the first corner of his house, Deborah came charging around the other side.

"She's fast," Jessica pointed out.

Kevin moved from the window and started toward the foyer. "This is ridiculous. I'm finding out what's going on." He pushed his feet into his sneakers and threw open the front door.

Jessica, Gerritt and April looked at one another, surprise written on their faces. "Should we follow him?" April finally asked.

"Absolutely," Gerritt said and extended a hand in front of him. "Ladies?" he said and motioned for them to precede him.

Jessica stepped forward. "Clearly," she said, her voice full of admiration. "Your Mother raised you right." She followed Kevin's lead out the door.

"I left my shoes in the kitchen," April called out. "I'll be right there..." Her voice trailed off when Gerritt placed a gentle hand on her shoulder.

"Listen," he said and leaned toward her, so close she could smell the licorice undertones of his cologne. "We were interrupted earlier, but I'd still love a chance to talk. Hear more about how it was when you grew up."

April swallowed and the sound seemed loud in her ears. "Oh," she managed, barely containing a squeak in her voice. "Okay, sure."

"Great." He smiled, his eyes kind and inviting. "Maybe we can set something up this week? Just the two of us?"

*Oh, God,* April thought, *please don't let my knees go beneath me.* "Sure," she said, again, hoping she looked pleased, as opposed to shell shocked.

The sound of raised voices outside broke the spell. Gerritt swallowed and straightened his shoulders. "I guess we should go and find out what's going on, huh?" He jerked his head in the direction of the door.

April took a breath and switched gears. "Absolutely. Forget about my shoes, I'll slip on some sandals."

He followed behind her as she walked to the foyer. They were both silent as they found their shoes and headed for the door. April dared to glance at him, just before they left the house and discovered him doing to same thing, to her.

*What are you doing?* she demanded of herself. *Playing with fire*, came the reply.

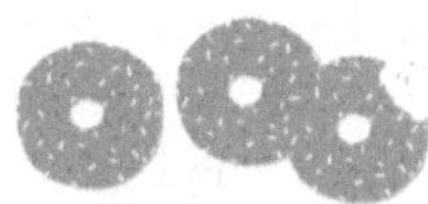

## 12:33 a.m.

"I am not making this up and I'm not crazy!" Deborah insisted, her voice so loud it echoed off the sides of the Noble's house.

"Deborah, please," Kevin tried to appease. "Have some respect for the neighbors and tone it down."

April slid in beside Jessica, Gerritt close at her heels. "What's happening?"

Jessica glanced at Gerritt and then narrowed her eyes accusingly at April. "Where have you been all this time?"

April looked at her sister's face, her pursed lips and watchful eyes, and wanted to laugh. She reminded her so much of their mother in that moment, it was comical. "I was getting some shoes. I left mine in the kitchen, remember?"

Jessica glanced down at April's feet in the grass and April kept the ball rolling. "You didn't answer my question, what's going on?"

"That woman," Jessica said, lifting her gaze and pointing a finger toward Deborah.

"Deborah," Gerritt offered, helpfully, and Jessica locked narrowed eyes with April.

"What?" April said, defensively, her hands palm side up as she shrugged. "In case you've failed to remember, he's been living here with us for a couple of days now."

Gerritt nodded. "Did she tell you about the whole garbage can incident?"

"See?" April shot Jessica a triumphant look.

"Fine." Jessica relented. "Anyway, your lovely neighbor, *Deborah*, has been going on and on about seeing someone in your yards. Something about suspecting they were prowlers." She shook her head. "I'm not exactly sure."

"Okay, please, just take a breath and calm down," Kevin said, attempting to reason with Deborah.

"No, I won't!" Deborah shot back, her arms folded tightly across her flat chest.

April frowned as she watched. What *was* the woman wearing? It looked like some sort of night gown, a very transparent sort of nightgown, and she felt slightly awkward looking directly at her.

"Whoa," Gerritt said, sharply, under his breath, when Deborah began to elaborate with accompanying, wild gestures and moved into the light being cast from the Noble's front porch. April turned in time to see him quickly avert his eyes from the skinny woman.

"Definitely not a sight a guy wants to see." He placed his hand in front of his mouth to hide his grin. "Anytime."

April couldn't help herself and giggled. "Way too much information," she murmured quietly and pressed her lips together to repress any further snickers.

"What are you two whispering about?" Jessica leaned toward them.

April jerked her chin toward Kevin and Deborah and hoped she wouldn't be detected. "That gown Deborah is wearing," she said, under her breath. "It's giving up way too much information."

"And," Gerritt added, with a grimace. "Not the kind I ever wanted burned into my brain."

Jessica glanced over and gasped. "Good God!" She tried to whisper, but wasn't doing a very good job. "She's practically naked when the light hits her!"

Bob suddenly stepped forward and April clamped her jaw closed. "Do you think he heard us?" she hissed at Gerritt between barely moving lips.

Before Gerritt could reply, Bob pulled off the robe he was wearing over his stripped pajamas and draped it around Deborah's shoulders.

"My guess is yes," he whispered back.

"I mean it, Kevin, and I don't care if the whole neighborhood hears me," Deborah reiterated, her voice nearly braying as she clutched at the edges of Bob's robe. "There was two of them and I think they have a connection to the dead animal in my trash."

"A connection? What kind of connection?" Kevin had his head cocked to one side and was using his I'm-being-patient voice.

"I don't know, *obviously*," she barked. "Maybe this time around they were planning to target one of our neighbor's pets."

The front light at Carol and Edward's went on, illuminating their porch as the couple stepped outside. Upon hearing Deborah's comment, Carol's eyes widened and she pressed a hand to her chest. April rolled her eyes. Oh, the drama.

"Hey, now," Kevin countered. "Before we get too deep into this—"

"Whatever the case," Deborah pressed on. "I won't give *that* possibility any attention. I'm not insane, or of a twisted mind." She pulled Bob's robe tighter around her stick-like frame, making herself look a lot like a awkwardly clad scarecrow. "All I wanted was to nab them before they got away and find out who the hell they were and what they were doing; skulking around your house in the dark."

Skulking? Her house? April cocked her head. Now Deborah had her attention.

"Are you sure they were actually intent on *this* house?" Jessica questioned, gesturing to Kevin and April's home.

Deborah turned sharply and narrowed her eyes. "And, *you* are?" she asked, her voice brittle.

April watched her sister's back straighten, her chin tilt upward and her eyes narrow. "Jessica," she replied, her voice cold and impersonal. "April's sister."

It was all April could do not to cheer. If there was one thing that she knew, it was that Jess could return, in equal measure, whatever Deborah believed she could dish out.

Deborah's gaze darted toward April, then right back to Jessica's unwavering stare. "Right." She nodded and her voice sounded remarkably less brittle.

"You were saying?" Jessica cocked her curvy hip to one side and folded her arms across her abundant chest. If she wanted to, she could probably snap the woman like a twig. "About the house?"

"Yes," Deborah said, straightening her shoulders. "I saw someone, I don't know who it was, from my house." She pointed toward her windows to indicate where she had been. "They were walking around your cars." She waved her hand toward Kevin and April's driveway. "Which I thought was very odd. Then—"

"They?" Kevin asked.

"There were two of them, from what I could tell," Deborah replied. "They crept in the direction of the house - more importantly the windows." She pointed a finger at the side windows on the house. "That was when I came rushing out to catch them." Her face screwed up in annoyance. "Clearly, I didn't meet my goal, but *next time*—"

"Hopefully, there won't be a next time," Kevin soothed. "It was probably just a mistake, someone lost and looking for an address, or something."

"Maybe, but I doubt it," April spoke up. "Deborah said they ran. Seems kind-of strange to run, if all you're doing is looking for an address, don't you think?"

Kevin turned to face her, his expression tight and severely pissed off. Oops. April stepped back a little closer to Jessica and Gerritt.

"You see," Deborah said, a small, smug grin on her face. "Even your girlfriend knows I'm telling the truth. It *is* possible there could be something else going on, that I interrupted."

"I never said there was no possibility," Kevin said, ever the mediator. "Of course, in life, anything is possible. *However*," he quickly amended, when Deborah's priggish smile widened. "Either way, there's nothing we can do about it. Not now."

Deborah opened her mouth to speak, but Kevin squared his shoulders and held his hand up, traffic cop style, to stop her. "*And,* yes, if they come back, which I doubt will happen, we'll all have you to thank for putting us on alert."

"They'd be nuts to come back," Gerritt whispered in April's ear, making her shiver. "Look at her face."

She looked. Just a hint at the possibility of the mystery people's return and Deborah's expression had changed from smug, to grim. The kind of grim that made April shuddered on the behalf of whomever might be caught by the woman, should they be so brave as to return to the neighborhood.

"Did you get a good look at either one of them?" Carol called out, from the protective covering of her porch.

Deborah looked up and squinted into the glare of the porch light. "Is that you, Carol?"

"Yes, me and Edward. Peaches is inside, getting her beauty rest," Carol replied, as though Deborah would give a darn as to the whereabouts of her dog. "We were worried, we heard you yelling."

Deborah nodded. "Yes. As a matter of fact, I did sort-of get a fairly decent look at the lurkers."

"And?" Edward asked.

"They were dressed in, what looked like, some type of camouflage wraps."

"Pardon?" Kevin said. "Camouflage? What sort of camouflage?"

"You know," Deborah replied. "The pants and shirts that look like foliage, so you can't be seen." She rolled her eyes, as though she thought Kevin was being purposefully daft. "And, not that I care one whit about nationality, but in the interest of full disclosure, one of them did look of Asian origin."

"Asian?" Kevin repeated, making Deborah roll her eyes a second time.

"Yes," she answered, her teeth clenched. "Do I have to describe that for you, too?"

Kevin frowned and shook his head.

"Good." Deborah cleared her throat. "As for the other one, I'm not completely sure of his, or *her* origin. I just know that he, *or she*, had particularly vibrant red hair."

Jessica turned her head slowly toward April and raised an eyebrow.

"No," April whispered when she saw her sister's face. "You don't think..."

"Denise and Heidi?" Jessica finished, in hushed tones.

"No," April said, a second time, and pressed her palms to her cheeks.

"Who else comes immediately to mind when you hear that description?"

April frowned. "But, why? Why would they be here?"

Jessica shrugged. "I have no idea. At least none that don't completely creep me out."

"I think we should say good night," Bob announced and placed a solid arm around his wife's boney shoulder. “It’s late and we could go round and round.” He gave them a lopsided grin and added, “In fact, we just did and still found nothing.”

Deborah refused to acknowledge his attempt at humor, wrinkled her nose and agreed. “Fine.”

“Thanks for trying to help,” Bob said to Kevin, sounding genuinely appreciative that he’d interrupted his crazed wife.

“No problem.” Kevin left the couple where they stood on the Noble’s lawn and walked over to where April, Jessica and Gerritt stood in front of his house. He turned and raised a hand in a wave. “Night all.”

Carol gave a small wave as she and Edward went back into their house and a moment later their porch light went out. Just like that, the front street went from lit, to dark.

Kevin yawned. “Shall we?” He indicated to the house and led the way.

They were quiet as they approached the porch and began ascending the steps, one after the other; as though following an imaginary string.

Last in line, April’s eyes had time to finally adjusted to the darkness. A movement to her right caught her attention and she paused on her bottom step to squint into the night. Her mouth formed a silent, *Oh,* and her eyebrows jumped upward in surprise when she saw Thomas, nearly invisible, leaning comfortably against his elegantly draping oak tree. Corkscrew sat sphinx-like at his feet and Thomas gave a small salute, the tip of his cigarette a red dot amongst the leaves. The cat blinked, his orange eyes luminous in the darkness.

April nodded her head in acknowledgment and wondered what his’ take was on the events of the last half hour. Had he seen the same thing as Deborah, but wasn't coming forward to tell? She wished she could approach him and find out.

She sighed and turned to follow the others into the house. It had been a very odd night and she had to admit to herself, seeing Thomas tucked into the depths of his trees seemed strangely fitting.

# CHAPTER 4 - Monday

10:15 a.m.

April stood outside the door of the antiques shop, *Back in Time*, taking deep breaths to steady her nerves. She was being ridiculous, she knew she was, making something out of nothing.

*Just get on with it,* she silently chastised herself. *Carpe diem.*

The shop keeper in the neighboring bookstore was beginning to shoot her irritated looks, and April figured she was only minutes away from security showing up to accuse her of lurking, so she took a final bracing breath, pushed open the door and stepped inside.

A bell, conveniently located above the door, jangled; however, April barely noticed. Her olfactory senses were being inundated by a combination of wood and candle wax, a hint of mustiness, coffee and well-worn books. It was intoxicating and stopped her in her tracks.

"Hey!" Gerritt called out, jarring her from her scent induced stupor. "It's you," he said, his face lit up with delight as he quickly crossed the shop to greet her.

"It's me," she agreed, unable to keep herself from grinning foolishly.

"You look gorgeous." He nodded appreciatively and April blushed. If he only knew the hell she had put herself through, going back and forth on what to wear. She hadn't wanted to look too contrived, but yet, still desired to look as though she'd made some effort with her appearance.

It had been exhausting.

After years of being in a relationship, she had discovered she'd lost her ability to throw together an outfit with ease. She'd also come to the surprising realization she spent way too much time in shorts and tee shirts. Consequently, the fact that Gerritt noticed how she looked in her slim-fitting, ruby red blouse and knee-length, denim skirt made her want to kick up her mules in delight.

"What brings you to these old, antiquated parts?" He swept his arm in a wide circle to indicate the shop.

"Well, I was in the neighborhood," April started, then stopped to laugh. "How cliché does that sound?"

Gerritt chuckled. "Very. But, hey, sometimes it's actually true."

"In this case, it is," she said, stretching the truth. "I was on my way to the library to finish my column and remembered Max's shop is here—"

"Why do you go there, if you don't mind me asking?"

"Where? The library?"

"Yeah." Gerritt straightened a lace doily atop a chest of drawers, giving her a chance to look him over without being noticed. He looked fantastic. Slim fitting jeans the color of charcoal, a black tee shirt and electric blue vest the color of his eyes, April had to catch her breath.

"Well," she said, forcing herself to focus. It was a good question and one that nobody had asked her before. "I've found it's a good place to get my work done without anything, or anyone, interrupting me." April cocked her head. "Why do you ask?"

He smiled. "Just curious, wondering what makes you tick."

April wasn't sure what to say to that, so she cleared her throat and glanced around the shop. "So, this is where you work, at least for the rest of the summer, huh?" She nodded in appreciation of the vibe that was created by the many table and standing lamps scattered in various locations around the space. There were no overhead lights to ruin the effect, giving the shop a cozy, intimate feel.

"This is it," Gerritt agreed. "Want a tour?"

April raised an eyebrow and he laughed. "Alright, it's all pretty straight forward, but there are some pretty amazing pieces that Max has found, tucked in here and there." His eyes lit up and he reached for her hand. "Actually, that reminds me, come here."

April felt as though a warm flame was working its way from his hand to hers, right into her veins. She let him guide her toward the chunky wooden cash desk at one side of the shop, the heels of her beige mules clicking on the well-worn, hardwood floors.

"Oh, this is nice," she said as she stepped behind the desk and ran her free hand along the polished wood. "You don't see this kind of furniture every day."

"I hear you," he agreed, then released her hand to crouch down and reach into a cubby hole next to the cash register. "If I had someplace for it," he added, with a grin, "I'd try to convince Max to sell it to me. Not that he would, but I'd try."

April watched him pull out a petite, sterling silver box, straighten up and place it gently on the counter top. "I think," he said. "This is something you'll really appreciate."

Immediately curious, April leaned in to get a closer look. Gerritt grinned and began pulling lifting the lid, just as her cell phone rang and nearly made her jump out of her skin.

"Jeez, sorry!" she apologized, while scrambling in her pocket for her phone. She yanked it out and looked at the display. "It's Jessica," she said, by way of explanation. "I should take it. Sorry, just one minute."

Gerritt shrugged and looked at her warmly. "No worries, we've got all day. Take your time."

April tapped the talk button. "Hi."

"You're not at home," Jessica commented. "I tried you there, before calling your cell. Am I interrupting?"

"No." April ran her hand along the smooth wood counter, enjoying the feel of the worn surface.

"Good. Because, I have something interesting to tell you."

"What kind of interesting?" she asked and shrugged her shoulders at Gerritt. He smiled and began making himself busy, sorting a pile of deep purple bags that had "*Back in Time*" stamped in gold script across their sides.

"I was in the shop this morning."

"I thought you were closed on Mondays."

"I am. I went in to get some inventory done.'"

"Oh."

"So, anyway, I was in the salon and guess who showed up at my door?"

"Even though you were closed?" April clarified.

"Uh-huh. Guess."

"I have no idea. The Queen of England."

Gerritt chuckled at her comment, even though he had no idea what she was talking about and April giggled at his response.

"Who's that? Where are you?" Jessica asked.

April felt cornered. She didn't want to lie, but at the same time felt pretty sure Jessica might not understand what she was doing with Gerritt, at his work, without just cause.

"April?" Jessica's tone was insistent. "Hello? Are you still there?"

"Yes, I'm here. I'm just doing a bit of shopping, then I'm going to the library to work on my column." It wasn't the entire story, but not a lie, either.

"Shopping where?"

"I was just near the bookstore," she started, then reached out to slap Gerritt on the arm when he mouthed the word, *Mommy*, at her. She wanted to shut him up, but it wasn't working. It just made him laugh harder.

"Okay, enough games," Jessica said, annoyed. "What's going on? What aren't you telling me?"

"Nothing." April sighed. "Jeez, you seriously sound like Mom." Gerritt winked at her, rewarding her for having the guts to say it. "If you must know, I was near the bookstore and now I'm not."

"Not *what*?"

"Near the bookstore."

"Okaay," Jessica replied, exaggeratedly. "So, that makes you *where*, exactly? On the way to the library? Why are you being so evasive?"

"For goodness sake, Jess!" April ducked her head, suddenly aware her voice could carry through the shop. "I stopped in to say hello to Gerritt, okay?" Her tone was measured and steely. "He's right next door to the bookstore."

"Oh." Jessica's voice became tense. "Right."

"Say hello to Jessica." She held the phone in Gerritt's direction, in a weak attempt to lighten the mood.

"Hey, Jessica," Gerritt sing-songed.

"April!" Jessica called out, tightly. "Are you still there?"

"Yes, I'm here." She swallowed a sigh, pressed the phone back to her ear and leaned up against the counter top.

"Do you want to call me back later?"

"No, I don't. I want you to finish your story and tell me who showed up at your salon, when most everyone knows you're closed on Mondays."

"Oh, that." Jessica hesitated.

"Come on," April pushed. "Spill it. You know you want to."

"Okay, fine, but we're not done with this yet. It isn't over."

April rolled her eyes. "Fine. Sure. Whatever. Just tell me what happened."

"Okay." Jessica's voice lifted and became noticeably more perky. "So, I was in the salon, doing my inventory, and I looked up and there they were. Denise and Heidi, knocking on my front door."

"No way! Seriously?"

"Honest to God. I was as surprised as you."

"What did you do?"

"I let them in, that's for sure," she said. "I figured the fates were smiling down on me and I wasn't about to turn them away."

April laughed appreciatively and shifted her weight from one foot to the other. While her mules were gorgeous, their comfort didn't match their looks. Gerritt came up beside her, pulled over a stool and motioned for her to sit. April felt a thrill of delight at his chivalry, smiled and sat.

"They said they were looking for Heidi's hat," she elaborated. "Supposedly, Heidi thought she'd left it in the salon."

"Did she?"

"Not that I had seen."

"Do you think it was legitimate?"

"I don't know, perhaps, maybe," she said, skeptically. "But, either way, I figured they were right there in front of me, I was going to take the opportunity being given to quiz them about their activities last night."

"No you didn't!"

Jessica laughed. "Of course I did!"

"My sister, ladies and gentlemen," April said, as though talking to a panel. "Takes the bull by the horns, every time."

Gerritt, on the other side of the counter straightening a bin of umbrellas, gave her a quizzical look. April just smiled and batted her eyelashes in return.

"It was very interesting, though," Jessica said. "When I started asking them questions about where they'd been last night, around midnight, they both got all cagey. Heidi clammed up and Denise answered me like some sort of double speaking politician, talking about the importance of exercise and walking. She made no sense whatsoever and they beetled out of there pretty darn fast."

"Oh, my, God. Seriously?"

"Seriously," Jessica replied. "It was all very strange. I'm of the mind that there's a strong possibility your neighbor's description was on the money and it was them outside your house."

April was blown away by the piece of news. What had those two women been doing sneaking around her house? She put the question to her sister. "But, what the heck would they want at my house?"

"I've thought on this," Jessica offered. "And, I have a guess."

April shifted the phone from her left ear to her right and turned her body away from Gerritt while she listened. "Which is?"

"The man you're talking to right now."

"Who Gerritt?" She lowered her voice, not wanting to draw his attention by using his name.

"Yes."

"How so?"

"Well, he said they were at his house yesterday afternoon, right?" Jessica reminded.

"Right."

"And, we saw Denise coming onto him at the grocery store."

April pressed her eyes closed. She'd been trying to forget that memory.

"So," Jessica concluded. "Maybe it's *him* they're following. Or, more accurately, *stalking*."

"Eww." April shuddered at the very suggestion. "Why?"

"That I don't know. It's anyone's guess. I've listened to them in the salon and those two are oh-double-D, odd. Quite creepy."

"Do you think I should say anything to him about it?"

"I wouldn't," Jessica replied. "At least, not until we have actual proof of something. I don't want to freak him out."

"Or," April added. "Have him thinking we're a couple of nut bars for our suspicions."

"Speak for yourself." Jessica laughed, then her voice grew serious. "I'm not the one hanging out with another man, while my boyfriend is completely in the dark, innocently getting ready for the approaching school year."

April cleared her throat and swallowed against a lump of guilt that felt lodged in her windpipe. "Jess, it's not like that—"

"Save it," Jessica said, abruptly. "We can talk later, when you don't have an audience."

"Fine."

"I have to go," she said. "I'll talk to you later."

"Bye." April hung up and swiveled her seat to face Gerritt. He'd finished sorting bags and was watching her, his head slightly cocked to the left.

"What?" She folded her arms across her chest, unnerved by his penetrating stare.

"Nothing." He shrugged. "Just you and your sister. It's an interesting dynamic to watch."

"She can push my buttons," April acknowledged and dropped her gaze to her shoes.

"So, anyway," her let it drop, rubbed his hands together and gestured at the waiting silver box on the countertop. "The box."

April unfolded her arms and slid down from the stool. She moved in closer, intrigued by his enthusiasm. The metal surface of the box was so detailed, she couldn't help herself and reached out to slide a gentle finger across it.

"The details are really something," he said, his voice almost a whisper as he, too, carefully caressed the swirls, flowers and cartouche embossed on the box.

"What is it?"

Gerritt eased open the lid, his face a picture of delight. Inside were six empty ring slots, lined in soft, green velvet. "It's been exquisitely preserved," he told her, his voice reverent. "Whomever Max got it from really valued it and it shows."

April glanced from the box to Gerritt, then back again, attempting to correlate the two. It was a delicate jewelry box and he was anything but delicate, yet, he was entranced. If she hadn't seen it with her own eyes, April might not have believed it. It dawned on her, in that quiet moment, that he held as much passion for his chosen profession as she did for her own. It was so attractive, it was unsettling.

Gerritt closed the lid and turned toward her, his eyes so clear April wished she could step inside them. "I had a customer come in on Friday," he said, his lips curving into a smile at the memory. "An older woman. She completely fell in love with this piece and that's why it's behind the desk. I'm holding it for her to pick up later today."

April nodded and looked around at the shop. "You've convinced me," she said, lightly. "This place definitely holds some interesting and amazing treasure. You just have to take your time and look for it."

"Exactly," he agreed and placed a hand on her shoulder. April's stomach flipped when he touched her and she caught her breath. "I'm pleased you understand. Sometimes, the most amazing things are right under your nose. You just have to take the time to notice."

April was at a loss for words and could only nod.

"I was going to ask you," he said, unaware of the effect his touch was having on her. "Do you want to meet for coffee, later?" Before she could utter a reply, he snapped the fingers on his free hand. "Or, even better, what would you say to coffee at my place - Max's house - after I'm done here and you're done at the library?"

April blinked. It was taking her a moment to digest what he had asked. His hand, warm through the fabric of her shirt, had muddled her thinking.

"If you don't want to, that's okay." He let his hand drop from her shoulder and his voice became guarded. "I just thought you might be interested to see for yourself the damage the trees from the storm caused to the place, but if it seems odd..."

Shit. He had misunderstood her silence for hesitation. "No!" April blurted, then quickly amended. "I mean, yes, I would love to come to your, or rather Max's, place. For coffee. To see the damage." She stopped talking and felt heat rise into her face. She was tripping over her own words.

Gerritt grinned and April reached out to clutch the edge of the desk. She was feeling a bit light-headed, it had been a long time since she'd been exposed to so much sexual innuendo.

"Excellent." He nodded, then turned his head when the bell above the shop door signaled the arrival of a new customer.

"I should go," April said, following his gaze. It was time she cleared her head and tried to get her work done. Flirting was not going to pay the rent.

"Right," he agreed and led the way, out from behind the high desk. "I'm done here by four, so do you want to meet me at the house at around four thirty?"

"Okay."

"Do you need directions?"

"No, I have a pretty good idea of where it is. This town isn't that big, after all."

He grinned. "You've got that right. Will that give you enough time for your column? Does the library even stay open past four?"

"It's open until five, so four thirty should be perfect."

April glanced the customer who'd entered the shop, a well put together woman of a *certain age*, heading directly toward a beautifully hand painted table. "Wow, that table is lovely," she offered, watching the woman lightly graze its surface with her hand. "I didn't even notice it until this minute."

Gerritt, also observing the woman, nodded. "Very nice and very pricey. It's a console table. Mongolian and all hand carved. Runs in the neighborhood of about twenty four hundred."

April turned to him, astonished. "Dollars? Really?"

"Yup."

"Well, then," she said. "I'll definitely get out of your way and let you get to that." She left his side and called over her shoulder as she walked to the shop exit. "See you later."

Gerritt was off to help the woman, but called back, "Looking forward to it."

April couldn't help herself and a large cheesy grin nearly split her face in two. She ducked out of the shop before she risked humiliating herself with a school girl giggle.

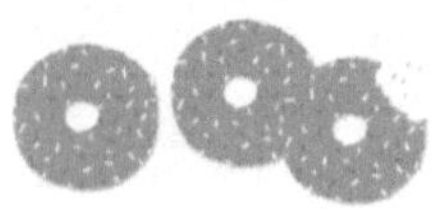

## 1:07 p.m.

April sighed and stretched her neck. She was working on her laptop at the library and what was supposed to be a straight forward column, about the joys of creating

throw pillows for a child's bedroom, had turned into a laborious chore. She was of the mind that she would've liked nothing better than to have one of those pillows in her possession; so she could smother and silence the hackneyed prose being typed across her screen.
"April?"

April blinked and looked up from her laptop. *Good God*, she thought and reflexively reached out a hand to grip the table.

"It's Denise," Denise said, then pointed to Heidi. "And, Heidi. You remember?"

April nodded, then coughed as the smell of Denise's pungent perfume hit her nostrils. Denise was standing quite close to the table, her pudgy form crammed into a pair of tan cargo shorts and a cinnamon-red tee shirt. The color of the shirt offset her sharply cut black hair and April wondered if it was naturally that black, or if Jessica did it for her.

"How *are* you?" Denise asked, leaning in slightly and placing her hand on the table next to April's computer.

April repressed the urge to arch away from the woman and, instead, affected her best Ms. Manners imitation. One of her favorite teenage expressions ran across her thoughts, '*When in doubt, bullshit your way out*', and she curved her lips into a tight smile. "Just fine, you?"

"You come here quite a lot, hmm?" Heidi asked, cocking her head to the side like an inquisitive pet.

April raised an eyebrow quizzically. How was it that *this* woman knew how often she was at the library?

"What I mean is," Heidi elaborated, her smile as sweet as saccharin. "I'm an avid reader and I'm sure I've seen you here a few times, *hunched* over your laptop."

April snapped her shoulders back. The sudden vision of herself as an aging, C-shaped woman came flying forward. Not a pretty sight.

"We're sorry to interrupt you." Denise took a step forward and sat down in the vacant chair next to April. Heidi took the other side.

April took a slow, shallow breath - they didn't sound the least bit sorry. A wave of claustrophobia rolled across her chest as the two of them closed in. "That's okay," she said and quickly snapped her laptop shut from their prying eyes.

"We won't keep you but a moment," Denise assured and laid a hand on April's shoulder. Heidi, still on April's right, nodded in agreement. April turned her head back and forth between them and had a vision of a tennis match, where she was the ball.

"We were just wondering," Heidi said, tilting forward as though she was about to share a secret in April's ear. "Gerritt Bond is staying at your place, with you and Kevin, correct?"

Ahh. Suddenly, the other shoe dropped. Jessica has been bang on. April leaned back in her chair and, thankfully, Denise dropped her hand from her shoulder.

April folded her arms tightly across her chest. "Correct."

Heidi waited a moment, her face expectant. April stayed silent. Heidi blinked and, finally, when the pause became awkward, asked, "Do you think he'll be with you for a while?"

April was taken aback. Talk about cutting to the chase. "You know," she replied, her tone stiff. "I really can't say. You'll have to ask Gerritt if you want that sort of information." She cocked her head and frowned. "If you don't mind *me* asking, why exactly do you ladies want to know?"

Heidi and Denise laughed in unison, their giggles pouring forth so effusively, April was startled. Heidi brushed a lock of her red hair back from her face and gave April a coy smile.

"Do you actually need to ask?" She shared a knowing look with Denise and lowered her voice suggestively. "The man is a serious dish, which maybe you don't really see since you have Kevin. That's understandable, but sweetie, let me assure you, he is yummy and we want to know where we can find him, day or night."

"Preferably night," Denise added, her grin lascivious.

April tensed and opened, then closed, her mouth. She was without words.

Denise reached out to pat her on the hand. "Don't look so surprised," she said, practically purring. "There aren't a whole lot of single men around these parts, at least not dishy ones like Gerritt."

"We certainly can't count your neighbor," Heidi added, her mouth curved into a smirk. "He has his own appeal, sure, in a rough and unkempt sort of way, but he's far too off beat to consider."

"My *neighbor*?" April frowned. Her neighbor? Did they mean Thomas? How did they know Thomas was her neighbor? She shook her head and turned to Heidi. "How do you—"

"Not to mention," Denise cut in, barely repressing her snicker. "We don't have a Daddy issue." Heidi cackled appreciatively at Denise's joke.

April blinked, almost going cross-eyed as she tried to keep up with their back and forth banter. The tennis ball feeling vanished and in its place surfaced a memory of the Disney movie about the dog living with two

Siamese cats. She felt very much like the wide-eyed dog in the film, stuck in the middle while the two felines - these particular ones substantially better fed - flexed their claws and licked their lips in anticipation.

"Well, ladies," April exhaled and pushed her chair back with such force it came close to toppling over when she stood up. She had to get away. Fast. "Since I don't feel I'm at liberty to give you Gerritt's itinerary," she told them, her voice brittle between tight lips. She was doing all she could to restrain herself from accusing them of being stalkers. "I suggest you ask him for yourself."

Heidi stood up and Denise followed. Heidi pursed her lips petulantly and stage whispered, "Oh, come *on*, April. Don't be such a spoil sport."

Denise nodded and chimed in. "It's difficult enough for us girls to get a bit of slap and tickle from the regular men we usually date." She sighed dramatically and ran her index finger across her bottom lip. "When a demi-god like Gerritt Bond shows up, we girls have to help each other out. How else will we find out if all of that sex appeal goes down under, if you *know* what we mean."

April averted her eyes from the Cheshire grin that curved Denise's lips and felt her stomach churn. *Where did they get their script from*, she wondered. *Soft porn? Uggg.*

"I'm sorry, but I can't help you," she insisted and made herself busy, swiftly tucking her laptop into its case on the table. "I've got a deadline and I need to get going."

Heidi pouted, pushing her bottom lip out in a babyish manner. "Well, if you change your mind and think you can tell us anything else..."

"I doubt it," April said, bluntly. "Gotta run." She scooped up her laptop and messenger bag and hot-footed it to the exit.

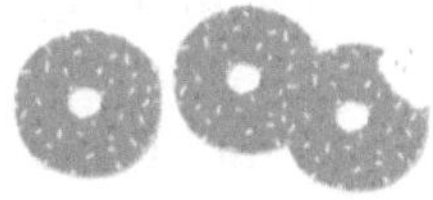

## 1:36 p.m.

April sat in the library parking lot and cranked up the air conditioning in Kevin's car. She wasn't sure what to do with herself. Her intention had been to work until on her column until her arranged meeting time with Gerritt, but after her strange encounter, she was feeling intensely hesitant about their agreement. While a part of her still wanted to go, there was a stronger side telling her to get a grip and not even think about it. The stronger side was winning.

While waiting for the interior of the car to cool down, April sent a quick text to Jessica, telling her she had a story for her about Denise and Heidi. She knew her sister would be equally creeped out and entertained when she told her about her interaction with the two women in the library. Just as she pressed "send" her phone rang in her hand, making her startle in the driver's seat.

"Hello?" she said, pressing the phone to her ear. She opened the middle compartment between the driver and passenger seat to search for the Bluetooth earpiece.

"Got your text," Jessica said. "What's up?"

April found the Bluetooth, turned it on and adjusted it over her ear. "I was accosted," she said as she pulled her seatbelt around her. "Denise and Heidi found me at the library and moved in like a couple of vultures; asking all sorts of creepy questions about Gerritt."

Jessica burst out laughing and as April checked her mirrors, then reversed out of her parking space, she joined in.

"God," Jessica said, continuing to giggle. "What did you do?"

April pulled out of the library parking lot onto the road and, even though her sister couldn't see her, shrugged her shoulders. "What could I do? I waited for my opportunity, like you did with your bad date and a snake fiasco, and got the hell out of there."

Jessica began to chortle all over again and April snickered as she drove. With a bit of space from it, she was starting to find the whole interaction more than a bit amusing. "They were like a couple of cats in heat!"

Jessica laughed harder.

"Anyway, the whole thing made my skin crawl," she said as the scenery flew by her windows. "And, they seemed pretty disappointed I wasn't free flowing with information."

"I can imagine," Jessica said. "Where are you now?"

"Just driving," April told her. "Kevin didn't need the car, so I took advantage of the chance to get to get my stuff done without having to try and haul everything on my bike. Where are you?"

"Home, getting prep done for dinner. You want to come by?"

"Um, I don't think so," she hedged. "I didn't tell Kev I'd be out and I'm not sure if he's cooking..."

"Right," Jessica said, and April felt guilty - not just for the white lie, but because her sister was all by herself.

"But, maybe tomorrow?" she offered, while turning left at an intersection that led her down a quiet back lane.

"Sure," Jessica agreed. "We'll talk and figure something out."

April slowed down and before she could start checking house numbers, saw the home with a huge, blue tarp covering up the entire right-hand front corner. She didn't need three guesses to know she was at the right place. "Okay, sounds good. But, listen, my battery is running low, so I should go."

"Did you manage to get your work done before the dynamic duo interrupted you?" The sounds of cutlery and dishes weaved their way between Jessica's words.

"Pretty much. Just a bit of a polish and off it goes."

April pulled the car in beside the curb, looked at the house and her breath caught in her throat. *What the hell?* Gerritt had opened the door and was standing outside on his step, a welcoming smile on his face.

"Good," Jessica said. "I'll let you go, safe driving and tell Kev I said hello."

"Okay, bye." April barely registered Jessica's last words as she ended the conversation. She swallowed, took a deep breath to quell her nerves and stepped out of the car. "You're already here," she said, by way of greeting.

"And, so are you," he bantered, his voice teasing as he watched her approach the house.

"I though you said after work," she said, slightly put out at being caught out front. Her intention had been to check out the place and leave; it had never crossed her mind that he might be there.

"Things got really slow after you left, so I decided to close up early and prepare for your visit." He gave her a penetrating gaze. "You sound surprised, like maybe you had other intentions?"

"I did." April stopped a few feet away on the path and looked up at him.

He raised an eyebrow and waited.

"I shouldn't be here, Gerritt. In fact, for all intents and purposes, we should agree I'm not." She wiped away a thin film of sweat that had formed just above her top lip - created by the combination of heat and nerves.

"Do you want to talk about this inside?" He stepped back and indicated the open doorway.

April hesitated for a beat, but the heat won. "Okay, but just in the entry way, no further. That way I'm not fully here."

Gerritt nodded and allowed her to brush past him, before stepping in behind her and closing the door.

"Ahh," April involuntarily exhaled as the cool air washed over her hot skin.

"Gotta be grateful for the a/c," he commented, grinning. "And, now that you're inside, are you sure you don't want to—"

"No." April cut him off. "I can't. I wasn't going to come here at all, in fact I don't know why I did, other than plain curiosity to see the house. Needless to say, you weren't supposed to be here and I was going to try and figure out some way to contact you and let you know I wasn't going to be coming by, after all."

"Okay, fair enough. But, now that you *are* here, you're not staying, why?"

April bit her lip. Was he really going to make her say it? What if she was wrong and there was no chemistry between them, just her own delusional ideas based on fantasy? She'd look like a complete ass.

Gerritt watched her and waited. He was really good at waiting her out, she noticed. It was intriguing, as well as bloody frustrating. "Fine," she said, folding her arms across her chest. "You want me to say it? I will. I think there's something more going on here, between us, than just an attempt at friendship."

April pressed her lips together and braced herself for his reaction. If he looked at her with pity, she was going to turn and run out the door. She'd be so fast, he'd wonder if she had been there at all.

"You're right," he agreed, looking her straight in the eye and shocking her right down to her sandals.

"I am?" April's eyebrows shot up in surprise. She was blindsided by his honestly.

"Uh-huh." He nodded and leaned his shoulder up against the wall, crossing one ankle over the other.

"Oh," she replied, grasping for her bearings. "So, umm, what does that mean?"

"To tell you the truth." He shrugged his shoulders. "I don't know. I mean, I know what I'd like, but this isn't a straight forward set of circumstances, so..."

"What would you like?" April asked, boldly. She was a little hesitant to the hear the answer, but not enough to stop herself asking the question.

He grinned. It was a slow grin that started at his lips and journeyed all the way up his face, to end at his eyes as they held her gaze. April's breath caught in her throat. Oh, dear.

"Let me rephrase that." She coughed and swallowed uncomfortably as the foyer suddenly felt a lot smaller. "What do you *wish*—"

Gerritt moved swiftly, taking just two steps to cross the floor and capture her mouth with his, rendering her mute and making her mind swim.

*Oh*, April thought, dazed as his kiss swept over her. She let her body melt into his for a fraction of a second, before her senses rallied and she pushed him back, hard, away from her.

"What the hell!" she blurted, the moment her mouth was free of his.

Gerritt raised his hands upward in a "don't shoot" gesture. "Sorry," he said, with no conviction.

"Like hell you are." April's words came out in a growl as she caught her breath and wiped a hand sharply across her mouth. "Why did you do that?"

"You asked what I'd like," he began.

"Stop." She held her hand up. "Seriously, please do not make light of this."

Gerritt cleared his throat and nodded. "Okay, you're right. Sorry again and this time I mean it."

April looked him in the eye and relaxed her shoulders. He'd dropped the teasing tone. "So? Are you going to tell me what just happened here?"

"I needed to know," he said.

"Know?"

"If this was just a flirty thing." He waved his hand back and forth between them. "Or, something more."

She waited. The question was burning in her thoughts, but on the heels of their kiss, she was too chicken to ask it.

Gerritt regarded her with soft, knowing eyes. "More," he said, his voice practically a caress.

"I have to leave!" April spun on her heel and yanked open the door.

"April, wait." He reached out for her hand and April recoiled when his fingers touched hers.

"No," she said, shaking her head firmly. "You don't seem to get it, Gerritt. I cannot do this. I made a commitment when I moved here, to Kevin, to this town, to this life. I can't just drop it because of some..." She paused, searching for the right words. "*Primitive attraction* to someone I barely know."

Gerritt's eyebrows shot up as he dropped his hand back down to his side.

"I'm sorry if I gave you the wrong impression," she apologized, feeling both foolish and teary. "It's just that, suddenly, I'm feeling really at odds with my choices. I thought I knew what I wanted and then you came along and everything feels different..."

Gerritt rubbed a hand across his chin. "Listen, April, regardless of everything else, if you need someone to talk to—"

"I have to go," she cut him off and turned her back to leave. "I hope you won't be mad," she threw over her shoulder as she jogged down the path to her car and pulled open the door.

"No," Gerritt assured her, his voice warm as it had been moments earlier.

"Okay, good." She looked up just long enough to meet his eye. "I'll see you later, back at the house?"

"You bet." He waved as she slipped swiftly into the car. "Drive safe," he called after her as she pulled away from the curb and the vehicle disappeared down the lane.

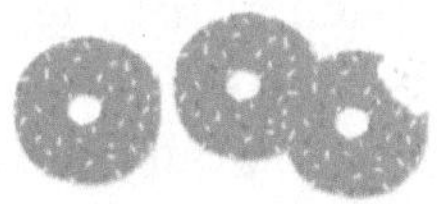

## 11:45 p.m.

April slipped ever-so-carefully beneath the covers, into her bed. Kevin was snoring gently on the other side of the mattress and the last thing she wanted was to disturb him. It hadn't been her intention to be so late, but once she had started driving she couldn't bring herself to stop. She'd needed the time alone to air out her thoughts, or at least try and out-drive them, and felt as though she'd traveled every road of Boxwood Hills at least twice.

Should she have called? Probably. Had she? No. The very idea had made her feel tightly bound by her own skin. Not the best feelings to be experiencing while attempting to explain to Kevin her absence and jumbled thoughts. It would only have caused discord, so she'd made the choice to simply go off the grid.

"Hey."

April froze. *Shit.* Maybe if she just pretended she hadn't heard...

"You're home," he said and moved closer.

*Oh, God, kill me now,* April thought. She didn't have the energy to deal with anything more at that point. Kevin let his arm settle comfortably across her hip and she stiffened. Trapped.

"Where've you been so late?" He breath was warm in her ear as he nuzzled his lips on her neck. "I texted, but you never replied, was your phone turned on?"

"I was working on my column," she replied, lightly, keeping her body turned away from him. Even though the bedroom was blanketed by darkness, she felt unease settle into her stomach at the idea of talking directly to him. Her thoughts and emotions were too tremulous and April was sure they would show on her face.

"This late?" He remarked. "Doesn't the library close?"

April knew he would say it. It was an obvious conclusion; however, guilt stepped in and began ruling her mouth. "Yes," she answered curtly, then shifted her midsection so he would be forced to remove his arm. He did.

"But, it had to get done, okay? It had to get finished, so I just kept at it until it was finished. What's with the questioning?"

"I wasn't *questioning*," Kevin replied, sounding a bit stunned. "I was just a bit worried when I didn't get any response back from you all night."

"I'm a big girl, Kev," she said, dismissively. "I *do* come from the city; a far cry from small town Boxwood Hills. The last thing you need to do is worry."

"Okay, fine." His voice was terse as he twisted away from her and threw back the covers. "Just do me a favor, the next time you decide to be a *city girl*, at least let your sister know. She called a couple of times tonight, looking for you. I felt like a bit of an ass, not having any idea of where you were, or how to get ahold of you."

Guilt rose in April's throat and she swallowed against it. Oh, God, she was making a hash job of things. Before she could form a response, Kevin had pulled his sweatpants on over his boxer shorts, picked up his pillow and stormed out of the bedroom, closing the door firmly behind him.

"Crap," April said to the empty bedroom. She sat up, punched her pillow a few times and flopped back down onto the mattress in exhaustion. Why the hell did Gerritt have to go and kiss her? It made a mess of everything. Did she tell Kevin? Was there anything even to tell? After all, Gerritt had kissed *her*, not the other way around.

April sighed heavily and pulled her covers up around her chin. She didn't need the drama, of that she was certain. She'd finally been feeling like she had her life somewhat on track and then, just like that, she was feeling on the verge of derailment.

Too tired to give it anymore attention, April started drift off. The last thing that swam through her jumbled thoughts, before she crossed over into sleep, was why did she feel as though she was being followed all night?

She was sure she'd noticed a blue, nondescript car on the roads around her, all during her travels through the winding streets of Boxwood Hills... had she been imagining it?

# CHAPTER 5 - Tuesday

8:00 a.m.

April munched on a piece of toast slathered in butter and jam and waited for the coffee pot to finish brewing. The house was quiet, both Kevin and Gerritt had cleared out early, which was fine by her. The less she had to interact with either of them, the better.

The telephone rang and she reached for the receiver on the countertop. "Hello?"

"Oh, what a surprise, you're home," Jessica said, sarcasm lacing her words.

"Good morning, to you, too." April bit noisily into her toast and tucked the phone between her ear and shoulder as she poured fresh coffee into her favorite, sunflower adorned mug.

"So, are you going to tell me, or am I going to have to barrage you with questions?"

"I have no idea what you're talking about."

"Okay, fine." Jessica exhaled into the receiver. April stuck out her tongue out, childishly, in return. "Did Kevin tell you I called?"

"No," she lied.

"He didn't? How late were you out?"

Bloody hell. Her, too. April felt like a child who had missed curfew. "Not that late, why?"

"When I called - because you didn't call me back like you said you were going to, I might add - it was pretty late. And, Kevin said he didn't know where you were."

April took a sip from her mug and wracked her brain for a reply.

"I have to tell you, it was a bit uncomfortable for me to have to hear the accusation in his tone. As though he was thinking I knew where you were, but wasn't telling."

April rolled her eyes. "Sorry for your discomfort?" she said, dredging up a sarcastic tone of her own.

"Very sincere, April Showers," Jessica responded. "So, where were you hiding?"

"I wasn't hiding, I was working."

"When I spoke to you yesterday afternoon, I thought you said you were done."

"Yeah, and I also said I had some polish left to do." She changed the subject. "So, any thoughts about Denise and Heidi at the library?"

"Actually, yes," Jessica said, switching gears with her.

April popped the last bite of her toast into her mouth and picked up her mug. "And?" she asked as she padded into the living room on orange, slipper clad feet. She was still in her pajamas, a pair of green baggy boxer shorts and a loose fitting, blue tee shirt.

"I said it before and I'll say it again, I had a feeling about those two when they came into the salon and started their double speak and I'll bet dollars to donuts I'm right."

"You won't get any arguments from me," April agreed, while she placed her cup on a side table. "I'm convinced you're spot on."

"Meaning?"

"Meaning, while I'm not one hundred percent sure, I *do* have a strong suspicion those two women may have been following me yesterday, after I left the library."

"What?" Jessica's voice was alarmed. "No, not really? Seriously?"

April was interrupted by the doorbell. "Hang on, someone's at the door." She walked into the foyer and pressed her eye to the peep hole on the door. "It's my neighbor, Bob." She opened the door.

"Hey, Bob," she said, cordially, shifting the phone away from her ear to rest on her shoulder.

"Hi!" Bob gave her a wide smile. "Sorry to bug you, April, but I, uhh, just needed to ask you a quick question."

April leaned against the door frame. "Shoot."

Bob reached down into a grey, plastic bag he was holding at his side and pulled out a sweatshirt. April blanched. It was her sweatshirt; the stained shirt that Thomas, the bugger, had put into Deborah and Bob's trash.

April pressed the phone back to her ear. "Jess? I'm going to have to call you back." She hung up the phone, gripped it in her hand like a pistol and squared her shoulders.

"Deborah insisted I ask the neighbors if they found this shirt familiar." Bob held it out for her to see. "I couldn't convince her, and believe me I tried, that it was a waste of time. So..." He shrugged his broad shoulders apologetically. "Here I am. Look familiar?"

"No." She was blunt.

"I didn't think so." Bob sighed. "I've already been to most of the neighbors in the cul-de-sac and they've all said the same thing."

April cleared her throat and hoped she sounded calm. "Really? Everyone?"

He nodded. "I just have the next two after you." He pointed in the direction of Thomas' house. "And, I'm hoping that's good enough to call Deborah off." He shook his head wearily. "She can be like a dog with a bone. A great trait in business, but a hell of a bitch in the rest of life."

April was taken aback by his frankness. He'd never spoken so freely, that she could remembered. The stress must have been getting to him.

"Well," she said, crossing her arms and tucking the phone between her bicep and ribcage. "You can tell her no one here recognized it. Completely foreign to us."

"Okay." Bob smiled and stuffed the sweater, *her sweater*, back into his plastic bag. "Thanks, April, I appreciate your patience." He made a motion to leave, then stopped. "Oh," he added. "One last thing before I go. I have to give you this." He handed her a small piece of paper, folded like a child's invitation. "Have a good day."

April smiled tightly as he turned and lumbered down the steps, then firmly shut her door. "Good God," she muttered to the empty house. "What next?"

The phone, still tucked under her arm, rang loudly and made April jerk with surprise. She snatched it into her hand and practically shouted into the receiver. "Hello?"

"Hey," Gerritt's deep voice slipped smoothly from the phone into her ear. "Are you okay? You sound funny."

"Oh-my-God," she replied as she shuffled into the living room to see if she could catch a glimpse of Bob over at Thomas's house.

"What's wrong?"

"This is too much," she stated, bending forward from the waist and peering through her blinds. Nothing. She couldn't see a darn thing.

"Is everything okay? Did something happen with Kevin?"

"No," she replied, ignoring the glimmer of hope in his tone. "Nothing like that. I just had a *lovely* visit with Deborah's husband, Bob. And, yes, if you're wondering, I am absolutely being sarcastic."

"I got that."

"He just showed up at the door, only a minute ago. With my sweatshirt!" April flung her free arm wildly as she talked, the folded piece of paper still clutched between her fingers.

"What?" Gerritt's voice was incredulous. "What was he doing?"

"Apparently, his nut job of a wife insisted he go door to door, pestering the neighbors to see if they recognized the damned thing."

"Jeez."

"I *know*." April began to pace back and forth across the living room as she ranted. "The woman is absurd, not to mention has a serious issue with obsessiveness."

"Okay, listen to me," Gerritt said. "This is nothing."

"Nothing!" April was beside herself. "Of course it's not nothing. I'm being hunted."

"No way." He started to laugh.

"It's not funny. I am."

He laughed harder. "You're *not* being hunted. She's just a loon, like you said. It will amount to nothing, I'm sure of it." He took a breath. "God, you really are something."

"Thank God it wasn't Kevin who had answered the door." April shuddered at the thought. "Can you imagine? He probably would have looked the damned thing over so closely, he would have said it reminded him of a sweatshirt of mine."

"But, he didn't," Gerritt soothed. "And, it didn't happen. So, don't think about it."

"You're right." April nodded and took a deep breath. "I dodged a bullet, it will all settle down and be fine. Also," she added. "Bob did say not one of the neighbors had recognized the sweater."

"There you go," he said.

"Okay, I'll let it go." She sat down on the sofa and tucked herself into the crook of one arm. "But, remember, Kevin knows nothing about any of it—"

"Don't worry, your secret is safe with me."

April smiled and felt grateful that her encounter with Bob had managed to annihilate the awkwardness with Gerritt. Small blessings. "Hey," she said, looking at the paper still clutched in her hand. "Bob also gave me some sort of paper, it looks like an invitation, or something."

"An invitation?"

"Yeah." She bent her neck to one side and tucked the phone between her cheek and shoulder. "Hang on, I'll open it." April pulled the edges of the paper apart. "Oh-my-God!" she yelped, letting the phone drop away and land in her lap.

"April?" Gerritt said, his voice tinny inside the receiver as she scrambled to catch it before it bounced off her lap, onto the floor.

"I'm here." April exhaled as she pressed the receiver back to her ear.

"What did it say?"

"It's an invitation," she told him. "To a block party." Gerritt started to laugh , again, and April tried to protest. "It's not funny," she began, and then gave up and giggled, too. "Okay, forget it, it is funny."

"Read it to me," he insisted, catching his breath.

"Dear friends and neighbors." April snickered at the very idea of *friends and neighbors* being one and the same. "It's time to recharge our neighborly batteries. Come on out and share in the good weather and good will of our cul-de-sac. Bring a friend and a treat to share—"

"Lots of sharing going on," Gerritt observed, amusement still lacing his voice. "When is this love fest scheduled to happen?"

"This coming Saturday," she said and leaned back into the corner of the couch.

"Can I be the 'bring a friend'?"

"Absolutely." April giggled and folded the invitation back together. "We'll make Jessica share in the ordeal with us, too. So, anyway, what's up?"

"Right," Gerritt said. "I was calling because I was wondering what you were doing for lunch this afternoon."

"Oh." April stiffened.

"Hear me out," he pleaded. "I just thought, considering how we left things yesterday, it would be a good thing to do to get us back to normal." He waited a beat for her reply. When he got nothing but breathing, he added, "*Or not.*"

"No," April said, decisively. "You're probably right. It would be good, clear the air and all that. I think it's okay for us to be seen in public, right?"

"Excellent." Gerritt nodded, even though she couldn't see him. "So, why don't you come by the shop at around twelve thirty this afternoon and we can pick somewhere to go."

"Looking forward to it." April smiled at the phone and felt like a teenager. A guilty teenager who wasn't telling her parents where she was going. "See you soon."

"Bye."

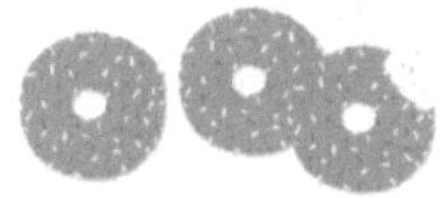

## 4:07 p.m.

"It was a *nightmare*," April moaned, from her prone position on the couch in her sister's staff room.

She had taken refuge at the salon, after her proposed friendly lunch date with Gerritt had turned into a disaster. Instead of the easy, one-on-one interaction she had imagined, it had turned into something resembling a three-ring circus. *No*, April thought. *Change that. A boxing ring.*

"It was like being at a boxing match," she groaned.

Jessica, sitting at a wicker, two-seater table across from the couch, attempted to sooth the situation. "It wasn't that bad," she said, while her face told a completely different story.

"It was. You know it was." April threw her arm across her eyes in an attempt to block the memory. It didn't work, it was too fresh. "I can see it so clearly," she muttered. "There we were, Gerritt and I, off to a harmless lunch and then, who walked merrily through the door? Kevin. After that, everything seemed to go in slow motion."

She pulled her arm from her face and sat upright, her hair jutting wildly from her skull. "I swear, when I saw Kev I nearly fainted."

Jessica nodded, but remained silent. She had already heard the tale once, from beginning to end, on the way back from the mall in her car.

"Thank goodness Gerritt was there to stop me from running and hiding behind the desk." April shook her head.

"Yeah," Jessica said, wryly. "*That* might have been a bit of a tip off that things weren't on the up and up."

"They were on the up and up! They couldn't have been more up! We weren't doing anything except going for lunch. It was Kevin who was the crasher and tainted it." She threw her hands up in frustration and glared at Jessica. "Why did you have to agree to come along?"

"Oh, nice," Jessica retorted.

"You know what I mean."

"I didn't realize, did I?" Jessica countercharged and folded her arms across her chest. "If you had taken a moment, just one simple moment, to call me back and fill me in on what had happened after you hung up this morning—"

"I was distracted by Bob," April cut in, trying to defend herself.

Jessica didn't stop, just steam rolled ahead. "*Then*, I wouldn't have been forced to call you on your cell and none of this may have happened."

"You still could have said no to Kevin's invitation to come along," April insisted. "You were on the phone, not even in person for christ's sake. How hard would it have been to say, 'no, thanks'?"

"Easy to say." Jessica's nostril's flared. "But, you *know* what Kev can be like. When he grabbed your phone away and started pressing and pressing that I join all of you for lunch, I knew he wasn't going to stop until I agreed."

"Fair enough," April conceded and raised her hands in front of her in surrender. She did know what Kevin was like. He was downright bullheaded and once he got an idea in his head, it was pretty much inevitable that whatever he set his mind to was going to happen.

"For the record," Jessica added. "You weren't the only one who was there at the table, suffering through it. I don't remember the last time I've been in such an awkward situation." She grimaced and April knew her sister was thinking of the four of them, seated round the restaurant table, making stilted small talk while Kevin shot intense looks at her across his menu.

"Ugg," April groaned, seeing Kevin's face in her mind's eye. She dropped back into the couch cushions and clutched her stomach. "Just thinking about it makes me feel ill."

"It could be all that bread you ate," Jessica commented.

"I had to focus on something besides Kevin's glares," she replied and rubbed her abdomen. "Bread was the only thing convenient."

"And, poor Gerritt." Jessica shook her head.

"Pah!" April exhaled. "Don't worry about him, he'll be fine."

"You seem suddenly all knowing on that front." Jessica's stare was penetrating. "When are you going to spill it?"

April sighed and sat up. "There's not that much to spill."

Jessica snorted and raised an eyebrow.

"Really." She shrugged and averted her eyes to pick at lint on her sleeve.

"Okay, if you don't want me to know—"

"Will you promise to keep an open mind?"

Jessica stared at her for a long moment. April did her best not to fidget. Finally, she nodded. "Yes. Of course. You're my sister, you can tell me anything."

April leaned forward and took a breath. "We kissed."

"April!"

"Liar!" April stood up, angry. "You said you wouldn't judge."

"Oh, sit down." Jessica pursed her lips. "I'm not judging. You just surprised me, is all."

April did as directed and sat down.

"When did this happen? And, for that matter, where?"

"Yesterday, actually," April admitted. "At his house."

"The demolished house?" Jessica's eyebrows shot up in surprise.

"Not all of it's demolished, just two big parts. That's why he can't live there until it's fully repaired."

"So, you kissed him, and?"

"He kissed me, actually," April clarified, hoping she would believe her. "And, it's the first time anything like that has ever happened to me. I mean, obviously I've been kissed, just not by another guy when I was in a relationship."

"How do you feel?" Jessica got up from her chair and crossed the floor to sit beside her on the couch.

"At first, I was confused."

Jessica nodded. "Understandable."

"And, I still am, just not about what I thought I'd be confused about." She took a breath. "Does that even make sense?"

"No."

"Well, after Gerritt kissed me, I was pissed off that he did it." April stood up and started to pace around the coffee table. "Then I drove around for a long while - that's why you weren't able to contact me, by the way. I just needed time to think and kept driving."

Jessica nodded.

"And, by the time I got home, I was still confused, but not about Gerritt. I was confused about Kevin." She stopped pacing and turned to face her sister. "I mean, I've made this commitment to this life and I'm starting to wonder if I really want it, or am I fooling myself..."

"God, April." Jessica sighed heavily and shook her head. "*Enough*."

"If this is about Kevin," April began.

"No." Jessica shook her head. "It's nothing to do with Kevin. I only wish it was that simple, but it's not. This is about you, April. You, you, you."

April frowned. "What about me?"

"You've got a problem, dear sister. A serious problem."

April folded her arms tightly, like a shield, across her chest. "This should be good," she said, her voice petulant. "I'm not ready to fall into holy matrimony with saint Kevin and now, all of a sudden, I have a *problem*."

"No!" Jessica shouted, startling them both. "Not suddenly, at all! You've had this problem for years. Years! Your life is living you, April."

"What the heck is that supposed to mean?" April said, the sneer on her face shifting, to be replaced by confusion.

"It means you don't live your life," Jessica repeated. "Just the opposite. You let your life live you. The only decisions you make are the ones that start things. From there, you just get swept along and then act so surprised when... *whatever* it is, doesn't work out."

"Oh, please." April rolled her eyes.

"Roll your eyes all you want," Jessica said, briskly crossing her legs. "But, it's true. Look at your track record and it's obvious."

"My *track record*?"

"And, then some. Where do I start? You wanted to be a writer, right?"

"No, YOU wanted me to be a writer."

Jessica raised an eyebrow. "Really? So, if I hadn't encouraged you and helped you to believe in your talent, you would have been off embroiled in some other career? Is that it? I interfered with you going after some unspoken dream?"

April shrugged and had the good grace to look uncomfortable. "Fine." She averted her eyes and raised her hands up in defeat.

"Seriously." Jessica wasn't about to be put off. "How many different jobs did you jump around with before you actually focused on writing?"

April sighed and gave Jessica a bored look.

"Too many to count, that's how many."

"Your point?"

"My point is that I did you a favor," Jessica said. "You wanted to be a writer and have your own column—"

"Which I achieved!" April cut in.

"And, which you more or less cannot stand!" Jessica swiftly retorted. "You do it not because you love it, but because it's better than the alternative."

"You congratulated me on my column when I got it!" April accused, incredulous. "Said you were proud of me!"

"And, I was." Jessica was quick to insist. "I was one hundred percent thrilled for you that you'd taken such a step in your goals."

"But?" April prompted.

"*But*, I didn't think you were going to sink in and stay there, April. I thought it was going to be a stepping stone, you know? That you were finally going to consciously take the reins and give your life some direction." She shook her head, disappointment written on her face. "You had such strong goals about the type of column you wanted to write, I just assumed you'd get that in motion once you'd gotten a foot hold and made a name for yourself. What happened to that dream? Instead of going for it, you got just close enough, then settled in and drifted along. Where are you going?"

April cleared her throat uncomfortably. "Fine," she said, flippantly. "Maybe I should have let my craft column be a stepping stone to other goals, but it doesn't mean I still won't."

"Uh-huh," Jessica murmured. "*If* you can give yourself more than five minutes to focus on it, before you distract yourself with another man."

April snapped her eyes toward her sister. "I knew it was all going to lead back to Kevin."

"Only because there's no other choice!" Jessica exclaimed. "In the past ten years you've been involved with, how many men? Eight? More?"

"Oh, come on." April pointed a finger. "You're one to talk, Ms. Serial Bad Date record holder."

Jessica gasped and April's eyes widened. She hadn't meant to sound so callous. "I didn't mean it like that," she began, trying to soften the intent of her words.

"No, it's okay." Jessica held up her hand. "I know what you were implying. And, you'd have a point, *if* I was actually doing so much dating because I was afraid to be alone; which I'm not. I just refuse to settle for the wrong person and it's fitting that you'd not understand that. I'm happy on my own, April, and now I'm looking for someone to share my life with, not *make* me a life."

"That's what you think I'm doing?"

"I don't think it," Jessica said, bluntly. "I know it. You've got some aversion to settling down, always looking around the next corner for something better. I could hypothesize that it has to do with the way Mom was, single and always with a new, temporary boyfriend; you learned at a young age not to be happy on your own."

"And, you didn't?"

"I dealt with that issue long ago. Why do you think I'm still single? As I said, I'm not looking for someone to give me a life..."

"Okay, okay, I heard you." April waved her hand dismissively.

"Well, it's time you woke up," Jessica told her. "Surely you've got to see that by getting involved over and over again, yet not letting any of your relationships get *too* involved, you've kept yourself distracted from taking any real direction in anything and you've missed out on a lot of wonderful opportunities for happiness, to boot."

"Yeah," April said. "But, if they weren't the right one—"

"I'm not saying every guy you were with was perfect, or *the one*, but that's the point, April Showers. No one is perfect and every time you get close enough to start discovering some depth with someone, you pull away. Just like Mom. She wasn't happy alone, but still wanted perfection from the men she dated. It was nuts. They were sunk before they began."

"I'm just going on a hunch here," April said, unable to temper her annoyance. "You're of the mind you have it all figured out and think I'm doing the same thing with Kevin?"

"I'm not saying Kevin is the one, either," Jessica replied, ignoring her sharp tone. "But, you're sure as hell not going to find out, if you repeat your same old pattern and throw Gerritt on the tracks in front of him."

April exhaled sharply. She'd heard enough. "I just said it wasn't about Gerritt. I haven't thrown him anywhere, except maybe away. I don't know what you want from me, Jessica."

"I want you to finally start living your life your way and not looking for someone else to create it for you."

"That's what I've been trying to do!"

"No," Jessica said. "You haven't. You've been avoiding and sidestepping creating a life of your own and, instead, have been letting yourself get swept along by the current; usually some guy. You've never put your ore in the water and made choices, on purpose, about your direction in anything. You've effectively been living your life by default."

April glared at her. "Fine, well, maybe so. And, I guess there's no time like the present to change, right?"

She marched away from her sister to the back alley exit. "Are you watching?" She yanked open the door. "This is me, making a choice, *on purpose*, to get the hell away from you!"

Jessica sighed, then winced as the door slammed shut, making the table rattle.

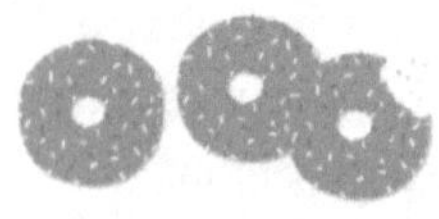

## 5:38 p.m.

April pushed open the passenger door of the taxi cab that drove her home and smiled at the driver. "Thanks," she said, handing him the fare and a generous tip, before lifting a box of jelly donuts sitting her lap. "Here," she said, holding the box out toward him. "Take these home to your family."

"Oh, no." He shook his shaggy, blonde head. "I couldn't."

"Yes, you could," April told him and pushed the box closer. "I thought we'd need them, but I've changed my mind. Silly for them to go to waste."

The cabbie grinned and took the box. "With that hard sell, how can I say no?"

April laughed. "You can't. Enjoy."

She stepped out of the car, closed the door and waved as he pulled away from the curb. *That's that*, she thought as she turned to face her house. She'd calmed down a bit since her argument with Jessica and after sitting for a bit in *The Bakery*, nursing a coffee and thinking, was no longer feeling the same need she had been for comfort food.

"Hi, April!"

April stiffened and stopped dead on her front path. It was Carol, or at least Carol's voice, beckoning. *I should have sprinted*, she thought, regretfully, as she glanced around for physical evidence of her neighbor.

"Yoohoo!" Carol called a second time as she rose up from the behind the tall blooms in her flower bed. The plants had grown so high, not to mention Carol was dressed in beige shorts and a flower print tee shirt, April had completely missed the woman crouched in their depths.

"Hi," April said, attempting to keep her voice polite and impersonal. Perhaps if she employed the strategy of appearing aloof...

"Have a nice outing this afternoon?" Carol asked as she stepped out from between her plants, Peaches tailing behind. "Was it a lunch date?"

So much for aloof. April's shoulders sagged and she jangled her keys. Maybe Carol would take a hint.

"Only, you look too dressed up for just shopping," she added, smiling and scoping her eyes up and down over April's outfit of knee length, yellow and blue patterned silk skirt, sparkly sandals and gauzy, blue blouse. Nope. Not even a chance of a hint taken.

"Yes." April nodded. "I was out to lunch, how astute of you to notice."

"Not a date, then?" Carol queried, her eyes bright with curiosity as she nodded her head in the direction of Kevin's car, in the driveway.

"With friends," April said, through teeth beginning to clench.

"Oh, look!" Carol raised her hand and waved enthusiastically. "It's Deborah." She waved again, as though trying to flag down aircraft. "Yoohoo, Deb! Over here!"

*Oh, dear lord,* April thought, inwardly cringing when Deborah looked their way. *This is why Jessica doesn't get what I'm saying. She doesn't live with this... this... set of neighbors! She'd cut me some slack about my misgivings if she experienced this.*

Deborah walked on carefully placed footsteps across the lawns and arrived to where April and Carol were situated, an almost pained smile on her face. April watched, curious as to whether or not the expression on Deborah's face was for Carol, or more likely, her.

"Lovely evening!" Carol gushed and patted her friend on the arm.

"Yes." Deborah nodded stiffly and smoothed her hands down her pristine, crease free, tailored shirt .

"It was so hot this afternoon, I thought I'd take the opportunity now to check on my garden," Carol said, her head bobbing back and forth to them both in her chatter. "Were you doing the same?"

Deborah raised a hand to cover her mouth and cleared her throat. "Yes, and I thought I saw something odd, a car not usually in the neighborhood, so I came out to have a look."

April raised her eyebrows, her interest piqued. "A strange car? Really? What color was it?"

"April was out for the afternoon, at lunch with friends," Carol blathered, before Deborah could answer.

April cut her eyes at Carol, then gave her attention to Deborah. "Yes, that's true, but you were saying, Deborah? About a strange car?"

"Um-hmm," Deborah murmured, her lips pursed in her thin face. "A blue sedan, older model, not one I've seen around here."

April gasped. Deborah's description was unsettlingly similar to the car she'd seen repeatedly the night before, when she'd been driving throughout the town.

Deborah looked at her sharply. "What? Do you know the car?"

*Oh, hell,* April thought. Thomas was right. With Deborah, you had to watch every word. Time for damage control. "Oh, uh, I don't think so," she hedged, reaching for a plausible excuse for her gasp.

"You seemed inordinately startled when I described it." Deborah folded her arms tightly across her flat chest and fixed April with a steady gaze.

A thin film of sweat broke out across April's top lip. God, the woman could be an interrogator, no problem. Even if you weren't guilty, she made you feel you were.

"Oh, look!" Carol blurted, again. April could have kissed her. "It's Thomas!"

April turned her head to see Thomas standing stock still in his yard, partially hidden by his large, leafy trees.

"Yoohoo!" Carol called out to him, in the same manner she had both April, then Deborah. "Thomas! Over here!"

April had to bite the inside of her cheek to keep from laughing out loud. Thomas's face was a mask of wide-eyed surprise at being spotted. April wrapped her arms around her middle to keep her giggles from escaping as she watched the situation unfold before.

"Thomas!" Carol called, again, her voice insistent as she waved her arm over her head.

Thomas slowly turned his head in their direction and April unclenched her sides to give a him small wave. She watched him audibly sigh, rake his hands through his untamed hair, then stuff them deeply into his pockets as he shuffled his way through his tall grass toward them. Dead man walking.

"Isn't this nice!" Carol effused, looking delighted at the turn of events. "We all so rarely get a chance to be together, it's like a warm up for Deborah's block party."

Deborah's lip curled when Thomas sidled up next to April. He nodded curtly and cleared his throat by way of greeting. A shiver ran up April's spine when the atmosphere in the space between her neighbors turned near glacial. Yikes.

Carol, still beaming, appeared oblivious to the unspoken hostility swirling around them. It fell to Peaches, bless her simple canine brain, to deftly break things up with a sharp bark in the direction of Thomas' yard.

"Oh!" Carol exclaimed as Peaches darted forward to stand at the edge of April's lawn; the last bit of cultivated land before Thomas's jungle of undergrowth began. "Sweetums, you stop right there!"

Thomas turned to watch the dog, rolled his eyes and offered, "Aye, the wee bugger probably noticed my pousie thar in the lea."

Carol's eyes widened measurably. "Pardon me?"

April snorted, while Deborah pursed her lips and looked offended.

Thomas pointed a finger at his yard, a wry smirk plastered on his face. "Over yonder, the pousie is faffing aboot."

April sputtered, coughed and took advantage of her opportunity. "He's talking about his cat, Carol," she said, disengaging herself and swiftly back stepping up her path toward her front door. "In the grass."

"Oh," Carol uttered, looking gobsmacked.

April spun around on the ball of her foot, skipped up the front steps and shoved her key in the door lock. "At least that's what it sounded like to me!" she threw over her shoulder as she pushed open her door, then waved merrily. "Gotta run! Thanks for the chat and see you at the block party!"

The last thing April heard before she firmly shut her door was Carol repeating herself. "Oh."

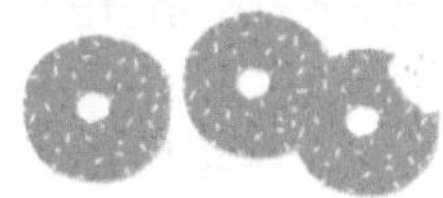

## 6:13 p.m.

April dropped her keys and wallet onto the bench in the foyer. *Jeez, that Thomas*, she thought, snickering to herself as she walked down the hallway toward the stairs. The image of Carol's startled face was hysterical and April's first thought was that she wanted to call Jessica and tell her about it.... Oh, right.

She stopped at the bottom of the stairs, torn between going up and taking a shower, or eating crow and calling her sister. She didn't get much time to ponder because the basement door flew open, jolting her from her thoughts.

"Ahh!" she blurted and jumped back, nearly falling over in her haste.

"Sorry!" Kevin reached out a hand to steady her. "I didn't hear you come in."

April pressed a hand to her chest and caught her breath. "God, you really startled me."

He dropped his hand from her arm. "You okay?"

"I'm fine." She waved away his concern and stepped back, acutely aware of how close they were standing and how little clothing he was wearing. After their strange afternoon lunch experience, she wasn't sure how to act.

"Working out?" She gestured to his shorts and tank-top that hid nothing and, instead, revealed everything. She'd give it to him, the man was buff.

"Uh-huh." He watched her take another step back and then followed behind her as she headed for the kitchen.

"Water?" April pushed open the kitchen door, trying to keep an even pace, even though she felt she was being stalked.

"Please," He spoke over her shoulder.

April reached into the cupboard for two glasses and busied herself getting water. The awkwardness between them was so thick, she was unnerved by it. In all of her time with him, they'd never been so uneasy.

Kevin sat down at the table and when she crossed the floor to place a glass in front of him, he reached for her free hand. "We have to talk."

April's pulse accelerated. Not the words anyone wants to hear from a lover, or otherwise. "Okay." She made an effort to keep her tone light and sat down across from him.

Kevin dropped her hand and leaned his elbows on the table. "I don't even know where to begin, just that we need to talk."

April took a sip of water from her glass and nodded. "How about starting with what's on your mind."

He rubbed at the stubble that decorated his chin and April watched the bicep in his arm flex.

"Something's happening," he said.

April waited. She didn't want to respond until she was certain where he was going with his thoughts.

"We've been out of sync for a while now and in the past week or so, it feels like its gotten worse."

April wiped at the condensation on her glass and continued to listen without comment.

"I don't think it's just me. I think that, if you were honest, you'd say you've noticed it, too." He ran a hand through his dark hair. "It's getting out of hand and I think we need to address it before it gets too big to fix."

Oh boy. April squirmed in her seat. He was giving her all the opener she needed and, suddenly, she was clamming up.

"What do you say?" he asked. "Have you noticed we've become two separate people in this relationship?""

"Well, we are technically two people." She attempted to infuse a smattering of humor to the situation. It didn't work. Kevin just stared at her and waited.

"Okay." April took a breath and exhaled. "I do know what you're saying."

Kevin nodded and lifted his glass to take a long swallow of water.

"I'm not sure if it's just started happening, this separation, or maybe its more like we didn't notice it until now."

His eyebrows knotted together. "What do you mean?"

"Well, until I moved here we had to have a separation, you know? We had no other option, so that's the way it was. And, now that I'm here, I don't think we ever really changed that way of being."

"So, you think we've always been this way? And, I'm just now noticing it?"

April nodded. It was a stretch and she couldn't help but see the huge holes in her theory. Apparently, he did as well.

"No." He shook his head. "I don't think so. We were doing great when you first moved. It's just been the past couple of weeks that I've noticed a change, or more accurately, a distance between us."

He sat back in his chair and folded his arms across his chest, waiting for her reply. Clad only in his shorts and barely-there tank top, he looked ripped and formidable. When she didn't speak, he leaned forward and rested his elbows on the table top.

"The real question is," he said, looking into her eyes. "What's happened to change things?"

*Help*, April thought. *Direct hit.* She couldn't squirm her way out of a direct question. She exhaled, knowing she was sunk.

"Okay," she offered, gently, feeling her way around the words. "If I'm being completely honest, I would agree things feel different - or changed, as you said."

"Right." He nodded.

"I don't necessary think it's you, so much as it's me." She paused and took another small sip of water. "I'll admit I have been having some thoughts about not feeling as connected to this, to us, as I did at first."

Kevin frowned and his expression became guarded. "Why didn't you say something?"

"I don't know." April shrugged. "I guess maybe I thought it would work itself out."

"April." He reached again for her hand. "These kinds of things don't work themselves out by magic. I know you've had a few failed relationships in the past, but this one is different." He looked at her imploringly. "*We're* different."

April felt sick to her stomach. She wanted to run from the kitchen and lock herself in the bathroom.

"Do you want to work this out?" he asked, his eyes intent on hers.

April met his gaze and blanched. She didn't know how to answer his question. Before she had a chance to sputter and stumble over her words, a loud scream vibrated the wall, causing the two of them to jump up out of their chairs as though they'd had an electric jolt.

"Jesus!" Kevin held the edge of the table. "What the hell was that?"

"If I was to guess, I'd say it sounded a lot like Deborah," April offered. "Do you think it could be her, again?"

"It can't be," he said, disbelievingly, and walked briskly across the kitchen to look through the window.

"Well?"

He exhaled heavily. "Holy hell, I can't believe it. Yes, it must be her. I just saw Carol chugging across her lawn in that direction."

"What should we do? Should we go over and see what she's carrying on about this time?"

Kevin stretched his neck from side to side. "I suppose so," he said. "Otherwise, we might have to hear it third person from another neighbor."

April nodded and followed him as he opened the kitchen door. "Um, Kev," she said, before they'd started out and down the back steps. "Do you want to put something else on?"

He looked down at himself and snickered. "Right, yeah. I forgot. Hang on." He turned and jogged through the kitchen, disappearing behind the cafe doors.

April continued outside and sat down on the back steps, readying herself for whatever was to come. Man, what a neighborhood.

"Ready?" Kevin asked, stepping outside to join her a moment later. He'd thrown a pair of black sweats on over his shorts and a white tee shirt over his tank top.

"As I'm going to be," she replied, wryly, as she stood up and brushed the back of her silk skirt. They descended the steps just as Thomas came sauntering over, a cigarette dangling from between his lips.

"Hey, Thomas," Kevin said.

"Another issue to tackle, do you suppose?" Thomas puffed on his cigarette and inclined his head in the direction of Deborah's house.

"I have no idea, but we heard her scream, so guess that means we should go over."

Thomas grinned. "Aye, she makes it difficult to choose another option, doesn't she?"

Kevin laughed. "That's one way of putting it."

"Have any idea what she might be going on about now?" April asked, shooting Thomas a pointed look.

"None, whatsoever, lass," he replied.

April watched his face and believed him. "Well, then." She shrugged and turned toward Deborah's, nearly tripping over Corkscrew as he darted out of the bushes and past her ankles. "Oh!" she exhaled and caught her balance.

"Keep yourself well out of sight, CS," Thomas addressed the cat. "Old lady McCaffey sounds right riled up and you don't want to find yourself caught in the crossfire."

The cat licked his lips and streaked back into the bushes, out of sight.

Kevin and April exchanged a look, but said nothing. Some things were better left alone.

"Shall we?" Thomas offered, gesturing gallantly in the direction of Deborah's property.

April grinned and the three of them crossed the yards toward Deborah's; unconsciously moving as one unit, as though sensing there was strength in numbers.

"Trouble?" Kevin asked, when they came to a halt beside Carol.

Carol turned wide eyes to Kevin. "Oh, it's trouble alright. Look."

She stepped aside and April gasped. There, on Deborah's back steps, was a very still and very dead squirrel.

"What's all this, then?" Thomas asked, smoke streaming from the tip of his cigarette with each word.

Deborah, standing like a marooned palm tree at the top of her stairs, glared at him. "Isn't it obvious? I'm being targeted!"

They all stared at her, speechless. Finally, Kevin spoke up. "Targeted?"

"Yes! That's what I said! Isn't it obvious?"

"For what?"

Deborah's face dropped some of its rigidity and twisted into a puzzled expression. "What do you mean?"

"I mean, have you *done* something?" Kevin asked. "Something to make someone angry enough to want to target you?"

April tensed and stole a sidelong glance at Thomas. He cocked his head slightly, his face a picture of curiosity as he waited for Deborah's reply.

"No," Deborah said, haughtily, the puzzled expression wiped from her face as she lengthened her neck and looked down the steps at him. "Absolutely not. I've been a friend to all."

She turned to Bob, whom April hadn't even noticed standing in the shadows next to the house. "Isn't that right, Bob?"

"Of course. Yes." Bob stepped forward and nodded his head rapidly up and down; as though the motion would cement his words.

"You all have to admit," Carol threw her two cents worth into the mix. "It *is* a little odd that first Deborah's trash can had a dead rodent in it and now, her steps are sullied?"

"Unless, of course, you've been putting oot that weed killer, agin," Thomas commented, his accent thick as molasses. "Making the wee vermin pop their clogs before they can get oot your yaird."

"*Excuse me*?" Deborah folded her arms stiffly across her abdomen. "What do you know about my using, or not using, weed killer?"

"Aye, come on, lass." Thomas chuckled smokily. "We all know you don'na like weeds, amongst other things, anywhere near your gairden."

"I'll have you know," Deborah's lips became thinner and thinner as she spoke. "I do not use any sort of poisons on my yard. They aren't environmental."

April was impressed. While the woman was a nasty piece of work, at least she was an informed nasty piece of work.

"Go ahead, check my garden shed if you must." She gestured toward a small outbuilding at the back of her property. "There's nothing in there that could cause any creature permanent harm."

April raised an eyebrow. It seemed to her that Deborah had put a bit of oomph behind the word "permanent". Or, maybe that was just her observation...

"I don't think that's necessary," Kevin said, attempting to placate her. "I'm sure Thomas was just trying to help, to offer a more agreeable solution to this issue than the idea of targeting."

A car engine caught April's attention and she turned to see, between the houses, Gerritt's vehicle pulling into the driveway. He stepped out of the car, saw them all in the backyard and gave a small wave.

"Hey!" he greeted the group cheerfully as he ambled into the yard. "Everything okay? What's going on?"

"We're not exactly sure," Kevin replied and pointed at the dead squirrel on Deborah's steps.

Gerritt's eyebrows shot up on his forehead. "Whoa! Having a bit of deja vu. What's that about?"

"What does it look like?" Deborah spat. "I'm being targeted."

"For what?"

"Oh, for Christ's sake!" Deborah said, exasperatedly, and rolled her eyes. "Not you, too."

Gerritt looked bewildered and April had to bite down on a giggle that threatened to overtake her.

"So, is there anything we can do, Deborah? Anything at all?" Kevin offered.

*Speak for yourself*, April thought, sharing a look with Thomas. His expression made it clear he was thinking much the same. The woman had been a bitch to both of them.

"Just be prepared for the police to question you all again." Deborah jutted her chin in the air.

Kevin crossed his arms and assumed his wide legged, Gladiator stance. "Deborah," he said, matter of fact. "I don't think calling the police, again, is going to do much of anything."

"You can think what you want—"

"Hear me out," he said, holding his hand up. "Bob, I'm sure you'll agree, and help your wife to understand, that the cops have more pressing matters to address than the occasional rodent kicking it in a person's trash, or on their property."

*Wow*, April thought, impressed. He wasn't pulling any punches. She could only assume he was fed up to his back teeth with it. That was the usual catalyst for him to shoot from the hip. It wasn't always pretty, but it was honest.

"I think, and I'm sure the rest of your neighbors do as well, you should just dispose of it and move on, Deborah."

"Amen to that," Thomas agreed, then turned sharply on his heels and walked away.

Deborah looked outraged. "Well, you're entitled to think what you want," she said, loftily. "All of you. But, as I said, if you find the authorities at your door once more, perhaps then you'll realize I'm not making something out of nothing. *This*," she said, stabbing her index finger in the direction of her steps. "Is not nothing."

With that, she imitated Thomas and spun on her heels. "Clean this up!" she barked at Bob, then disappeared into her house.

"Sorry about that." Bob shrugged his shoulders and rubbed his neck.

"No problem, Bob." Kevin shook his head. "Have a good evening."

Bob gave a small wave as they disbanded, Carol to her house; Gerritt, Kevin and April to theirs. Gerritt walked close on April's left side and Kevin, at a distance, on her right.

"So," Gerritt said, oblivious to the physical separation between the couple. "You'll have to fill me in on what I missed."

April glanced toward Kevin and noticed the thoughtful expression on his face. When they arrived at the back door, she was acutely aware of how careful he was not to touch her as they entered the house.

"Yeah," she agreed, with a sigh. "I'll bring you up to speed."

# CHAPTER 6 - Wednesday

6:45 a.m.

April hit *send* on her email and breathed a sigh of relief. Her work was in the hands, metaphorically speaking, of her editor and she could relax for a day or two, until she had to begin her next column.

There was a knock on the bedroom door. "April?"

"It's open."

The doorknob twisted and Gerritt pushed back the door. "Sorry to bother you," he said, his grin so welcoming it made her stomach flip. "I'm making some coffee and I wanted to make sure I'm doing so to your specifications."

April couldn't help herself and smiled back at him. She knew he was being cheeky, but didn't care. The cool, almost glacial atmosphere that had descended around Kevin since their kitchen talk made her pathetically willing to bask in the warmth of a man's attention; even if it was the wrong man.

She raised an eyebrow and Gerritt gave her an innocent look. "*Please*," she said, with a laugh as she pushed herself off the bed. "Like you can't make coffee."

"Sure." He continued to feign innocence. "But, every coffee maker is unique."

April rolled her eyes and dared to slap him playfully across his bicep as she brushed by him, through the doorway. He grinned down at her and she saw the flicker of something more move like a shadow across his face. Yikes.

"Follow me," she said, moving swiftly down the stairs.

"My pleasure," he bantered.

*Watch it*, a small voice in April's head warned, reminding her how easily the teasing could move into other territories. "I'll bet you say that to all the girls," she shot back, her pulse kicking up as she ignored the voice.

Gerritt moved rapidly down the stairs behind her and was almost on her tail as she pushed her way through the cafe door into the kitchen. "Wouldn't you like to know," he said, his voice silky and teetering on the edge of intimate.

April turned on her heel, causing him to stop short, and met his eye. In that moment she had to admit to herself, yes, she would like to know. He watched her closely, his dark pupils dilated in his bright blue eyes, and April caught her breath. She knew she had no business flirting with him, but...

A thumping sound from outside jarred her from her less than stellar thoughts. She frowned and looked toward the kitchen window. "Did you hear that?"

Gerritt nodded and went toward the window. "Uh, huh. I did."

"Did it sound like heavy footsteps?"

"That's exactly what it sounded like," he agreed as he leaned across the countertop and peered between the slats of the blinds on the window "What the hell?"

"What?"

"I'm not completely sure, and I don't want to freak you out, but I think there was someone outside."

"What!" April stared at him, wide-eyed. "What do you mean? Like a prowler, or something?"

He shrugged and massaged his forehead with his fingertips. "Let's not overreact," he said, his hands out in front of him, patting the air in a calming gesture. "At least not until we know for sure what that was."

"And, how do you suggest we do that?"

"Hang on."

He walked over to the back door, opened it and disappeared outside. April thought about following him, but the chairs at the kitchen table looked more inviting. She needed to get off her feet for a moment; she wasn't feeling very steady.

Gerritt came back inside and closed the door. When he didn't say anything for a moment, she prompted. "Well?"

"Yeah, no question. There was definitely someone there."

"Oh. My. God!" She exclaimed, glad she was sitting.

"And, from the amount of footprints in the dirt, I'm pretty sure it was more than one person," he added, then braced himself for her reaction.

April looked at him, stunned. "What do we do? Something? Nothing?" She stood up, then sat down, then ran her fingers through the layers in her hair, at a loss.

Gerritt sat down in the chair opposite her and shook his head. "No idea."

Finally, in a measured voice, she said, "What the hell is happening, and where the hell am I living?"

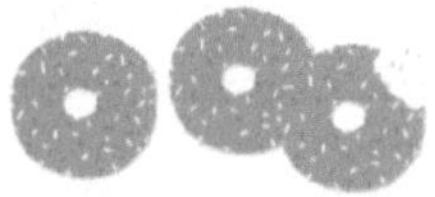

## 6:54 p.m.

Jessica moved from station to station in her salon, straightening up. Her stylists were in charge of keeping their areas clean and tidy, but she was like a mother hen, clucking behind them.

April spun in lazy circles in the chair she'd dragged in from the reception desk and watched her sister fuss. She hadn't intended to be the first one to cross the imaginary line they'd drawn and hold up her metaphorical white flag, but after the freaky peeping tom incident... Well, she had to talk to someone about it. Someone who wouldn't immediately turn it into a reason to call in "the authorities".

"They're grown women, you know," April commented as Jessica moved a container of styling wax from one station to another. "And, don't they pay rent on their chairs? Meaning, they understand you have an image you want upheld?"

"I know," Jessica admitted. "But, I don't mind. It makes them feel valued."

April raised an eyebrow, but offered no return comment. She wasn't about to argue with that logic. Instead, she moved the conversation back to where it had begun. "So, what do you think? I mean, don't you think I have legitimate reason for concern here? Someone was looking, or trying to, in my windows - in broad daylight!"

"I'll admit, it's unsettling," Jessica agreed. "Did you tell Kevin about it?"

"I haven't had a chance." April leaned back and watching the ceiling blur as she spun the chair slowly with her foot. "The whole thing spooked me so badly, I threw myself together and took off to the library for most of the afternoon. I didn't want to be in the house."

Jessica nodded, looked at the order she had created and brushed her hands together in satisfaction. "But, you're going to tell him, right?"

"I suppose." April stopped spinning and sat upright. "But, I can't even begin to imagine that conversation. 'Hey, Honey, I think I'm being stalked. Or, maybe, Gerritt is being stalked and I'm being lumped into it by default.'" She shook her head. "He's going to think I've lost the plot."

"Maybe, but even so, you have to say something." Jessica walked to the front doors, checked that they were securely locked and gestured to April. "Chair, please."

April stood up, slightly unsteadily from all the spinning, and pushed the chair toward her.

"Get Gerritt to back you up," Jessica said, catching the chair, tucking it behind the reception desk and then flicking off half the lights in the salon.

"Yeah," April agreed, half-heartedly.

"What?" Jessica asked, her voice cautious. They were getting dangerously close to the territory they had just left in their previous conversation, from the day before.

"Nothing," April assured her. "I'm just keeping my distance in that regard, you know? Since a little bird told me I have a habit of being a serial monogamist—"

"I didn't use those words," Jessica cut in.

"No." April acknowledged. "But, it's what you were leading to, amongst other things."

Jessica looked ready to defend herself and April held up her hand. "I'm not trying to start things up again, Jess. Honest. You had some valid points, I've been thinking on them, so let's just leave it, okay?"

"Okay." Jessica bit her lip and looked as though she was having a hard time meeting April's eye.

April sighed. "Say it."

"I'm just worried for you, April Showers," she admitted as she lead them into the staff room and opened the door to the back alley. "Yes, Gerritt is beautiful and I can see the attraction, I'm not blind. And, I know I sound like a broken record, but, the old adage is true. Act in haste, repent at leisure."

"Don't worry," April said, following her into the evening air. "I'm so shell-shocked by everything, I'm not acting at all."

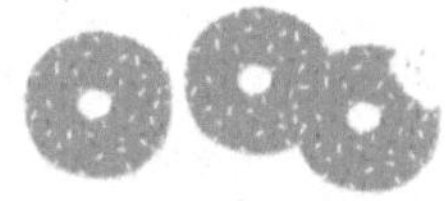

## 7:44 p.m.

April stood at the curb in front of her house and waved Jessica off. *I have to get a car sorted out,* she thought as she turned away from the street. The transit system in Boxwood Hills was far from ideal and it wouldn't be summer forever.

Head lights illuminated the front of the house and she watched as Gerritt pulled his vehicle into the driveway and parked it beside Kevin's.

"Hey," he said as he stepped out of the car.

April smiled and felt like a goofy teenager stealing a moment with her forbidden boyfriend. *Stop it,* she chastised herself.

Gerritt pressed the button on his key fob, locking his doors, and walked across the lawn to meet her on the walkway to the house. "Nice night," he offered. "Going inside?"

"Just about to," she began, then stopped when she heard a loud, "Pssst!" She raised an eyebrow at Gerritt and glanced around. "Okay, that wasn't me. Did you hear that?"

"Yeah," he said, frowning.

"Pssst! Over here."

April immediately recognized the Scottish inflection and looked to her right. Sure enough, the red tip of a cigarette bobbed in the shadows and standing directly behind it, was Thomas.

"This way," she told Gerritt and cocked her head in Thomas's direction. He gave no reply, just followed her across the lawn. As they got closer, she could see the smoke rising lazily from Thomas' cigarette, wrapping around his head.

"Hey," she said, by way of greeting. "What's up?"

Gerritt reached out and offered his hand to shake. "Good to see you, again, Sir. How're you doing?"

"As good as can be expected, I'd say," Thomas replied, then indicated with a jerk of his head for them to move in closer.

April decided to cut to the chase. She was finding it awkward, not to mention just plain odd, that the three of them were tucked between the branches of Thomas's oversized oak trees.

"Is there something you needed?" she asked.

"No, not me," he said, shaking his head. "But, there is something I think you need to know."

"What's that?" Gerritt crossed his arms and waited.

"This afternoon when your house was empty I saw someone, two of them to be exact, sneaking around your property."

"What?" April involuntarily reached out to clutch at Gerritt's arm, her fingernails pressed against his skin. "Are you sure? Who was it?"

Thomas shrugged. "Don'na know. Didn't recognize them. Two women, I'd say aboot 10 years older than you, April. One of them Asian, the other pale with red hair."

"Holy shit," Gerritt said, immediately identifying with Thomas's description.

"It's you," April blurted at him and dropped her hand from its clutch around his forearm.

"Me?" he said, his voice surprised. "What are you talking about?"

"That wasn't just anyone, those women were Denise and Heidi," she blathered. "They have a thing for you and they're stalking you."

Thomas nodded. "Ahh," he said, as though what April said was more than obvious.

"What '*ahh*'?" Gerritt frowned at Thomas.

"Well, look at yerself," he said, waving his hand up and down at Gerritt. "You're a fine lookin' man, aren't you? Of course you'd be making some of the ladies a bit barmy."

"That's it, exactly," April insisted. "You've made them crazy and now they're stalking you."

"How do you know that?" Gerritt asked. "Did they come up to you and say, 'Hey, April, we're hot for Gerritt'?"

"*Actually...*" She shrugged, hesitantly.

"Oh, come on!" He crossed his arms defensively across his chest.

"No, listen," she elaborated. "When I was at the library, the day I came out to Max's house, both of them were there, too."

"So?"

"*And*," she kept talking. "They came up to me and started asking me questions about you and how long you were staying with us and..." She took a breath as a shudder ran up her spine at the memory. "Generally said they thought you were a dish."

"So, based on that, albeit unsettling encounter, you think they're *stalking* me?"

"Didn't Thomas just say the women lurking around the house were Asian and a redheaded? *And*," she added, pointing her index finger at him. "Remember the night we all went out for dinner and Deborah was running around, insisting she saw two people with the exact same description around the property?"

Gerritt cleared his throat and frowned. April nodded and crossed her arms. "Uh-huh. Right? Coincidence? I think not."

"She's got a right convincing argument there," Thomas offered, with a shrug, the glow from his cigarette tip bobbing in the darkness.

Gerritt nodded and continued to frown.

"I didn't want to say anything about them before," April said, her tone apologetic as she explained. "Because I thought, if I was right, it would creep you out."

"Bang on, I'd say," Thomas commented.

"Okay, fine, that aside," Gerritt said, to Thomas. "Can you tell us what they were doing when you saw them?"

"Right. That's what counts." Thomas nodded sharply. "They were sneaking aboot as I told you, standing next to windows, trying to get a look inside, that sort of thing."

"Did you do anything?" April asked.

He started to chuckle. "Aye, I did. I sent the cat after them."

Gerritt raised an eyebrow. "Meaning?"

"I sent CS into the shrubs there." He pointed to the bedraggled hedges growing between their property lines. "And then, on my signal, he darted oot quick as a shot, making 'em yell and jump oot their skin and tripping 'em up in their eagerness to make haste."

He chuckled some more and the smoke from his cigarette puffed vigorously, creating a haze around them. "You should have seen it, it was priceless."

"Did it do the trick?" April asked, thoroughly amused by the picture he was painting.

"And then some." He ran his fingers through his hair, a grin on his face. "The two of them yelped like they'd seen a ghost and tore oot the neighborhood as though it was right behind them."

"Hopefully that's the last we'll see of them," Gerritt said.

"Thanks for telling us." April smiled at him. Even though there was no question the man danced to the beat of his own drum, he was turning out to be a lot more personable than she had originally thought.

"Yeah," Gerritt chimed in. "Thanks. A lot."

Thomas nodded. "Aye, no trouble. Have a good night."

He ducked under the branches of his tree and shuffled through the long grass in the direction of his backyard. Corkscrew dropped from one of the tree branches above, landing almost directly beside him; accompanying him to the backyard.

"Evening, CS." Thomas's voice drifted by them on the breeze as he and his cat disappeared around the side of the house.

April grinned. They were becoming quite the amusing pair.

"What?" Gerritt asked.

"Hmm?" She said. "Oh, nothing. I just find those two intriguing."

He nodded and looked into her eyes, holding her there for more time than was necessary. April felt the darkness settle around them like a blanket.

"Want to know what I find intriguing?" He said, taking a step closer to where she stood.

*Uh-oh*, April thought, watching him come closer and inhaling his scent of licorice and vanilla. "Umm," she murmured, as a conflict of emotions beat through her. She wasn't going to do this, had made the choice to deal with her *issues* without a man muddling up the process, but *jeez*, the Universe wasn't playing fair.

Gerritt took another step forward and closed what was left of the gap between them. His eyes were still on her, watching her reaction for his cue. When she didn't flinch, he bent forward, grazed her cheek with his fingertips and gently lowered his mouth to hers, giving her a kiss sweeter and more knee trembling than she'd had in a long time.

*Push him away!* The voice in April's head was loud and insistent. Against the instinct of her body she obeyed, placing her hands on his chest and giving him an almighty shove. "Gerritt!" she hissed, when they'd separated.

Gerritt inhaled sharply, his chest rising and falling beneath his tightly fitted tee shirt. His eyes were almost black, the pupils were so dilated, and he released his breath slowly as he fought to regain his composure.

"You have to stop doing that!" She hissed, again, keeping her voice at a whisper, so as to not draw attention to their presence in the quiet night. She rubbed at the back of her neck and glared at him, angry that he made her want to respond when she knew it wasn't an option.

Gerritt held his hands up, palms forward and nodded. "Sorry. But, seriously, you don't seem to get what I'm feeling and I don't know how else to tell you."

"Whatever it is," she said, placing her hands on her hips. "You can't tell me. Do you understand that? Can't. I have other stuff, big stuff, that I have to deal with and *this...*" She pointed her index finger first at him, then herself. "Can't happen."

"Ever?" he said, bluntly.

April stopped short. Could she really say that? That they would never, *ever* explore the option? It was a valid question and she was dismayed to find herself hesitant to offer a concrete reply.

"Okay, then." He nodded, as though her silence was her response. "Not now. I get that. I can live with that."

"Well," she began, feeling she had to offer something other than silence.

He stepped out of the shadow of the trees and fixed his eyes on hers. "Not *now,*" he repeated, before turning his back on her and walking toward the warmly lit house.

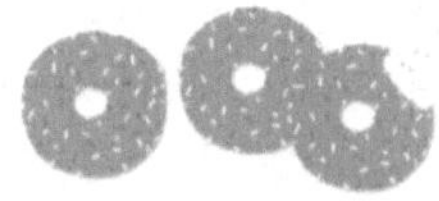

## 9:17 p.m.

April clicked the page turning button on her Kindle and tried to ignore the twitch of Kevin's foot on the couch. He wasn't prone to fidgeting, so it was a pretty obvious indication something was on his mind. She sighed, put her eReader into sleep mode and tucked it beside her in the armchair. "You okay?" she ventured.

He moved his gaze from the TV and rubbed a hand across the five o'clock shadow on his chin. "Yeah, just thinking."

Crap. April shifted in her chair. She had a feeling a "talk" was about to ensue. "About?"

Before He could reply, Gerritt came down the hallway from the guest room. "Hey, do you guys mind if I make some coffee?" he asked. "I've got some stuff I need to do for an exhibit when I get back home and it could be an all-nighter."

"Of course," April said, grateful for the interruption. "Go right ahead. Do you need help with the coffee pot?"

Kevin's back was to Gerritt, so he didn't see the smirk form on his friend's face as he looked at April. "I'm sure I'll be fine."

"*Okay.*" She smiled, innocently. "But, I know that coffee pots can be tricky, so if you need help, just ask."

Gerritt raised an eyebrow and then quickly dropped it when Kevin stood up. "Be right back," Kevin said and left the room to go downstairs to the basement.

April snickered at the inside joke she was sharing with Gerritt and he rolled his eyes at her before walking away, into the kitchen.

"Hey, April?" Kevin called out, figuratively smacking her out of her silliness.

"Yes?" she called back.

"Could you come here a moment?"

"I don't know," she muttered under her breath to herself. "Do I really want to?"

She stood up, stretched her arms above her head and let them drop back down to her sides. *Face your fears and do it anyway*, she thought, counseling herself as she walked down the hallway to the basement stairs.

"Coming," she said and descended the steps.

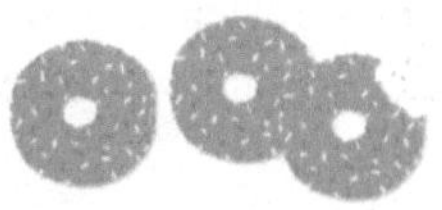

"In here," Kevin called when April's feet hit the bottom step. He was in the workout room.

She pushed open the door and stopped short in the doorway. He'd stripped down to only his boxer shorts and was steadily lifting weights on his machine.

"What's up?" April asked, warily, leaning against the door jam and watching the muscles in his arms flexing and releasing with his movements. Quite the show.

Kevin slowly eased the bar he'd been pulling, back to its resting position, returning the weights to their stack. "I wanted to talk to you, pick up where we left off before," he said, turning to face her. "Without interruption."

He meant Gerritt, that was obvious. "Okay," she said and moved from the doorway to sit on the stationary bike. "Shoot."

"You said you've been feeling out of sorts, but that's as far as you got," he said.

April placed her bare feet on the pedals and pushed slightly, unsure of how to respond.

"What I mean is," he said, then stood up to stretch his arms above his head. Impressive obliques. "You said you've been feeling distance between us for a while, but thought it would pass." He dropped his arms back down and placed his hands on his waist. "Is that the truth? That's how you feel? Nothing else?"

April shrugged. At that moment she felt like she wanted to throw up, but didn't think it would go over well to share that tidbit of information. She was such a coward. She had to get a grip.

"I do feel something else," she said, finally. "Confused."

"Confused?" he repeated, nodding thoughtfully. "Okay. That's okay. We can work with that."

"I don't know," she said, trying not to wince, or wimp out. "I think this goes past working it out. I have some stuff that I have to address, Kev, and dragging you along with me..."

"Whoa," he said, bluntly. "You're hardly dragging me. I asked you to move here, remember?"

"I do." She nodded. "And, maybe that's part of it. I came because you asked."

His face twisted in confusion. "What are you saying? You didn't want to come? What the hell does that mean? Why would you, if you didn't want to?"

"No," April said, shaking her head. God, he looked like she'd kicked him. Hard. "I didn't mean that. I *did* want to come. Really."

She slid off the bike seat and walked over to stand beside him, placing a gentle hand on his arm. "It's just that I think I have some issues with commitment. Some stuff I haven't face up to yet. Jessica gave me a whole wheelbarrow of crap about it, in fact..." She fell silent and watched him.

Kevin ran his hand through his hair and exhaled, releasing the air slowly from his mouth. April," he said, his voice tender as he wrapped his hand around hers on his arm. "Sweetheart. From the first time we kissed, there wasn't any confusion about how we fit together."

He placed his other hand gently on her neck and slid his fingers into the base of her hairline, massaging the tension beneath her skin. "We can work this out."

*Oh, dear,* April thought. Things were not going in a direction that she'd intended.

He kept massaging and she found herself hypnotized by the heat in his voice. When he moved closer and pressed his torso against hers, she let out a small sigh. He was still her boyfriend, after all...

"Can't we?" he whispered and slowly moved his mouth toward hers.

# CHAPTER 7 - Thursday

10:27 a.m.

"Thank you for helping me with this," April said, to her sister.

They were standing side by side at April's kitchen island, ten muffin tins lined up in front of them on the granite counter top, methodically scooping cupcake batter into waiting yellow and orange paper liners.

"I've had a lot going on and this block party thing snuck up on me. If I didn't have cupcakes to deliver on Saturday, I seriously think Deborah would find a way to make me pay."

Jessica laughed, but kept her spooning hand steady. "No problem, I was taking the day off, anyway. It's kind of nice to spend some of it this way. We haven't baked together in a long time."

April considered what she said, it was true. "You're right, you know," she said.

"Yes, I do know."

April smirked and nudged her hip with her own. Jessica snickered.

"*Anywaaay*," April said, setting down her scoop and wiping her fingers on her blue apron. "You're invited to the block party. You know that as well, right?"

Jessica laughed. "Even if I wasn't, after helping to make the food, I'd show up. Scary neighbor be damned."

The timer on the oven chimed and April reached for the oven mitts. She opened the door, pulled out two tins and nodded with satisfaction. "Perfect." She placed them on a rack on the counter, slid two more tins of unbaked batter into the empty space and closed the oven door.

"What now?" Jessica asked as she reset the timer and wiped her hands on a tea towel.

"Once these are done and cooled, we can start on frosting," April replied, straightening her green tee shirt beneath her apron.

"No." Jessica shook her head, making her gold star earrings glint in the overhead lights and folded her arms across her chest. "I meant, what's going on with you, now."

April raised an eyebrow.

"You didn't chime in about your scary neighbor, which you always do, so I can only surmise that something has you seriously distracted. What is it?"

April sighed. Busted. She picked up a cloth and began to half-heartedly wipe the countertop. "I've been a wimp."

"What happened?"

"No, that's not what I mean." April dropped the cloth on the counter. "I mean, I've done some soul searching and you were right, Jess. It's time I faced up to how I've shaped my life, or rather let my life shape itself, and actually consciously set my course for once."

Jessica's eyebrows shot up on her forehead, a stunned expression on her face.

"I don't want to end up like Mom," she continued. "An endless string of decent guys that I never fully commit to; a job that is only good enough; getting involved just enough, but being fearful of fully jumping in. I need to grow up, quit fudging around and make choices; or life is going to pass me by."

Jessica put down the tea towel still clutched in her grasp and wrapped April in her embrace. "I am so proud of you," she said, into the top of her sister's head.

April inhaled Jessica's flowery scent and tears welled up in her eyes as she tightly returned her hug. "I couldn't have taken this step without you." She sniffled, her voice muffled as she spoke.

Jessica laughed and released her, swiping at the dampness beneath her own eyes with her fingertips. "Of course you could have. You're a strong and smart woman, April Showers. You just needed a push, that's all."

April nodded and straightened her shirt. "The most difficult part is going to be setting things in motion."

Jessica pushed the sleeves up on her pink blouse and nodded in agreement. "It always is. But, if you just concentrate upon taking it one step at a time—" She paused and frowned. "Do you hear that?"

April cocked her head. It was shouting. Coming from outside. She frowned and asked, "Is that coming from the front yard?"

"Sure sounds like it." Jessica walked around the island and pushed open the cafe door. The voices got louder. "Okay, definitely coming from that way."

April quickly untied her apron, pulled it over her head and dropped it on the counter top beside her discarded cloth. She was about to follow Jessica into the family room, when the timer on her oven signaled.

"Damn it," she exhaled and grabbed the oven mitts. "I'll be right there," she called out as she yanked open the oven door, hauled out the cupcakes, then slammed the door shut and plopped the trays onto a rack.

"Oh, my, God, April. You've got to see this!" Jessica yelled, causing April to fling the oven mitts from her hands and sprint across the kitchen and out to the family room.

"What? What is it?" she said, as she joined her sister at the window. Jessica pointed and April jolted as she looked through the glass. There was a small crowd on her driveway. "What the hell?"

"I don't know," Jessica offered. "But, from here, they don't look very happy."

"God," April huffed. "This neighborhood. It's always something around here." She gestured to Jessica. "Come on, let's go and find out what's going on *now*."

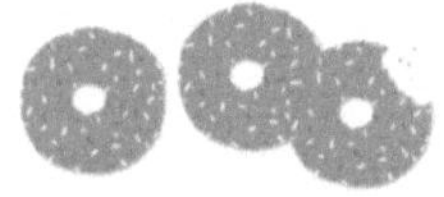

## 11:08 a.m.

April opened her front door and she and Jessica stepped onto the front porch, their astonished faces mirroring each other as they took in the display before them.

"What on Earth?" April said, trying to make sense of the chaos as they descended the steps and walked into the yard.

"Do you *know* these people?" Jessica asked.

April squinted, she'd left her glasses inside. "Well, yeah, over there on their porch is Carol - the one with the dog - and her husband, Edward. And, on the driveway is Deborah - the dragon lady - and her husband, Bob. And, next to Bob is... Oh-my-God!"

Jessica clutched April's shoulder at the same moment and squeaked, "Denise and Heidi! What the hell are those two doing here in your neighborhood?"

"What seems to be the issue?" Thomas asked.

April jumped at the sound of his voice in her ear. He'd come up behind them without warning and, as she turned her head, she noticed he was staying slightly behind them, as though using them as a shield. She would have called him cowardly, but under the circumstances, she didn't blame him.

"No idea," she told him. "We just got here, too."

"That Deborah woman seems to be in charge, wouldn't you say?" Jessica pointed at Deborah, who had a very firm hold on both Denise and Heidi's shoulders.

"Isn't she always?" Thomas quipped, a wry grin across his face.

"Look who else is here." Jessica pointed down the street.

They watched as Kevin walked briskly toward them, probably coming from the school; then as Gerritt drove his car slowly into the cul-de-sac.

"Good lord," April exhaled. "It's a freakin' gong show."

Kevin didn't so much as glance in their direction and, instead, kept walking purposefully toward the larger, more vocal group. They were shouting and making a such a general ruckus, it made sense to April why they would grab his attention.

Gerritt, on the other hand, parked on the street. *Smart move*, April thought. *Stay well out of it.* He got out of his car, looked at the commotion on the driveway and immediately walked across the lawn to join their small group.

"What's going on?" he asked.

"We have no idea." Jessica shrugged. "We heard yelling, came out to see what was happening and that's about all we know."

"Or, want to know, really," Thomas added.

"It's like a scene from a badly written movie," Jessica commented. "And, the only part I want solved is, how in the hell Denise and Heidi got in the middle?"

"What?" Gerritt said, his face alarmed, then shifting to angry as he peered at the group on the driveway. "Denise and Heidi? Are you God-damned kidding me?"

"Nope." April shook her head.

He exhaled and ran a hand across his hair. "This is too much. It's time to get to the bottom of things with those two..."

"There! See!" Heidi shrieked so loudly, she drowned out the rest of what Gerritt was saying. She pointed insistently toward April, Jessica, Gerritt and Thomas. "They're even together now, we're not making this up! I swear it, we've *seen* them."

April's stomach dropped and she looked sharply at Jessica. Her sister had gone still, her eyes wide.

"Oh, oh," Jessica muttered under her breath when Kevin turned swiftly to face them. "This doesn't look good."

April flinched when she saw the thunderous expression on his face. Jessica was right, it did not look good. The feeling swept over her that she was in the direct path of the storm brewing behind his angry eyes and she swallowed nervously against the panic rising in her throat. If she'd had a rock nearby to crawl under and hide, she would've done so willingly.

No such luck.

As an alternative, she reached out with her left hand to grip Jessica's forearm. Jessica responded immediately and covered her hand with her own, making them a united front as Kevin walked with firm, measured steps toward them.

"Brace yourself," April advised. "I have a hunch this could be brutal."

"Jesus," Gerritt said, squaring his shoulders. "He looks pissed."

"What were those two gels yammering about?" Thomas asked, not yet up to speed on the change in atmosphere coming at them. "I'm pretty sure they're the ones I saw last night, by the way."

April didn't offer a reply. She wanted to keep an eye on Kevin and stood as still as a statue until he stopped directly in front of her.

"Is it true?" he said, his frown deep, his chest heaving up and down and his breath coming in short gasps.

"What?" Her eyebrows knotted together.

"I *said*," he repeated, his voice increasing in volume as he fought to control his emotions. "Is it true?"

"Is what true?" April implored. "I don't have any clue what you're talking about, Kev."

His eyes slid toward Gerritt, then back to her, and he spoke through clenched teeth. "Him and you. Is. It. True."

"Oh, God, Kev," she began, then clamped her mouth shut and gripped Jessica's hand when his eyes filled with something akin to rage.

"You've got to be *fucking* kidding me." He almost growled as the words left his mouth. "Jesus, after last night..." His nostrils flared as he fought to contain his emotions.

April's knees begin to tremor. Never, in all of their time together, had she seen him so angry.

"Wait a sec," Gerritt said, holding up a hand.

April instinctively leaned into her sister when Kevin turned to face Gerritt, his expression murderous. She was seriously concerned he was going to try to do injury to the man.

"Who the fuck are you?" Kevin spat, squaring his shoulders and puffing out his chest. "Huh? Who the FUCK do you think you are? You back-stabbing, son of a bitch."

Jessica gripped April's arm and tugged her aside, away from the two men. Thomas stepped back a couple of paces, giving them space, and the group on the driveway fell silent; watching with wide, startled eyes.

April turned and glared at Denise and Heidi. She wanted to do damage to them for causing such a mess. Denise caught her stare and snapped her eyes away. *Cowardly hag,* she thought.

Gerritt exhaled and raised his chin to meet Kevin's rage head on. "No way," he said, shaking his head firmly from side to side. "You aren't taking some gossiping biddy's point of view over mine."

He looked Kevin in the eye. "You have to listen to what I have to say, to what April has to say, before you believe the lying trash those two are spewing."

"How do you even know what the lies are, huh?" Kevin took a step forward toward him. "And, how is it that there are even lies being spewed in the first place? Huh? Have an answer for that? They have to have *some* grounding to have even been started."

Gerritt opened his mouth to reply, but shut it fast as Kevin took a broad swing at him. Everyone gasped in shock as Gerritt jerked backward, Kevin's fist narrowly missing his jaw.

"Kevin!" April shrieked, while Jessica kept a firm grip on her arm, restraining her from moving forward into the middle of the two men. "Stop!"

Kevin barely even registered her voice, he was focused upon Gerritt. "You're a two-faced, prick, you know that?"

He started moving toward Gerritt, again, but Gerritt was too swift, taking a step to counter every one he put forward.

"Kev," Gerritt tried again. "Please, let's stop and talk this out." He moved lightly on his feet, watching Kevin's body with a practiced eye.

"He moves like he knows what he's doing," April whispered, of Gerritt, to Jessica.

"He should," Jessica whispered back. "He's a third degree black belt in Kung Fu."

"What?" She turned to Jessica, shocked. "Are you kidding me?"

Kevin swung violently at Gerritt a second time, halting her inquiry in its tracks. All she could think was that she was suddenly worried for Kevin. He was no match for that sort of training.

"What kind of an asshole makes moves on his friend's girlfriend?" Kevin raged, throwing a third punch that was nowhere near close enough to touch Gerritt. He was so frustrated and angry, he just wanted to keep on swinging until he, hopefully, wore Gerritt down and was finally able to belt him.

"Men!" Thomas piped up, making April jump. She'd never heard his voice so commanding. "Kevin, that's enough!"

April watched, astonished, as it worked. Thomas' harsh bark broke the spell. Kevin stopped the slow dance he was creating around the lawn, his stance softened and the tension left his face.

"Okay?" Gerritt dared to push for more. "Will you hear both of us out?"

Kevin was nothing if not fair. His fairness and ability for reason were what made him such a great teacher, amongst other things. He took a deep breath, looked over at April and nodded.

"Fine," he stated, holding her eyes with his own. "You're right. Here-say causes more trouble than facts ever do."

Jessica exhaled the breath she'd been holding and released the grip she had on April's arm. "Thank God," she murmured, before narrowing her eyes and turning to face Denise and Heidi. "Now, *those two*, they need to be dealt with."

Thomas pulled out a cigarette and lighter and April noticed his hand was slightly shaky as he lit the flame. He inhaled deeply and glanced her way. She had no concrete proof he knew the lay of the land, but had her suspicions he was privy to a lot more than he let on.

"Well," Deborah spoke up, her voice loud and firm. "Before you deal with *that* mess, I want some answers."

"We told you," Denise said as she tried, in vain, to shake off Deborah's claw-like grip. "We don't have any idea about any dead squirrels."

"You've got a serious obsession going, Honey," Heidi said, smoothing her hair back from her face. "I'd see someone about it."

April bit her lip to keep from grinning. While she was royally put off by the two women, Heidi's comment was ever so slightly hilarious.

"You would, too," Deborah said, through clenched teeth. "If you'd had not one, but *two* dead squirrels show up on your doorstep. I'm being targeted."

"Not by us," Denise shot back swiftly.

"Deborah, *Sweetheart*," Bob began, soothingly, before being loudly interrupted by a commotion coming from Thomas' yard.

In the next instant, Corkscrew shot out from behind the trees; launching himself directly at them. The cat darted between the many pairs of legs on the driveway to arrive with a hard stop, smack dab in front of Deborah.

"Good God!" Deborah shrieked, pulling her hands from Denise and Heidi's shoulders and holding them out in front of her like a traffic cop.

"Wow," Denise commented. "Some speed on that animal."

"What's that in its mouth?" Heidi asked, peering at the cat.

Bob stepped in front of his wife, hands curled into fists and placed on his hips, making him look like a chubby super hero. "Stop!" he bellowed, unnecessarily, at Corkscrew. The cat, already stopped, didn't so much as bat an eye. Instead, he sidestepped Bob and dropped a limp squirrel carcass onto the driveway beside Deborah's feet.

"Ewww," Denise wrinkled up her nose. "Call me crazy, but I think you've got your answer to your question. If you're being targeted, it's by that cat."

Corkscrew yawned widely, displaying his perfectly pointed sharp teeth, blinked, then darted back across the yards to disappear back into Thomas's foliage.

"Well, will wonders never cease." Thomas shook his head, his face a picture of surprise. "Looks like you've got yourself an admirer, so you do." He puffed on his cigarette, a wide smirk washing across his face. "No one was targeting you at all, lass."

"Excuse me? An *Admirer*?" Deborah peeked out from behind Bob and looked wide-eyed at Thomas.

"Aye." Thomas nodded confidently as he turned and began to amble away from the rest of them. Before he imitated his cat and disappeared into the depths of his yard, he spoke one last time over his shoulder. "The most flattering thing a poosie can do fer ya, is bring you a present."

"That's true, Deborah," Carol offered, from the safety of her front porch. "I saw it on the National Geographic Channel."

Deborah looked poleaxed and Bob looked jubilant. "Well, there you go!" He smiled cheerfully. "Mystery solved. No madman, just a cat who thinks you're something special. The *cat's meow*, if I may," he said, cheekily.

Deborah narrowed her eyes as him, unwilling to join in on his attempt at humor. She took a deep breath and straightened her shoulders. "Well, be that as it may," she offered. "Get rid of it."

Bob dropped his joyful smile and nodded. So much for making light of a tense situation. Deborah gave him a dismissive wave of her hand and turned her attention back to Denise and Heidi.

"As for you two." She fixed them with a fierce glare and they both flinched. "I recommend you stay well away from this neighborhood. You have no reason to be here. Ever. These are good people." She gestured to the group at large. "Not anyone you need to concern yourselves with."

She raised her chin and looked down her nose. "In fact, I would hate to have to find you here, again. I honestly don't know what I might be forced to do, if I did."

Denise and Heidi looked genuinely alarmed and April didn't blame them one bit. The woman could be flat out scary. However, when she was on their side, it was rather pleasant.

"Leave," Deborah spat, pointing a stiff finger at them.

Needing no extra encouragement, they took off and began to speed walk down the street as though the Devil himself, or Herself, was following them.

"Now," Deborah said, with an near royal dip of her head. "I think you all have something to work out. It's none of our concern, so we'll respect your privacy and depart." She gave one last glance at the dead squirrel and then raised an eyebrow at Bob. "I *said*, get rid of it."

April was speechless. The woman could hold court, that was clear.

"Damn," Jessica muttered.

"Absolutely," she agreed.

"Okay," Kevin said and crossed his arms, making him look like a warrior. "I don't want to drag this out with a lot of talk. What's the deal?"

"First," Jessica said. "Tell us what the *Witches of Eastwick* told you."

He took a bracing breath, then jerked his chin first at April, then at Gerritt. "That these two have been getting together behind my back."

Jessica and April exchanged a look. April had begun talking the talk, would she step up and walk the walk?

"Let's go inside, okay?" she said, gently. "I don't want to have this discussion out on the front lawn."

He stared at her, his jaw clenched. She held his gaze until, finally, he nodded. "Fine." He shrugged and turned toward the house. "Whatever."

"Um, listen," Jessica said, hesitantly, glancing at her car in the driveway as Kevin walked away. "We had a few more cupcakes to bake, but I think I should probably go..."

"That's fine, Jess," April said, reaching up to give her a quick hug and looking across her shoulder to see Kevin slowly ascending the steps, his posture slumped.

"I'm going to clear out, too," Gerritt said, awkwardly, taking a few fast steps backward toward his car. "I think you guys could use some privacy."

April shot him a grateful look. "That would be good. I'll call you in a bit and give you the all clear, okay?"

He nodded, left the property and slipped into his car. April watched he and Jessica drive away, took a deep, bracing breath and followed Kevin into the house. She'd only moved into the neighborhood a few months ago, it was time to finally start getting things sorted.

# Epilogue

4:05 p.m.

Kevin yawned and stretched his arms above his head. He was beat. He dropped his arms back down and rested his elbows on his desk, reveling in the silence of his empty classroom. While he loved the energy of his students, the quiet was always welcome at the end of the day.

Snow began to fall gently outside his windows, large tumbling flakes drifting lazily toward the ground, and he felt amazed at how swiftly the first leg of the school year had passed by. It was his last day before winter break and, yet, it seemed a blink of an eye since the summer had ended and he'd been welcoming his students into his classroom on their first day.

Summer.

Kevin ran his fingers through his hair as memories rushed forward, unbidden. It had been such a jumble of chaos, from his neighbors to his personal life... He took in a large breath and exhaled.

At least he could finally think of Gerritt without wanting to slug him. That was a good thing. Progress. It had taken him a few months to get there, but he had. He'd finally come to the understanding that Gerritt wasn't trying to personally hurt him as a friend, he was just driven by his own agenda that had nothing to do with anyone else. Anyone, of course, except April.

*It's in the past*, Kevin silently counseled himself. He'd grown from the experience, taken both April's and her sister's wise words of comfort, and accepted that sometimes the most difficult experiences turn out to be the most beneficial. It may not seem that way at the time, but in the end, there it was.

He tidied the papers he was grading into a folder and tucked the entire thing into his briefcase. Homework for the holidays - for him. He never assigned anything to his students, but he was the teacher, after all. A whole different ball game.

A light knock at the door made him raise his head up from his task and he grinned. "Be right there," he called out, quickly zipping his briefcase and taking a last quick look around his desk to make sure he hadn't left anything behind.

He pushed back his chair, grabbed the handle of the case and walked toward the classroom door.

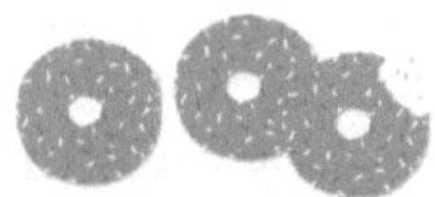

"Hey," He said, his face lighting up as he walked out into the hallway where she was waiting. "Just have to grab my coat from the staff room and we can take off."

"How was the last day?"

"As good as can be expected." Kevin chuckled as they strolled down the empty corridor. "The kids were over excited, we had their party, played lots of games, went to an assembly and that was that. Freedom for the next two weeks until the new year."

"Sounds like you're looking forward to it, too."

They arrived at the staff room door and he held his hand up. "Hang on, hold that thought," he said, before slipping inside. He was in and out in a flash, leather jacket in hand.

"Yeah, I'm really looking forward to it," he said, continuing where they'd left off. "The past few months have been a blur, but I feel like I've turned a corner, you know?"

He stepped ahead of her and held open the main entrance door. They stepped outside into the fresh falling snow and Kevin quickly pulled on his jacket, a hug smile lighting up his face. "Perfect. Snow for Christmas. I wasn't sure I'd be looking forward to the holidays, but..."

Jessica turned to face him, the snow making her auburn curls sparkle. "But?" she prompted.

"But, I am." He smiled down at her and reached out for her hand. "And, the new year, too."

Jessica grinned and squeezed his hand back. "I spoke to her today," she said, her voice careful, testing.

Kevin led the way to the parking lot, the snow swirling around their shoes. "How is she?" he asked, genuinely curious.

"Good," she said, relieved he sounded so unaffected by the news. He had been telling the truth. He'd finally moved forward. "She's busy, her new column has taken off like gangbusters."

"What was it about, again?" He opened the passenger door of his car.

"It's a city beat sort of thing. She's all over the place, reporting about all sorts of things. Never the same thing twice, lots of excitement, right up her alley."

Kevin nodded, a small smile playing on his lips. It didn't surprise him that April was happier back in the city, chasing down stories. It was who she was and, in his haste to make things work between them, he'd ignored that. It hadn't been fair to either of them.

"Well, I'm glad she's happy," he said, then hesitated, forcing himself to ask. "Is she on her own? Or...?"

Jessica slipped through the open door into the passenger seat and looked up at him. She was as proud of him as she was of her sister. Both of them had faced a hard road and had landed firmly on their feet.

It had been touch and go there for a while, for Kevin. She'd worried he wasn't going to be able to pull himself out of his funk, but he had. It had come as a shock to her that during the process, their feelings for each other had deepened; so much that they had crossed the boundary from friends, to potential.

April, when she'd found out, had insisted she wasn't shocked at all by the turn of events. She'd even gone so far as to claim that she was more surprised she hadn't put the idea of them together, sooner.

Kevin closed the car door and slipped around the other side of the vehicle. When he'd tossed his briefcase into the back and settled himself into the driver's seat, Jessica answered his question.

"Yes, she's been dating, again. Nothing overly serious at the moment, but she's hopeful."

Kevin started the engine and nodded. He was okay with it. Life moved on. He shifted his shoulders to face her and grinned. "Good," he said, picking up her hand and kissing her open palm. "Everybody deserves to be hopeful."

The End

# About the Author

Kathleen began storytelling in grade school and has many fond memories of passing summer afternoons, out on the swings in her backyard, creating tales that entertained her neighborhood friends.

Many years later, too many to talk about without seeming rude and nosey, Kathleen has channeled her imagination to the pages of her novels. She hopes you enjoy her tales and encourages you to feel free to read her stories on the swing set in your own backyard.

Kathleen now spends time in her backyard with her beloved husband, adored son and silly dog. They let her tell them stories and always laugh in all of the correct places. She's lucky, and she knows it.

Please visit Kathleen's website to find out about her next novel, *Favorable Conditions.*

**Connect with Kathleen Online**

Website: www.kathleenkole.com

Facebook: www.facebook.com/KathleenKoleAuthor

Twitter: www.twitter.com/kathleenkole